# AMONG
# THE
# KINGDOMS

# Among

# The

# Kingdoms

JacQueline

Vaughn

Roe

RONA
Queen's Tower
King Purnell's Castle
Lord Colin
Sir Reginald
Castle of Silver Birds
Maer
Illyan Sea
Kabir Island
W
N
S
E

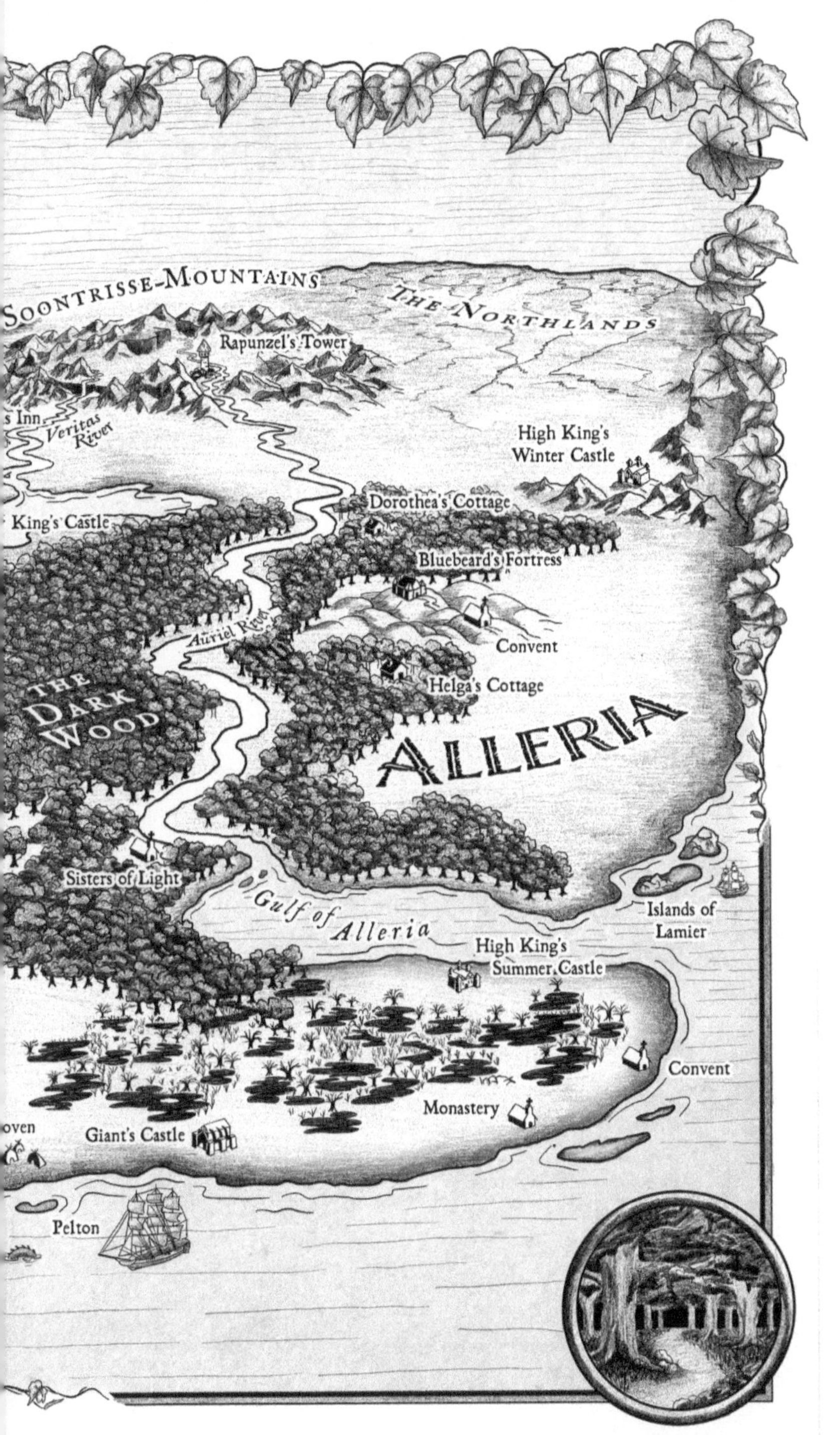

Soontrisse-Mountains
THE NORTHLANDS
Rapunzel's Tower
's Inn
Veritas River
High King's
Winter Castle
Dorothea's Cottage
King's Castle
Bluebeard's Fortress
Convent
Auriel River
Helga's Cottage
THE DARK WOOD
ALLERIA
Sisters of Light
Gulf of Alleria
Islands of Lamier
High King's Summer Castle
Convent
Monastery
oven
Giant's Castle
Pelton

CONTENTS

# PROLOGUE

Camilla had been waiting. She'd been listening. It had taken time to locate another source of power she could manipulate, but at last she had found the young maid. Deep in the swamps, she had collected again what little strength she could still summon. She would need to go out to deeper waters soon. But not yet.

Nofra was sitting on a mossy log, silent tears wandering down her lovely brown face. Her curly dark hair, braided to the side, was resting over her shoulder. Her dark eyes were unfocused. Unaware of the patchy light straining through the dim trees. Unaware of the sorceress as she rose to the surface. Camilla's sleek eel-like body morphed into a towering woman with auburn hair streaming water. The maid turned and stared at the sorceress.

"You know who I am?"

Nofra nodded, mouth agape.

"You were sworn to my sister, and she used you—but I will never use you like that. You will be my vessel and I will grant you power, as long as you bind yourself to me. Do you understand? Only me, never to Amee again—or any other," she added.

The girl nodded, ringlets at the tail of her braid bobbing.

"You will be more powerful than you can fathom. Just imagine, together we will make the kingdoms crumble. You want to be a queen? You can be. You want to be a sorceress? You will be! But you must be mine. At all costs."

The maid's dark eyes filled. "Will I never see my mother again?"

Camilla's voice thundered, and the maid shrank into herself. "You call her that? After all, she abandoned you. She betrayed you, betrayed us all! How can you—" She broke off when the maid lifted a tentative hand.

"But she's all I've ever known."

"Until now." Camilla's lips split into a sneer. "Come, let's gather our people together. It's time for war."

# AN UNEXPECTED QUESTION

"*Y*ou can't be serious! Do you have a death wish?"

Prince Edmund stood up carefully beside his bed, balancing his weight on both legs. Better than last time. He looked down into Gwynndolen's stormy face. Couldn't she see?

"Don't smile at me like that!" she spat at him. "You're in no condition to—"

"To what? Represent my kingdom after I drowned everyone else at sea? Oh, and sent our gifts for the High King under the waters as well? You're right, I should just stay here, act the part of an invalid and let the High King finally have the excuse he's always wanted to take over my island."

To her credit, Gwynndolen didn't answer right away, but her eyebrows drew together.

Edmund reached for her. "Help me," he conceded slightly. He allowed her to come under his left arm and help him walk, something he hadn't been able to do since being struck down a week earlier.

The Summer Castle's stone walls were draped in ornate tapestries celebrating the lineage of the people of the Eastern Ports. But the bright hues of the woven threads no longer comforted his eyes. The walls were closing in, reminding him of his impotence if he didn't take action soon.

"I need to get out of this room, go to court. Many of the royal families from the kingdoms have gathered and that means the gossip has begun. You know how dangerous that can be."

"Not as dangerous as entering a tournament your body cannot withstand. If I was taller, I could hide beneath your armor and fight for you."

He chuckled and instantly regretted it. The cracked rib on his right side stung and he gasped in pain.

"Did I hurt you?" Gwynndolen turned her chin to look up at him, and he forgot about the pain. All he could think about was her pink lips. He brushed a kiss to her mouth, and she yielded slightly. He kept the kiss soft, not allowing his growing passion to overwhelm him. This powerful woman, a source of wonder and frustration, mesmerized him. That she could love him gave him hope, even amid a loss so great he could barely stand. They had barely survived, while most of their family lay at the bottom of the Illyan Sea. But at least Edmund had helped divide the sisters of sorcery, Camilla and Amee, when he gave his life to Jesu, the Son of the Most High God.

In truth, Edmund wasn't sure what it meant to be a follower of the Christ, but he was grateful for the chance to learn. If he could save his throne at the same time. He hated the thought that their families might have died for nothing. He had to make things right, and the only way to do that was to see that the ridiculous High King didn't snatch his throne and ignore the threat Camilla still posed.

After a lengthy kiss, Gwynndolen pulled away from his embrace, leaving him to balance, holding onto the frame of the grand bed. But she stayed within reach, just in case. "Edmund," she began, and he smiled. At last, she was calling him by his name, and not his title. "Edmund, I don't feel you are paying attention to me."

He blinked and straightened up. "I'm sorry. I'll try to do better."

"See that you do," Her tone was playful. "But, I suppose we need to have some sort of plan. You are not well enough to fight in the tournament, and we can't send for someone to fight in your stead."

When she paused, lost in thought, he almost kissed her again, but just as he leaned in, she straightened up and he jerked back with a wince just in time to keep from knocking heads with her.

"Why couldn't I fight for you? I've heard stories of the women warriors in the Eastern Ports. Terrifying women!"

"I've heard tales of them, too. Aren't they raised to fight for God?"

"They are. I used to dream of becoming one of them. But my training hasn't been lacking, you know. My family has trained me practically since birth!"

"I know." That much was true, but . . . "It doesn't feel right—"

"Of course it doesn't feel right to you, but it feels much more right to me to save your throne. You can spend your time convincing the king of the threat he is determined to ignore. We know Camilla is still out there. I admit, I don't feel quite safe, even if Amee is in the dungeons. It's simple —I fight, you bargain."

"It's not that simple, Gwynndolen."

"It is!" As her dark Ronan eyes flashed, her skin turned rosy, almost matching her hair.

"But there's only one way for you to fight for the island . . ." He trailed off, unsure of how he felt at this turn in conversation.

"I'm willing to do anything! Just speak it!" She wet her lips and grinned. But he wasn't sure it would last.

"You must be in line for the throne if you are to fight."

"You mean . . .?"

"Yes, you could only do so as the princess or queen, if I'm remembering correctly."

"But I'm not the—"

His heart thudded at the thought. "But you could be."

Did she mean to step back?

"What are you saying?"

"I'm saying that your determination to fight for Rona will require you to become queen to do so. You are of a noble house and—"

"But I'm not of noble blood. I'm adopted—my parents were commoners."

He nodded, but caught himself with a shake of his head. He needed to articulate the details clearly. "The nobility has accepted you. You only need marry a prince or a king and no one would question your right to—"

"Marry you?"

"Marry me."

Gwynndolen's mouth opened and shut once, and then again without saying a single word. She paced, biting her lower lip. Finally she faced him, but this time from across the room, too close to the large wooden door for his liking. "But, we're not betrothed."

"No." He leaned back against the bedpost and crossed

his hands over his chest. "But didn't you say it was my mother's wish?"

She took a few steps back in his direction. "It was. She felt I alone could handle you—you would never be able to manipulate me with your wish." A smirk overtook her mouth, and he laughed. If they had children, they would have dark Ronan eyes that glittered with sarcasm, but would they have his sandy brown hair or her bright red curls?

He straightened as he hobbled forward, stepping carefully across the lavish purple rug. "And she was right."

"But queens sit around all day gossiping!"

"Have you met High Queen Pasca yet?"

Gwynndolen frowned slightly. "Not yet."

"The High Queen is not one to sit around gossiping. She leaves that to her husband and is more likely to see a thing get done than any other queen I know."

"How many do you know?"

Edmund lifted one shoulder, but grimaced in pain when he tried to take another step. Would he need a staff? He cringed at the thought. "Not enough, I admit, but that will change as soon as I can leave this room. Besides, my mother didn't fit that description, did she?"

Gwynndolen frowned at this.

"Exactly. She was her own woman. Why not make your own way? We have an island all to ourselves—make being queen something that suits you." The prince gestured, and she came back to his side so he could continue to walk around. He would have to get stronger, and he knew he could do so as long as she was by his side.

"I thought I might never marry." It was almost a whisper, but he stopped and looked down into her face.

"You could probably do without me, my lady, but I

could never do without you. You are my perfect match. Whether we marry here, now in the king's court or in a few years' time, it makes no difference to me. I want you for myself and for my kingdom—if I have a kingdom."

"I think I'd like it better if you didn't."

He laughed at first, but the pain in his side sliced through him like a knife's blade. Taking a breath, he spoke calmly. "I'm learning to say, 'As God wills it.'"

She was quiet for a moment, looking at the floor. He never knew what to do with her when she was quiet. "Do you think God wills us to marry?"

He nodded, but then realized she didn't see. "I think he does."

She stopped moving and turned to face him. She wasn't wearing the face of a woman besotted and blinded by love, but a face of determination. This was a choice she was making—a choice he hadn't wished her into. "Then, I say yes, so long as I can fight for you. You may not have left the room, but I've seen the pampered princes preparing for the tournament. It's not that none of them are good, but they will underestimate me. And you know how fast I am."

"I do." A niggling feeling tainted his momentary triumph. He didn't like to think of her fighting instead of him. What kind of man was he if— But they were in the Eastern Ports, not Rona, not even Alleria or the Northlands. Perhaps if she could find a trainer who could help her make the most of her skills against the nobles . . .

But his legs wobbled, and he nearly went down as one foot failed to lift out of the thick rug.

She steadied him, redirecting to the bed. "Lie down, silly prince, before you fall down. Let me make sure your servant brings you something to eat and then you can rest. I'll go scout my competition and strategize."

"Of course you will." But he pulled her close for one more kiss before she could leave.

# THE CAT AND THE MONSTER

Katterina wished she could pounce on something, on anything. Whatever it took to get rid of the extra tension building in her neck. She shrugged her shoulders up and down, breathed in the heavy fragrance of frankincense and myrrh that hung in the air. Still, she felt jittery. There were times she missed having a tail. After all, she had been a cat almost as long as she had been a woman. She remembered the feeling of anticipation filling her lungs as she would lie in wait for a mouse. As she crouched low, belly to the ground, her tail would swish back and forth, counting off the moments till the mouse emerged to meet his doom.

*His doom.* That sounded dramatic, and she pulled a saucy grin.

"What are you thinking?" Jacob asked, his tonsured head bending toward her ever so slightly. His wide brown lips didn't stretch in a smile yet. His smiles were rare. She had grown to love seeing his face, normally stern, light in happiness in those rare moments. What could she say to him now to earn such a smile in this solemn place?

Katterina stared at the altar, a glint in her emerald eyes. If she were still a mischievous calico cat, she would have bounded up onto the platform and then the table where the sacramental elements lay during Mass. "I was thinking of when I was Cat. Some of that life was simple by comparison. I would find shelter and food. All of life revolved around those basic needs. I have to say, I miss that —and having a tail." She flipped a lock of black hair over her shoulder.

Yes! His broad lips split into a smile, and he chuckled, the deep sound of his quiet laughter reverberating in the wooden nave.

Rapunzel entered at the back of the room, coming up the center aisle with Prince Paul at her side. Helena sat on her hip, bunching Rapunzel's pale blue surcoat and navy cotehardie gown up enough that Katterina could see a couple of inches of the white chemise beneath.

"Kat!" Helena giggled, dropping the fabric and stretching for her grandmother. Katterina's heart swelled with joy.

"Give her to me, please." Rapunzel's rosebud mouth pursed in a sigh as she handed over the squirming toddler. There were faint shadows on her pale skin beneath her own emerald eyes. Poor thing. "What have you been doing, little one? Causing much trouble?"

"Kat-kat!" The little pink-and-white cherub pounded her chubby fists together, her cloud of dark hair curling about her round face. Rapunzel said Helena's eyes were deep blue, but Katterina agreed with Paul that they were violet, containing the joyous mirth they had prayed would fill her. She looked nothing like the golden-haired Rapunzel or hazel-eyed Paul, since she was adopted, but her laughter was something they had passed down to her through their daily love.

Rapunzel frowned. "It doesn't seem fair that her first word is *Kat*. Shouldn't she be saying *mama* or *da* or something about us?"

Katterina laughed, her own joy resounding off the walls. It had only been a few days since the one-toothed child had chattered her first word. "Well, she took this long to speak. She obviously wanted to say the right thing first. And you chose well, didn't you, my sweet Helena?"

"Kat!" Helena proclaimed, and laid a wet, sloppy kiss on Katterina's cheek. For a moment, Katterina forgot all about why they had come to the monastery and how soon they would have to return to the High King's court.

"Did Father Iohannes . . .?" Rapunzel looked up at Jacob and then at her mother.

"Did Father Iohannes what?"

"Has he come out yet?"

Rapunzel and Paul had elected to walk around the grounds for a short time since they had been told that Father Iohannes couldn't speak with them right away. Jacob had wanted to come inside, saying that he would rather wait inside and listen—but listen for what, he hadn't explained.

"No, he hasn't yet—"

The sound began with a slow and steady beat, thumping on the floors somewhere nearby. Then another beat began a counterpoint. The beats escalated and a bass voice sang words Katterina heard, but didn't understand. She had never been very good at understanding the Latin liturgy most priests used. Next, a baritone joined, and at last a tenor, the voices intertwining, weaving a spell of wonder on the little group. Jacob joined the song, his bass blending perfectly. Something in Katterina ached to hear the yearning in his voice, the longing mirrored in her own heart. Though she didn't know the words, she knew the truth. All of creation waited, longing for things to be put right by the Creator. When would he return and make all things new?

AMEE RECOILED after hitting the wall of the dungeon. Her form morphed again, but she fought it, determined to gain control over her own body. It was no use. Her body spasmed out of her control. When Dietz descended moments ago into the dungeon where she was being held, she looked reptilian. When she strained to become a woman so that her son could recognize her, the morphing had taken over into something else. Something hideous she couldn't stop. Why couldn't she control herself?

"What do you want?" she asked now, touching her cheek with care, but turning to her confused son. What must she look like to him? She certainly wasn't improving his impression of her. If she could just transform back into a woman—but if she did, then the bruise would swell and purple within minutes.

Had she ever been a woman—a normal woman—at any point in her life? The power sparked through her like electricity, trying to change her again into something else, and she resisted with what little energy she had. But then she relented. Maybe it would change her back to someone he could tolerate. At least, as long as he was down here with her.

"I wanted to—" But the young man halted. He sucked in his full, tan lips. She could see so much of his father in him. Why? Why did he have to hate her? She knew it was her own fault, but if he could just understand . . . Her body shook, the violent transformation raging within her at once. "Stop that!" he lashed out. His bold voice echoed against the stone walls. It looked as though it surprised him. He stepped forward, as though to come at her, but stepped back. He must have felt the invisible wall that kept her in the back portion of the dungeon.

"I can't—I don't know why, but I can't." Her body shook, and she fell backward this time, hitting the back of her head on the same mildewed wall she had hit earlier. She would be a mass of bruises soon. It was only getting worse. She needed to sink down inside herself, ground herself, reach deep into the earth for the power. But she couldn't look away from her son's face. So like his father's! Her body trembled, and she sobbed. The ache of all she had done, all those she had betrayed, this one person she had tried to save—but he stood before her, hating her. "I did it all for you."

"But you—I—I'm the reason—" A torrent of emotion scrunched up his face, confusing his ability to speak.

A tender memory surfaced. "Your father would stumble over his words when he felt things too deeply. He was a good man, always caring for others. You remind me of him."

Dietz swallowed, straining for control. "When did he die?"

"Shortly after I sent you away. I lost everything—everyone."

"You didn't lose my brother. You—you sacrificed him for more p-power!"

The pain rattled her frame. Half of her sprouted the

hind end of a centaur, but she fell over, having no front legs to rest on. Then she trembled and transformed again.

Dietz shook his head in disgust. "What is wrong with you?"

Where was her power? Where was her control? What —or who?—had ahold of her? "I honestly don't know."

"It's been a week of this and they said if I didn't come see you—well, I'm here. S-s-so, s-stop!"

She gave up trying to stand and lay sprawled in the musty hay that littered the moist floor. "I don't know how to. I haven't slept for more than a few minutes in over a week. I just needed to see you."

"Well, here I am—see? What—what do you want?"

She closed her eyes in exhaustion, hysterical laughter accompanied by sobs. Tremors caused pieces of her to continue to shimmer and morph. She rotated as her body changed into that of a mermaid, her tail shining and flipping in the cell on the dirty floor. Then she shook again. Suddenly a minotaur, her weeping changed into a guttural sound of woe. "I just want to say I'm sorry," she cried when her body finally returned to that of a desperate woman, stretched-out gown hanging loosely on her frame. "But it's too ridiculous, isn't it?" She dug deep into what little strength she had left. She must hold still or he would leave. He would never know how dearly she loved him. "Please know, everything I have done since you were born was to protect you. To give you a better life than—"

"Than my brother? Oh, I see that. I know that." His voice was clear for only a moment as he looked straight into her eyes. "But why d-d-didn't you love him enough?"

"I didn't know he was the price. I didn't even know I loved him until Eufemia took him from me. I had been living so long with my hatred and my fears—"

He turned his back, yelling up the stairs. "Guard!"

"No, please don't go! Please, stay! Listen to what I have to—"

He looked over his shoulder, his face contorted as he lashed out. "N-n-nothing you have to s-say is worth listening to. I should have been the one s-sacrificed, n-not him."

The trembling began again. Amee shook as the power overtook her body and the sounds of her sister's laughter filled her ears. Or was that her own laughter? Hysteria raged in her body, tightening like a fist around her throat. Would she never be free of the pain she had caused? The pain set in motion long before she ever drew breath? How could she have ever thought to free herself?

# THE FATHER'S DECISION

The fool clapped his hands as he drew near the group after exploring the monastery. He could feel the clap make his blue jester's hat waggle. "Brother Jacob, isn't the likeness amazing?" He raised his bushy dark eyebrows, certain that his blue eyes were now sparkling with happiness.

The last strains of the monk's worship was lingering in the halls, and Jacob looked quizzically at Amis. The jester gave a wide grin. Amis made certain that he always kept the self-assured man a bit off-balance.

"I haven't been able to find a difference between this monastery and the one they tricked us with."

"Tricked?" A deep voice came up from behind them, and Amis whirled to greet the stately priest. Yes, this was the one. The man was as tall as Jacob, though not as broad in the shoulders, and his coloring was more olive and not as deep a brown. Like Jacob, he had a clean tonsure shaved into his hair; but where Jacob's hair was close-cropped, black, and curly, Father Iohannes's was white, though his eyebrows were still black and thick. The man had a long face that seemed longer because of his floor-length robes that were made of white silk and threaded with little gold crosses.

"Hello!" Amis bowed low, with as much reverence as he could muster as a jester. "It is great fun to be here at last and meet with you."

The man could easily have dismissed him, pushed them all aside in favor of speaking with Jacob alone. The warrior monk was the only one who had a right to an audience with Father Iohannes, but the pious man stopped and looked at Amis. Really looked at him.

Amis felt a grin grow across his face. "We were to meet you some time past, but sorcery got in the way."

Jacob stepped forward. "What my friend the fool is trying to say—"

But Father Iohannes held up a patient hand and looked at Jacob. "I would like to hear what your friend has to say about sorcery. We may live in a monastery, but rumors have reached us." He leaned his head closer to Amis. "Is it true that one sister took my shape and deceived you? Did she even sound like me?"

"More or less. I, of course, had never seen you or spoken with you, but her guise took even Brother Jacob in."

"We have also been told that you escaped and bound her by the name of Jesu the Christ."

Amis nodded, again making certain his jester's cap shook atop his head. If it had been time to perform, he would have worn the one with bells on the tips, and they would have jingled merrily. "You have heard rightly. What glorious news has traveled to your ears!"

"So, she is in the dungeon of the High King?"

"Yes."

"And a threat no more."

Amis halted his nodding, glad to at last correct the priest. "The High King thinks that to be true, but you must know it is not so."

"Why must I know that?"

Amis cleared his throat and deepened his voice. This was a tale of drama. "They say she is shifting all the time now, cannot hold still in the week since we bound her. Her sister roams at large. Rumors abound that she commands a fleet of pirates from the Land of Midnight. These are things that have us a bit worried, your Holiness." *Holiness*—was that the right way to address Father Iohannes? He hazarded a quick glance in Jacob's direction, but the man gave no outward sign that Amis had misstepped.

"You have, all of you, come to warn us of the threat?"

"We seek your aid, Father." Jacob spoke at last.

"Is that so?" The man's dry voice left a question of whether he understood the gravity of the situation. He should, shouldn't he? How else could he be Father Iohannes, the man who was patient, slow to act but decisive when he did? He leaned forward. "Before we go further, I would like to know your companions. Tell me why you have traveled all this way to bring news—most of which I have already heard." His words hung in the air as Jacob made the introductions.

Amis shifted on his feet, taking a deep breath. He wanted to do a flip to shake off the weight of tension, but there just wasn't room in the nave.

"And so you traveled this spring, all the way from the Northlands, to tell me of the demise of Ute, only to be stalled by her sisters. Do you know what they are now planning?" His eyes glided over the forms of the little group, resting at last on Lady Katterina, who had kept quiet so far. Amis knew that wasn't always easy for her. "Lady Katterina." His tone lowered. "We have heard of you as well. Were you not once a cat?"

"It wasn't her fault," Jacob interceded.

But Katterina stepped forward, handing Helena to her daughter. "That's not entirely true, I'm sad to say. It was my fault for betraying my sister."

"You didn't deserve to become her feline messenger." Jacob stated, but he said it while looking at Father Iohannes, as though measuring the man's reaction. The holy man gave a slow nod, his long, tapered fingers weaving themselves together as he listened. What a pair the monk and Father Iohannes made. So alike! Amis imagined the man was picturing the misadventures in his mind's eye so that he could make his judgment once they were through speaking.

Katterina was not one too shy of her past wrongs. A sly smile split her lips, and she looked at Father Iohannes, undaunted. "I freely admit to you I was the messenger that brought word of the plans from Ute to Amee, the centaur. They had me spy in different places, compelled to obey, though I did my best to cause some mischief along the way. But how could I free myself? I couldn't. It was my daughter whom God used at last to help me."

The priest inclined his head. "Magic has marked you, many of you. Perhaps that qualifies you to help destroy those who want to crush the kingdoms. But it also makes you of greater risk."

Rapunzel drew in a sharp breath, and Helena shifted with a whimper when she held her more tightly.

Amis appreciated how the priest appraised the group and then turned back to Jacob. "What is it you need?"

"The High King does not believe the sisters of sorcery are still a threat."

"Yes, well, he may be our sovereign, but I fear that prayers for moral sense on the throne will only be answered if the High Queen asserts her authority."

"Which is why we sought an audience with you," Jacob confirmed. "We know by the spiritual nature of this war, we need your help—but how do we address the royal household as to the danger?"

Father Iohannes looked much too contemplative for Amis's liking. Things were too quiet.

"What if!"

Jacob turned at Amis's interruption. "What if?"

Amis bounced in place. "Yes, what if I used my powers of storytelling?"

"What do you mean?"

"Well, Her Majesty is reasonable, isn't she?"

"Yes, but what does that have to—"

"I could go to her, tell her of the danger, you see? And then, we shall find our way to tell the High King!"

Jacob had that look on his face, and Amis laughed.

"Never mind, you don't see! It's just as Father Iohannes said, things will only turn out well if the High Queen asserts her power. I will return and get the High Queen to meet with me. Perhaps then she can even get me before the High King and tell him and everyone the story of what we have been through. The Tale of"—he searched his mind for something appropriate—"the Unlikely Rescuers." But the look on Father Iohannes's face clouded, so he explained, "Because we are told to be like Christ, are we not? So he allows us to assist in his rescue mission when we help those in need."

Father Iohannes lifted his brow. "This plan, though

simple, seems appropriate. But how will you get her to meet with any of you?" He tilted his head slightly as he gazed on Rapunzel, causing Amis to laugh.

"You've just recognized her, haven't you?"

"We met once before, haven't we, princess? Though I can't seem to recall—"

"It was right before you became the Father." Rapunzel pulled Helena's chubby hands from grabbing her blue wimple off her head. "I was at the abbey helping my mistress, Adeliza, before she gave birth. And your wounded nephew found us, and we helped him recover."

"I remember now. It was right before Father Razin died and I officially took my new orders. How strange that our paths have crossed again."

Amis clapped his hands. "Strange? Not at all. Predestined! It makes the tale that much better."

Father Iohannes almost smiled, but stopped, and his eyebrows drew down. "There is more at work here than we can understand without prayer and fasting. You will leave today. None of us will join you in traveling to the Summer Castle right now. We will remain here and continue to ask God for wisdom." Amis noted how his eyes lingered on Katterina and then back toward Jacob. "This is all I can say for now, and that you, Brother Jacob, should join us in prayer and fasting during this time."

Jacob looked as though he wanted to urge the man to take action, but he bowed with reverence. "Do you wish me to stay here?"

The priest nodded, once again looking at Lady Katterina, as though something about her was a cause for concern. Well, maybe he didn't like cats.

# THE KING'S CHALLENGE

$\mathcal{H}$e was stupidly stubborn, Gwynndolen thought to herself as she watched Edmund struggle to his place, unused to using a staff. She stood near the guards next to the door, waiting to be addressed. Formality required her to hold still and be quiet. Still and quiet? The combination felt impossible. She bit her lower lip and tried to keep from shifting. *Hold still*, she reminded herself.

High King Zakarriyya wasn't wearing his day-clothes yet, but a silk robe. Of course, he had his ornate crown perched on his head which covered much of his dark, textured hair. He had seated Edmund next to himself at the table in his personal dining room, lit by only candelabras on a serving table behind the king. Thick tapestries covered the windows to keep the light from irritating the king's notorious morning headaches, but even Gwynndolen could see the pouches beneath the king's eyes darkening his brown skin. The man looked a bit too besotted for Edmund to make much headway.

But Edmund was nothing if not stubborn.

The king stared at the prince with his watery, bloodshot eyes and then swigged the hot brew in his mug before addressing him. "We see you are healing, Prince Edmund. You might even wish to be crowned following the tournament, is that right?"

Edmund gripped the staff that Gwynndolen had found for him. "I would not presume on the kindness of the king. That is for you alone to decide, Your Majesty."

The king's face became a study of interest. He inclined slightly, a little unevenly. "What do you mean?"

Gwynndolen frowned, wondering if this was a good idea.

"Well—" Edmund plunged ahead. "I understand that you may have other ideas about my father's island."

The king laughed out loud and then shuddered at the volume of his own voice. He pushed back from the table and turned in his seat to better view Edmund. "Is that so? Our advisers tell Us We should, but Our wife, oh, Our wife, she says you would make an excellent king."

"I have learned to heed the voice of your wife."

"We usually do, but there are times a man must decide for himself." The king tugged on his robe's belt, which seemed hung up on the oversized belly. "You know, you should take care not to die in the tournament. You would leave your island without an heir."

"I have thought about this while recovering. What if, instead of fighting in the tournament myself, I were to name an heir and allow such a one to fight in my stead?"

The bland food began arriving, the smell of rice porridge and strong coffy wafting in as servants filled the room. The king pulled himself back up to the table with the help of an attendant. From the frown on the king's face, Gwynndolen surmised the noise of dishes being brought evidently jarred the king's sensitive ears. "Oh yes? An heir? We would look favorably upon such an arrangement—that is to say, We *might* look on such an arrangement with favor, should such an idea appeal to Us in reality —in the very throes of the tournament."

Edmund nodded agreeably, but Gwynndolen could not puzzle it out. What on earth was the man saying? Did he even know himself?

"Exactly, Your Majesty."

The High King looked pleased with himself and nodded for Edmund to continue.

"I would like to present my heir to the king, if it would please Your Majesty. This morning, in fact."

"He is here?" The king looked into the dark corners of the room. "We thought all those who accompanied you on the ship had died on the sea."

"All but Lady Gwynndolen."

The king's hand halted the path of his dark brew to his lips, and instead set it down, sloshing the contents on the purple table runner. "Pardon? Are you putting forward a woman as your heir? Do you think that wise, considering how fickle women are?"

"Your Highness, her ladyship is anything but fickle. We would like you to listen to her and better know for yourself what kind of woman she is."

The king blinked his dim eyes before turning his gaze on her as she stepped before the table. She tried to make the most of her height by standing up straight. Was she smiling? Gwynndolen's mother had always said she should endeavor to smile more. If she didn't, she was likely to glare.

"Why is she looking at Us in such a way?"

Oh, enough was enough! Gwynndolen was tired of

having others speak on her behalf. "I beg Your pardon, Your Highness. My mother says that if I'm not careful, my face forgets to smile."

"Not becoming in a lady of the court."

"Perhaps not, but in an heir to a kingdom beneath the watchful gaze of Your Highness, it might be best." Where had that come from? Was she learning to speak more diplomatically from Edmund?

The king laughed and then took another long gulp from his mug. He had yet to eat the mushy rice that filled his trencher, but moved it around with his spoon. "You know, We hate morning chats. We can barely stomach them, but Our wife insisted on this one. There have been many things We have refused her of late, but speaking with the two of you has been something We've been glad to have agreed to. So you want to fight in the prince's stead? Unusual, though not unheard of. You know, We don't favor women ruling, much less fighting. We've had too many trying to rule Us, you know."

How could she answer that? She almost nodded, but saw Edmund give a slight shake of his head. "I'm sorry, Your Majesty. I don't know what you mean . . ." Her voice trailed, and she tried to smile again. Perhaps time to change the subject? "My father always saw promise in me, and when he became ill, I cared for and trained our horses so that they could continue in Your service. My regret for this summer is not being able to bring you the steeds our kingdom promised."

He waved this away as though it was of no matter. "You have more horses at home."

She swallowed. Those horses were spoken for, but of course His Majesty would have what he wanted.

"When you return to your island, you will send them to Us."

She nodded, hoping no pirates would come in the way of yet another shipload of horses.

"So, you are to be heir? Does that mean you will marry Prince Edmund?"

"I—yes," she stumbled, as her cheeks heated.

He laughed. "Marriage is fraught with things you can't plan for, things you can't see. What We will do is this— bless your marriage to the prince. We will then allow you to fight the tournament for your island. Win, and We will crown him and yourself. Lose, and things will go differently." He held up both hands as though to hold them off. "Do not try to change Our mind on this. Only Our wife gets to do that." At this, the king chortled.

"I have no intention of changing your mind, Your Majesty. I think your plan a grand one." She tried not to notice the pinch between Edmund's eyebrows. "But if the tournament should be delayed—"

The king's brow creased. "Delayed? Why should there be a delay? We will have the tournament when We have said! The christening will be in a week's time, and then the tournament. Woe to those who have not come to attend to Our affairs this summer!"

It was nearing evening again when Camilla abandoned hope of finding the power she needed in the depths. Light from the surface had dimmed the topmost waters, but when she broke the surface, the sky was lit with a brilliant sunset, blazing orange and gold. For a moment, she gazed at the colors, wishing they could infuse her with the power she needed. She floated on the waves, letting the tendrils of her tentacles reach out, searching, seeking any little inkling of an energy source that could rejuvenate her.

There. But was it close enough to harness? Did she have the strength to . . .? But she would push herself. She must. Dipping just barely into the waters again, she found a current and let it pull her along its aquatic tunnel. The last bit of the way she had to swim, but at least the current had allowed her to save enough of her energy that she found the strength to transform back into a woman.

"Ahoy!" Her deep voice rang out into the gathering dark.

A lantern lit and came over to the side. She could barely make out the face of a woman peering down at her. "Who are you?" the pirate's voice grated.

"Camilla, now drop me the ladder."

Nothing more needed to be said. The ladder rolled down, and she climbed up as the waters splashed against the hull.

The pirate queen, Hadijah, was at the helm, as she had been the first time Camilla had met her. The woman stood tall, though not as tall as Camilla. Her nearly black skin would blend into any night. She was considered "pure," her blood never mixed with those outside of the Land of Midnight. Camilla appreciated that these women regarded their race as untainted, but she needed to teach them to bend, or they would never work well with Amee's covens from the Eastern Ports. And she needed them to work together.

"What do you want?" Hadijah snarled, and Camilla smiled. Yes, here was the attitude that would aid their cause.

"Have you enjoyed the plunder I allowed you to discover at sea?"

"The Ronan king's ship had mostly horses, not much booty. I lost more of my sailors than it was worth."

"I saved your life and gave you a new ship, a new crew, and even more treasure than you imagined."

Hadijah's eyes shifted away for a moment, then locked back on Camilla's. "I've been wanting to ask why you did that."

"Because I need you to command these ships. Block the port entry once all the kingdoms' ships have arrived. No ships will leave and seek reinforcements, you understand?"

"Trapping the kings and princes in one grand castle? Are you planning a siege after all?"

"So much more than that."

The whites of Hadijah's eyes glittered. Her white teeth seemed to snap. "Good. I hate the High King and his kind."

Camilla rubbed her hands together and then stopped. She steadied herself with a breath and lowered her voice. "There's something else I need."

"What is it?"

"I will move my sister's covens to meet with all of my people. We will come together before you move to block in the ships."

"By 'all of my people,' you mean us pirates, don't you?"

Camilla looked up at the sky, now glowing a deep purple with pinpricks of stars. She turned back to Hadijah. "You are mine, aren't you? I provided for you, gave you the cure so that you could live. Before me, you had nothing."

Hadijah gave a firm nod, but Camilla could see it did

not thrill her to owe her life to anyone. Camilla could understand and use that.

"Whom did the plague hit hardest?"

"What do you mean?"

"And whom did my cure help most?"

Hadijah's eyes hardened. "Those strong enough to follow you."

"And those you couldn't save? What have you done with the weak ones?"

The pirate queen shrugged, refusing to meet Camilla's gaze any longer, but Camilla stepped closer.

"Tell me."

"Don't you think we left the weak at home in the Land of Midnight?"

Camilla lifted Hadijah's chin and breathed the words into the woman's face. "I don't. Don't you think I know you and your superstitions by now? I know you brought the ones hit hardest with you."

"What does it matter to you?"

"I need power, more than I have now in order to bring our forces together—and I don't have long. You will supply that power."

The pirate queen didn't speak, but gave another tiny nod. Camilla stepped back, and the pirate queen snapped her fingers. A younger pirate came to take over at the helm. Camilla followed the queen belowdecks and found, to her delight, a new source of power.

# MISGIVINGS

The trip back to the Summer Castle was uneventful, which should have heartened Rapunzel, but it didn't. As soon as she had returned, the head housekeeper had reminded the princess that one of her duties was to select a maidservant.

Rapunzel knew duty must be dealt with, but first, a walk for her little one. She roamed the outer gardens with her mother and Helena, marveling at the vibrant colors of the Eastern Ports. She hadn't seen such colors since she was a little girl and the witch worked her magic in their Northland garden. Helena lunged for a bright orange blossom blooming between bright green stalk-like canna leaves. Rapunzel pulled Helena back and wondered if she should take the little girl with her. Did selecting a maidservant even matter right now?

"There is a sorceress beneath the castle, another roaming about somewhere planning our demise, and Father Iohannes won't come to talk the High King into taking action. Instead, here we are. Just acting as if this is a normal summer gathering, a time to discuss the cut of our dresses while the men speak of trade agreements between kingdoms. Isn't it ridiculous?" She frowned at her mother.

Katterina's mouth tipped up, and her un-plucked eyebrows lifted.

"What?" Rapunzel looked over at one guard who seemed like he was lounging rather than guarding. "It makes me so—so frustrated! You know what? I could scream."

Katterina smirked. "Except you won't."

Rapunzel scowled. But she knew her mother was right. She shifted Helena's weight to her opposite hip.

"You are a princess, about to be crowned queen, and though you might deny it, you have responsibilities. Set down Helena and go select a maid."

Rapunzel huffed a laugh as she set the child down next to a bench. Katterina bent down and held out her hands. Helena stretched out one hand toward her and teetered on chubby legs. "I know you're right, but it all seems pointless in the face of—well—everything." She swallowed, hoping no one had overheard her tirade. But no, the guard was watching a dragonfly buzz over the pond's surface.

Why was it so hard to calm down? Usually, she kept such heated thoughts to herself. Smoothing her dress as she sat, a small smile played around the corners of her mouth. Too bad Lady Gwynndolen wasn't nearby. She would have encouraged Rapunzel to scream.

"Well, it will suit me much better, knowing you won't be asking for help with your hair or your gowns anymore. You don't want the War of Sorcery to begin again while your hair is such a mess, right?"

"Mother."

Katterina laughed. They just weren't the sort of women to worry over such details. "Rapunzel, I know you don't want to do it, but if you allow yourself to find a trustworthy maidservant, maybe even a lady-in-waiting, they can help guide you during your time at court."

"I'm not sure it works that way. I think you have to grow up with ladies and then select one. But, you know I did not." She took in a deep breath, imagining for just a moment the isolation of her tower from days gone by. How her life had changed from one of solitude, to one of service, and now to one of the state. She felt cold despite the warm humidity of the garden. Would people know just by looking at her she was common born? "I used to be a maidservant, Mother. Surely all who meet me here will know that."

Katterina glanced up from watching Helena's wobbly steps. The little girl finally landed on her backside and abandoned walking for her speedy bear-crawl across the bright green moss. "Perhaps—or perhaps they will know how you heroically helped defeat Ute and how you escaped the power of a witch who had imprisoned you most of your life. Your life is much more interesting than the lives of most of the ladies and princesses and queens about. Besides, the High Queen herself wants us to meet with her. How many of these nobles can claim her personal acquaintance?"

Rapunzel looked away.

"What? What's wrong?"

"She has every right to ask me to attend her, but I have no desire to be in that woman's presence. There is something about her . . ."

Katterina laughed. "There is!" Helena sat down and laughed along as though she agreed. "I know exactly what you mean, though I can't quite put it into words. But, you aided her, aided her entire house when you solved the mystery of the tattered slippers. And if you have aided the queen, she is in your debt."

Rapunzel shrugged.

"Don't worry about that yet. We will go together when it is time. But first, go select your maidservant. And don't worry about Helena here with me, she and I will have such fun!"

Rapunzel shot a glance behind her as she made herself leave. She trusted her mother to take great care of Helena, but some weight pushed upon her heart at the thought of leaving her little one behind. When she had gone to rescue Jacob and Amis in the marsh, she had left Helena behind with her mother to keep the little girl safe. But in her heart, she didn't want to let her go again. The child had been through so much, too much, and only Rapunzel understood what that was like. Only Rapunzel could care for Helena the way the girl needed.

DIETZ STEPPED FORWARD, his staff crashing into Paul's, but he yelped in surprise when Paul's pole slid upward and Dietz's fingers got crunched.

Paul halted the training bout. "Are you—"

"I-I'm fine!" He jerked his staff back toward his mentor, hoping to shake off the sting.

But Paul was ready for him, feinting to the side and letting Dietz stumble forward, his staff useless. It might as well have been a walking stick for the good it was doing him this morning.

"Dietz, let's st—"

But Dietz spun around, trying to use his staff to trip the prince.

He heard the prince sigh as he stepped out of the way, and with a quick move of his own, tripped Dietz. "Stop."

Dietz jumped up, heat filling his face. The temptation to ground himself and pull energy up from the earth—

He dropped his staff. Bending over to pick it up, he wondered where that thought had come from. Using magic to manipulate and get ahead of his enemy wasn't something he wanted to do anymore. He shook his head. What was he thinking? This was Paul. Paul wasn't his enemy. Paul had never embarrassed him before. If he was doing it now—

"Dietz, are you all right?"

Dietz shook his head again, trying to clear it of the strange longing to feel as powerful as he had when he was learning sorcery. For just a moment, it was as though he could hear voices from his past—the voices of his coven brothers mocking him. The only thing that had shut their mouths was when he commanded the power from deep below. "I-I'm fine," he lied.

Paul reached over and rubbed his head playfully. "Sometimes it's hard to learn how to handle yourself with a weapon in hand while you're still growing into your full size. But don't worry, you'll probably be as large as I am in time, perhaps bigger."

Dietz wanted to smile at this, but couldn't quite manage it.

"C'mon, let's put these away and go for a ride."

"A ride?"

"Yes, a ride. To help clear your head."

The young man shook his head. He needed to practice his form. "I c-can control my frustration, I c-can!"

Paul put his hand on Dietz's shoulder, so much thinner and narrower than Paul's. "Of course I know you can, but sometimes it helps to have a change of pace. Come with me."

Dietz followed Paul, putting away the staff in the armory and heading to the stables. Paul wasn't much older or taller than Dietz, but he was stronger, sharper, smarter. He had once confided in Dietz of his own troubles with his family, how he had struggled with anger toward his own father. Could this man help Dietz sort through his own inner mess?

The High King's stables were massive, and the open stall doors wafted the sharp scent of manure and hay. The stable hands were quick to attend them. Soon they were on horseback, walking alongside each other. "I found a spot that's good for just running—follow me." And quickly the two of them were cantering side by side through the grounds specially laid so they would not sink into the marshy land of the Eastern Ports. Here it was safe for knights to exercise their horses.

Dietz focused on the rhythm of the hooves beating the ground beneath him. *Th-th-thump-th-th-thump-th-th-thump.* His body moved as though it was one with the horse, leaving no room to think of sorcery or mothers who betrayed their children. Dietz pulled back on his reins when he realized Paul was stopping. He looked up into the crystal blue sky, where the sun had lowered past midday. The horse was thoroughly lathered. He should have been paying better attention. He followed Paul at a trot over to the trough where the horses could drink. "Do you feel better?" Paul was patting his horse, but he looked at Dietz with concern.

Dietz nodded. He still didn't have words for his pain, for his fear. But Paul seemed to understand. He wouldn't make him talk before he was ready.

"You know you aren't alone. We think of you as part of our company. If you need something, we will take care of you."

Take care of him. There was always someone having to care for him. But he should be a man, he should be— He gripped the horn of his saddle, the lack of words and the inability to communicate the gnarled frustrations rooted deep inside him. A vice of pain clamped around his head, a piercing needle in the back of his left eye. He was wrong. Paul couldn't understand. No one could.

# EXPECTATIONS

Rapunzel sighed. It was time to act the part of a noblewoman—a queen, in fact! But her hip felt unbalanced without the weight of Helena. She straightened her back. There was no time for weak thoughts. She had gladly chosen Paul and therefore the life before her.

A steward directed her to a wide hall with a vast, brightly threaded tapestry depicting a great hunt. Beneath it stood a few women speaking in low tones. She wanted to walk away before they noted her, but she refused to play the coward. She forced a smile to her mouth and stepped forward, wishing she had brought her mother with her.

Katterina had never met a stranger, of course, and she didn't seem to mind whether anyone liked her. So why did Rapunzel care so much? Why couldn't she simply be grateful for the life she had chosen and remember that when all this was said and done, she would return home safely with her child and her husband?

Of course, that was if they could stay out of harm's way.

She suppressed a smile. Since she had left behind her

tower, she had never stayed out of trouble for more than a few months at a time, even before she had knowledge of the sorcery that entangled the kingdoms.

"I'm sorry, what is your name?" a dark woman in a black cotehardie and purple surcoat asked Rapunzel in Latin, snapping her attention back to the task at hand.

"I am Princess Rapunzel from the Northlands."

"Ah, yes, I'm Luciana. We have matched you with a maidservant we think will suit your needs as you visit with us. It will be easy for you to see if she serves you well. If she does not, we will find another for you. She'll be here momentarily. But first, let me introduce you."

Rapunzel looked at the other women. Neither of them was the maidservant—that had been clear by their lovely silk dresses of bright yellow and green. So why were they here?

Luciana retained her crisp reserve with a frosty smile. "Your Highness, both of the women you see before you are nobles of lesser households. They are ladies-in-waiting, quite ready to wait on and help you. Your king was most insistent that you get to know other nobles who would be amenable to your particular upbringing, those who understand how the court works and can guide you through proceedings. If you suit each other, they too can return home with you and serve you in the Northlands."

Rapunzel's stomach fluttered. "You have chosen these women to guide me?"

"Yes. Princess Rapunzel, Lady Bazzu," she said, gesturing to a dark-complected woman whose textured hair was oiled and braided into a crown around her head. She was wearing yellow gowns that were enhanced with embroidery, but she did not wear the jewels Rapunzel had seen on so many other noblewomen. Her broad smile stunned Rapunzel with her gleaming rows of white teeth. As she gave a deep curtsy, Rapunzel attempted a smile.

"Princess Rapunzel, Lady Florese." This woman was taller and of a lighter skin tone, with liquid brown eyes that did not light with a smile when she gave her short curtsy, her light green dresses barely touching the ground as she bent. Her hair was smooth, also pulled back into a braided crown. Rapunzel almost touched her wimple, self-conscious about what expectations were concerning the hair that had constantly been a struggle for her to maintain. "They will dine with you and help you so that by week's end you can join the rest of the court in the Great Hall at mealtime."

"But I already attended mealtime before I left for the monastery."

"Yes, well, that shouldn't have happened, and I apologize. It was only recently brought to my attention that you were not born and raised as a princess. No one faults you, but we have precious little time to rectify things before the royals finish gathering for the christening and tournament.

"The Ladies Bazzu and Florese will help you walk and talk with grace so that we can present you before the court." The woman paused momentarily, looking her over. "They won't have much to do in that regard, as you already hold yourself quite well." But then she frowned, dismissing her own compliment as she went on, "That will leave more time for the most important bit of all, knowing how to conduct yourself during the tournament itself."

"During the tournament itself," Rapunzel repeated, her mind grasping for understanding. "Don't I just watch?"

Lady Florese took a step forward. Had she had eyebrows, they would have shot straight up, judging by the wrinkles that appeared in her forehead. "Of course not. A princess never just watches. She knows what is polite to comment on and how to show her preference at the appropriate time."

Rapunzel felt her shoulders round, but she fought the shrinking feeling. "My preference is for my husband. I will show him that when I speak with him to encourage him to do well."

Lady Florese sniffed, but Lady Bazzu, coming closer, patted Rapunzel on the arm. "There is so much more than that, especially since you will be Queen of the Day in less than a fortnight."

"Queen of what?"

"Oh, this will be a treat!" The lady nearly clapped her hands in delight. "Queen of the Day! And you will knight one victor from among the young lords."

"I thought only a lord or king could knight—"

Luciana shook her head. "This is why we will advise you. We know you need guidance. You don't know what to expect or what is expected. You don't want to bring dishonor to your husband's family or the kingdom, do you?"

Rapunzel shuddered at the thought. Still, shouldn't it matter more who she was and how she loved her family rather than polite decorum? She couldn't imagine that the Fisher King had desired they speak to her in such a way.

Or had she been displeasing him with her coarse manners and ignorance all along?

Rapunzel blanched at this speculation. His wife had died long ago and so the princess had never gotten to meet her. If Rapunzel were to be the next queen, they would compare her with the woman and all the other queens attending the tournament. People would desire certain things from her. The thought made her want to run back to the gardens and cuddle her daughter.

Why couldn't Paul have been a simple hunter?

Nofra entered the hall quietly, her feet making no sound on the stone floors. It helped her remember why she was there to have her hair down, no longer braided in the style of the coven. She stood in the shadows and flipped a curled lock back over her shoulder. Now she was a servant to the princess and a spy for Camilla.

Watching the princess for another moment, she took her measure. The young white woman seemed frail, uncertain. Look how she bowed her head as the ladies began advising her! Camilla said it would be easy to ingratiate herself to the young woman, and Nofra realized that was an understatement.

Keeping her head bowed in subservience, she stepped forward to show she was ready.

Luciana clapped her hands together once. "Ah! Your maidservant is here, princess! Now, she will prepare you. I believe you and your mother will attend the High Queen later this week?"

"Yes." Even with her eyes lowered, Nofra could tell the princess was uncomfortable. What must it be like for her to have lived such a strange life? First imprisoned in a tower, but now surrounded by those of the highest station, with the highest expectations? A shadow of a frown hovered near her own lips. Perhaps she and the princess had something in common. Nofra understood what it was to be ill-used, didn't she?

"Now the Fisher King has done well with your clothing, but your head must be uncovered here in the Eastern Ports, ready to accept your crown. Nofra knows our ways and will help you. Take her now and attend to the lessons when Lady Bazzu and Lady Florese meet with you. I will send a servant to collect you and your mother when the time has come for your attendance with Her Majesty."

Nofra trailed after Rapunzel, impressed at how efficiently the young woman navigated the massive castle back to the guest chambers. She must have a wonderful sense of direction. Once the princess entered her chambers, Nofra realized they were not alone. Katterina was playing on a grey rug with a toddler.

"Mother, may I introduce you to Nofra, my new maidservant?"

Nofra curtsied, but looked up in time to see how Katterina would receive her. Would she be able to sense Nofra's duplicity?

For a moment, Katterina appeared cat-like and sniffed the air as she rose to her feet, but then the woman swayed, eyes unfocused for a moment. Rapunzel reached out to steady her. "Thank you! That was odd." But she laughed, dismissing the wobble. "Nofra, we are so glad to have you. I'm afraid you'll see why I'm so glad in a moment's time. Rapunzel, show her your hair."

Rapunzel sat down at the dressing table before the silver glass and uncovered a mass of tangled curls.

Nofra didn't mean to gasp, but as soon as she did, Katterina chuckled. "What happened?" Nofra asked.

The princess could not meet Nofra's eyes in the reflection. Instead, she stared down at her hands clasped together. "Well, I had a maidservant quite a while back, but then I lost her. And I could take care of my hair for a time, but I think I forgot to care for it on my journey here.

I was too busy tending my daughter. I used to have such long hair and kept it in a long braid. I had so much time to care for it, but now—well, it was easier to just cover it while traveling through Alleria and put off worrying about it till later."

Nofra stepped forward and put a comforting hand on the princess's shoulders. Inwardly, she scorned the pitiful creature. What kind of woman, much less royalty, didn't keep up with her appearance? Wasn't that a chief concern of any queen? Her eyes tallied the princess's features. Rapunzel had light skin and emerald eyes, a slender form that was quite becoming. But her hair! Her hair was coarse and curly, so thick Nofra wondered if she could even find a way to pick through it in a few hours' time.

"I hadn't noticed what a mess it was until we arrived in the High King's court and I sat in front of this beautiful mirror. I mean, I knew it was a little unkempt."

Did Katterina snort? Nofra tried to keep a straight face. "Well, there isn't much I can do to make this easier, but I know a great deal about caring for thick, curly hair." She pulled a lock of textured curls over her own shoulder. "I know our hair isn't exactly the same, but you still must keep up with it daily."

Rapunzel nodded, as though receiving a reprimand.

Nofra frowned. "But that's no judgment on you, princess. You simply should have had someone attending to you all this time. And perhaps someone to care for your daughter so that you could—"

"I alone care for my daughter."

Nofra removed her hand and stepped back in surprise at the hardness in Rapunzel's eyes.

"I'm sorry, it's just that my daughter needs me. No servant, no matter how wonderful, could replace me."

But Katterina came over and knelt beside the princess, taking one of her daughter's hands in her own. "I know you don't want to hear it, Rapunzel, but even good mothers receive help. No one is trying to take her away from you."

Nofra glimpsed the pink hue that filled the young woman's pale cheeks. Weighted silence filled the chamber. "Shall I begin, Your Highness? I would like to have you looking your best when the ladies come to meet with you."

Rapunzel turned back to the looking glass and flashed a grateful smile at her. Dear! Was the princess so change-able? Camilla would be interested in hearing about Rapunzel's state of mind. If she could just earn the woman's trust.

# THE CAT AND THE MONK

Katterina wound her way down the stone staircase into the bowels of the castle, following the flaming torch she held ahead of her. The guard—if the inattentive attendant could even be called that—had paid her no mind when she announced she needed to see the prisoner. He had simply yawned, opened the door, and given her the torch. Shadows scurried away from her as she descended, even as the smell of damp and urine rose. Was it wise to travel down into the dungeon alone? Katterina knew it probably wasn't, but she did it anyway. Something in her spirit compelled her to come, leaving Rapunzel to her maidservant's ministrations.

Amee was part woman, part monster. Her streaked-grey hair was limp, her long neck and torso covered in fine fur, her hind end reptilian. Katterina placed the torch in its iron ring at the bottom of the stairs, staying well away from the invisible wall that the name of Jesu had bound Amee behind.

"Have you come to mock me?" Amee's voice trembled with fatigue, and Katterina held a hand to her chest where her heart was aching. This woman—was she still a woman?—was so lost.

Katterina cleared her throat, thinking of how easy it had been to find her way down here. No one knew where she was; no one really needed her. Once again, she wondered why she had left behind the Northlands to come to this grand castle. Her daughter had wanted her, but she felt useless now that Jacob was no longer with them. "I came to see."

A shimmer wavered over Amee's body as it transformed into some sort of winged creature, but the reptilian tail remained.

"I think that will prove cumbersome during flight," she said, pointing.

"So, you came to mock."

"No, I—"

"What then?"

"I didn't know you had children." She licked her lips. "Before, when I was bringing messages to you from Ute and Eufemia, back when I was Cat, I didn't know about your sons. I just thought you were a monster. Like my sister had become."

Amee's tone was flat. "Look at me—I am a monster."

"No more than I."

The creature jerked her head up and opened her beak with a shrill cry. The sound bounced off the walls, but no guard came down to check on them. "Stop it! We are nothing alike."

Katterina put her hands in her pockets, but pulled them back out and rubbed them together. "I think we are. I think you are a prisoner in the same way I was a prisoner. Sin is a strange thing. You think you want something, and while you're reaching for it, you hurt someone." She couldn't tell if the mother before her understood. Was she stupid to try to reach her? "Your sisters, they were hungry for more and more power. Maybe you were too. But you're a mother. That changes a woman, doesn't it?"

The creature didn't reply, but she didn't move away or morph into something more hideous. She actually held still.

"It's something I learned, about the way God made women. After sin entered the world, we were cursed, but there was a seed of blessing in it. God makes us mothers, and he uses that to transform us. In a way, God used my daughter to rescue me, change how I understood him and the world. Perhaps he will—"

"Don't!" Amee croaked. "Don't give me hope. My son hates me. He *hates* me. And he should. God would never want to save me, not after all I've done."

"I once thought that, too. But you see—"

Amee shook and shriveled into the form of an old woman. "Please stop!" She wept, and then howled, pushing herself forward as though to rush at Katterina. But she hit the invisible wall and fell backward. "Leave me now!"

Katterina backed away, but before turning she spoke her prayer: "May God change your heart."

JACOB KNELT ALONE in the nave in quiet prayer. His body craved food, but he pushed it away from his thoughts. In the stillness, his spirit stirred, searching for some inkling of what God wanted. Scriptures reminded him of what God desired: for a man to have a thankful heart, to be a cheerful giver, to do justly, love mercy, and walk humbly with God.

But in this moment, with a sorceress set loose on their world and a king ignoring the danger, what would God desire of them? Surely God would speak to them soon in that inaudible way he had. Jacob had heard it before, as though with an inner ear. Soon God would guide him in how to convince the High King—

"Brother Jacob, there is something I must speak with you about."

Jacob looked up, surprised he hadn't heard Father Iohannes's approach. The older man was standing next to him, his shoulders, once broad and straight, now slightly curved by age and the cares of his station. Jacob stood and followed Father Iohannes into the pews. Father Iohannes motioned the monk to sit on one end while he sat on the other, and they turned on the hard wood to face one another.

"Have you heard from God about—"

Father Iohannes held up his hand. "It is a personal matter we must discuss."

Jacob kept his face blank, but leaned forward.

Father Iohannes attempted a smile, and his deep voice was gentle. "You have been gone from us for a long time, my son."

Jacob nodded.

"Is it good to return to the Brotherhood?"

Jacob nodded again.

"And yet . . .?" The man appeared to be waiting for Jacob to say something, but Jacob could think of nothing to complete the sentence that hung in the air between them.

"I don't understand. Have I done something wrong?"

"I can't say. Do you feel as though you have?"

Jacob shook his head slowly. "I have done nothing against our Lord and Savior."

"But what of the Brotherhood? What of your vows?"

Jacob looked up, but said nothing.

"It is a conversation I have with all those we send out into the world. The accountability that we who live cloistered together experience is largely lacking from your life. There are many who fall away into temptation. Some who even willfully pursue a life of sin."

Jacob continued to sit in silence, and the older man nodded at him.

"I do not mean to imply that you have given in to a life of sin, but it is important that we must each search and purify ourselves during this time of fasting and prayer in order to be pure vessels to follow God into the battle ahead. It is time to answer some very hard questions." He folded his hands in his lap together, steepling his index fingers.

"I see."

"Have you looked out for the oppressed while you've been away, or have you become an oppressor?"

Jacob thought through his life in the Northlands. He had helped the Fisher King develop a more charitable heart toward those struggling in his kingdom. They had given the poor bread after Mass each day, and the taxes had decreased. "I have championed the downtrodden, but I am certain I can always do more."

Father Iohannes nodded with a smile. "Yes, my son, as can we all. Have you given of what you have, freely, to God and the Church, or have you coveted, in your heart of hearts, the gold of your betters?"

Jacob weighed his heart. "Sometimes I did long for

more for myself, but God is good and showed me how to give him that desire and rejoice in what I had."

"I appreciate your honesty, brother." He nodded to himself, tapping together his long, tan index fingers before turning his eyes back on Jacob. "Finally, as to your vow of chastity, have you kept yourself from all women and devoted yourself only to God, even in your heart?"

Jacob had known the question was coming from the moment Father Iohannes had looked on Katterina. "Though I have not physically given into temptation, my heart now belongs to the Lady Katterina."

Father Iohannes sat up straighter. "Have you told her this?"

"No."

Father Iohannes's face was somber, eyes downcast for a moment. "I was afraid something like this had occurred," he said at last. "It happens to more of our brothers than we like to admit." Then he lifted his eyes to Jacob, the lines in his forehead pressing up. "You must purge these feelings, lest you act on them and leave God behind."

Jacob looked away. "In the Bible it says that it is not good for man to be alone, and this was why our God created woman, for man, from man, was it not?"

Father Iohannes held up a hand. "You must not forget that the apostle Paul also spoke that it was good that people be as he was, chaste and free to serve God alone. The coming of the Christ set many of us apart to live such lives in service to God alone, and not to be divided by the care of a wife and children. You have taken a vow of chastity, brother, and you must honor that vow."

"Would God want me to honor the vow if I took it without comprehending his mercy and forgiveness? I took that vow in the wake of discovering about my mother's sin in practicing sorcery. Looking back I can see I was young and naïve, trying to earn my salvation and hers by taking that vow."

Father Iohannes's lips thinned for a moment. "I—I did not know that."

"Nor did I. I was ashamed, so inexperienced with his love and grace, I thought only of his judgment."

"But Christ came to set us free of the sins of past generations."

"He has made that clear to me, but I did not grasp that then."

Father Iohannes shook his head. "This does not change the fact that you made a vow to God. And you know that the Scriptures say you must honor the vows you make before God."

Jacob looked into the eyes of Father Iohannes, wishing he did not have to admit his weakness. "I know—but the Apostle Paul also said it was better to marry than to burn with passion."

Silence filled the nave.

"No wonder the Lord has not spoken. How can you hear him above your sin?"

Jacob looked down at his own hands, unable to meet the gaze of his mentor. "The love I hold for the Lady Katterina is not a sin."

Father Iohannes shook his head. "Brother Jacob, I fear for your soul. You must recommit yourself, put this—*love*, as you call it—away from you. Fast more, pray harder, that you may purge yourself. Only then can you hear from our Lord and Savior. Only then will you know what he is saying." The man stood and placed a hand on Jacob. "We will redouble our prayers for you as well."

# DARKNESS MEETS

amilla watched as the pirates came ashore, lowering smaller boats from the side of the seafaring vessels. The sharp tang of salt air filled her nostrils as Amee's covens left behind the trees to fill the shoreline, also watching the pirates. When the sisters had reunited in the spring, Camilla had looked forward to this day, when they would finally unify her pirates with Amee's covens. Convincing Mauro and the other coven leaders throughout the marsh that it was necessary to come together had been more difficult than Camilla had at first realized. Without the centralizing figure of Amee to guide them, the covens scattered, as though they had lost sight of their purpose. Would they give up and settle for practicing their sorcery in secret in the marsh, as they had for the last fifty years? Camilla shook her head. She would bring them together, convince them of their need for the freedom to do as they pleased.

Now that they were gathering on the shores of Pelmont, Camilla watched as the pirates came forward, sloshing through the waves to stand and stare. Such an odd combination of magic-wielding warriors, having a similar purpose, but untrusting. She turned to face the crowds gathered, musing how the heritage of these darker-skinned peoples was similar—but could she teach them who they could become *together*?

The sound of the breaking waves receded as she focused on the task before her. If only her weak sister had focused, had not lost sight of what was most important. How was she to find the power she needed to win this war with such a divided force? She wanted to laugh at the absurdity, but it really wasn't funny.

Hadijah walked over to Camilla, staring down her nose at Mauro. Her harsh voice rang out and seemed to startle the man. "This is who you would have us align with?"

"You know the ways of the sea, but they know the secrets of the lowlands and the marsh. There are forces here they have been gathering to prepare for the war. They have spies within the High King's castle who report on all the kingdoms who are arriving, even now. Treasures are being brought into the High King's storehouses, and soon, they will be ready for us to blockade them."

Camilla knew that Hadijah's clipped nod was a sign of respect. The woman's words also held a trace of excitement as she murmured, "Then, we will destroy them without losing all the plunder."

Camilla laughed. "They will be at our mercy and will have to agree to our terms."

The old man stared hard at Camilla. "And will we be rescuing your sister from the enemy's dungeon when we take the castle?"

Camilla stared at Mauro, Amee's loyal servant. How

simple he was. How blunt, like a man. His wrinkled eyes blinked at her, his dark skin contrasting with the whites of his eyes. Now that Amee was a prisoner, Camilla could see he imagined he understood what they needed to reignite and win the war.

Her lips split into a snarl. "My sister who betrayed us? My sister, who should die in the pit?" She laughed, her throaty cackle disturbing causing an uneasy ripple in her sister's followers. Good. They didn't need to love her, they needed to fear her. "We will not free her, but we will take hold of her. She is a power source that I must tap into if we are to make headway with the forces."

The man's mouth opened. But Camilla would book no opposition. "Amee taught you to sacrifice and then did not complete her own sacrifice. Did she share with you what she had done long ago to her firstborn son?" Camilla looked the man in the eye. "No. She trusted none of you."

Camilla turned to face the crowds on the marshy banks of the southern Illyan Sea and raised her voice. "Amee doesn't deserve your loyalty. Why all this effort if we do not see it through? We will find our way, together, but only once we have secured the forces we need." Her voice resounded. She would convince them she was as strong as she needed to be. But she wasn't. Camilla would need more sacrifices to replenish her strength. When she had those, then she could strike and at last access the power that had eluded her all of her life. The power her sister had been too weak-minded to attain.

*Little Sister, succumbing to the temptations of motherhood, risking all we have fought for.* Camilla wished she could simply leave her sister forever to languish in the dungeon. But need was driving her to desperation.

Is this what Ute would have done? Did it even matter? Camilla flung the thoughts from her mind and instead thought of her father, the Grand Sorcerer. He had taken what he needed, supplemented by the strength of the three sisters for the war. Perhaps they had been too hasty in dividing themselves from his power after all. If only she could go back, could keep them from rebelling against him. They could have had victory fifty years ago, rid the land of the hateful god that missionaries from the Land of Midnight had brought so long ago.

But what they had done was past. As the pirates from the Land of Midnight had cast off the weak god, so would they. She could not go back and change the past; she could only move forward. Without the help of her sisters. With only herself to rely on, she would fuse the covens from the swamps with the pirate women and at last claim victory.

Mauro need not know it, but she had plans for Amee. She would find her way to Amee when it was time. She would. And begin what would give them everything they needed to win the war at last.

GWYNNDOLEN LAUGHED RIGHT out at the princess, not helping Rapunzel at all. "You look terrified. There is nothing to worry over, Princess. You will do well, you know you will! You have a husband who loves you and a king who believes you can do this."

"Yes, he believes it so readily that I'm to be trained right here and now."

Rapunzel sat in the chair opposite her friend, her scalp still sore from Nofra's combing. No matter how gentle the maid had been, it had still hurt and taken till the midday meal to get through first the bath and then the knots and tangles. Then, of course, her ladies-in-waiting had corrected every bite she took while served in her private chambers.

She was leaning too far forward, then she was sitting too far back, then she was sitting too rigidly. Rapunzel had barely eaten anything with the ladies looking on. How on earth was she going to master the art of eating correctly by the week's end? It only made matters worse with Helena sitting nearby, smacking at her food and making a mess. The ladies clucked their tongues, reminding her she should have brought a nurse for her daughter. But the princess wanted to care for Helena's needs herself, even though she suspected Nofra would love to help.

By the end of the meal, she was more agitated than ever. Why had no one ever told her before she needed correction? Surely the summer she spent in Rona traveling with Prince Edmund's family, she should have learned to do better.

Her stomach churned, but not from hunger. The entire day felt a mess to Rapunzel. Possibly the complete trip. And how selfish was she being right now? Gwynndolen had barely asked how she was doing when Rapunzel felt the need to launch into her own troubles. Great friend she was being, always thinking of herself.

She looked around the room at the gauzy netting draped over the bedposts, so different from the heavy blue curtains that were in her chambers at home. Little Helena was now sound asleep in the middle of the enormous bed, surrounded by pillows, the sight filled Rapunzel with a homesick feeling.

Her one moment of calm, of doing something right,

had been to sing to her little one. Strains of the song God had helped her rewrite filled her mind:


*ACCEPT HIS PEACE, it is yours my child,*
   *As long as you keep the truth . . .*


AND HELENA DID LOOK as though she had accepted his peace; it was Rapunzel who was struggling. If only she could be in the Northlands, singing her to sleep there, at home.

Home. She really thought of the Northlands as *home.* How long till she could return there with her husband and child? Her throat tightened at the thought.

"But . . .?"

She looked up, confusion distracting her from the sudden pang of longing. "I'm sorry?"

"You were going to say, 'But . . .'"

Was she? What had she been about to say? "I just—I don't know what's expected of me. Or what I should expect of others. But I want Paul to rule successfully—I don't want to embarrass him or the kingdom when he's crowned."

At this, Gwynndolen giggled. "I have worried about this very thing, myself."

"That you would dishonor your family?"

"No, the kingdom of Rona—!" She clamped a hand over her mouth.

"Why would you be an embarrassment to the kingdom of—wait! What happened while we were with Father Iohannes?"

"Well, I got Edmund to agree not to fight in the tournament—"

"That's wonderful! We worried about—"

"—as long as I agree to marry him."

"Wait, what?"

"And the High King will crown Edmund, as long as I win a competition in the tournament."

Rapunzel blinked. "I don't understand—you marry Edmund, then fight, then the High King crowns Edmund? I'm really not sure that I follow."

Gwynndolen shrugged as though it were of no importance. "My dear princess, I will be his champion and I will win. I know it."

"But this is ludicrous! There shouldn't even be a tournament. We should have had Father Iohannes return with us to stop these ridiculous proceedings. It's not time for tournaments and jousting, it's time for war!" Rapunzel realized she was pacing. How long had she been walking around the chamber? She looked over at Helena, who was stirring. She needed to lower her voice and settle down or the little one wouldn't get a good nap.

Gwynndolen stepped quietly over to Rapunzel and whispered, "You seem agitated. Much more than I've ever seen you before."

"I just feel like everything is spinning so fast here. I don't know why I feel that way. Perhaps I should have eaten more at the midday meal, but I could only seem to do one thing right for the complete meal, and that was drink cups of—"

Gwynndolen's left eyebrow arched. "You drank the dark brew of the High King?"

"Yes, his coffy. I wasn't feeling adventurous at first, but

I was so tired that the ladies suggested I try some. Why? Was I not supposed to?"

"Well, I heard King Tasufin brought enough for the whole kingdom to sample, but I would sip slowly."

"It was bitter, but I rather liked it!" Helena stirred again, reminding Rapunzel to quiet down. She walked to the other side of the chamber where the table sat, Gwynndolen close behind. "What's wrong with it?" ·

"The king thinks it helps his morning headaches, but Edmund thinks it makes other people excitable. Be careful how much you drink."

"Oh! But it's delightful! It was the only thing the ladies didn't criticize all day. I enjoyed a couple of cups."

Gwynndolen covered her laughter with a hand. But it was no use. Helena was waking up. Rapunzel walked over to her daughter as she sat up. "No wonder you're so agitated!" she heard Gwynndolen say. Turning, she saw her holding out her hands. "Come, get Helena ready, and let's find Katterina. You can come watch me train, and that should use up some of your energy."

"I would that we could, but I'm afraid I have more lessons on proper decorum. I need to be ready for later this week when the High Queen wants an audience with us."

"'Us'? All of us?"

"Well, just my mother and myself for now, but Amis is trying to find his own invitation."

Gwynndolen laughed again. "Does that man ever allow anyone to tell him where he can go and what he should do? He is a merry servant, but he's his own master."

Rapunzel bit her lip as she brushed her little girl's dark curls. "Gwynndolen, would you come with me?"

"To see the High Queen?"

"Yes." Rapunzel pressed her lips into a firm line. "I think you have a different perspective that I can't share. You have many more dealings with Camilla."

"That may be true, but it's Prince Edmund who knows her best. Besides, I can't go if the High Queen hasn't asked me."

Rapunzel nodded. She would have to get them all into an audience with the High Queen soon.

# THE TALE OF THE GOOSE GIRL

*A*mis smiled to himself. What a simple thing it had been to convince the pretty maid to let him deliver the queen's tea to her. It had only taken a few coins, coins he didn't need since he began serving the Fisher King again. A simple nod to the guards, and they opened the doors.

This was a sitting room? Amis wanted to clap his hands in delight. Yes, he could see how it would be appropriate to call it a *sitting room*. The queen had fashioned the vast room into a place of gathering. There were several ornately carved mahogany chairs that boasted cushions of purple and silver. Like much of the grey-stone castle, brightly threaded tapestries covered the walls. But these tapestries showed off women and their everyday lives. Amis stepped closer to one and almost upset his tea-tray as he stared at the brown girl with long tresses of black hair the wind had blown toward a gaggle of geese in the field behind a castle.

"Who are you?" the queen snapped from her cushioned chair that was seated before a crackling fire.

"Just a simple jester ready to serve you."

The queen's eyes shifted to the young, pinched woman sitting in the chair next to her. "What do you think, Princess Qasmuna, is this man to be trusted?"

"Men should never be trusted. Not anymore."

The queen tilted her head. "But you might just be bitter. You don't like the man you're married to."

"I was a prize, Mother, and he claimed me. That does not make for a happy marriage."

She looked at her daughter and waved her away. "Well, take your lack of happiness elsewhere. We want to hear what makes a jester play the part of a maidservant."

Amis set about serving the queen with grand gestures, which earned him the smallest of smiles. He moved around the chairs quickly, but not even his finest back handspring followed by a double flip seemed to truly please her.

"Is that all you came to do? Move my things and play the fool?"

"Well, I am a fool, but I've actually come to tell you a tale."

"Oh, is that so?" She set the tea saucer and cup delicately in her lap, but her eyes were anything but gentle.

"It is."

"Tell me, what's the tale about?"

"Two sisters."

She took another sip of tea and swallowed. Amis waited, trying not to bounce in anticipation. Finally, she looked him in the eye. "You may proceed."

He raised his voice in favorite storytelling tone, but instead of focusing on Her Majesty, he stared at the tapestry and smiled. "Long ago, but not so long that one could forget, there lived two sisters, Itr and Princess Pasca —half sisters, to be exact. They both resembled their father, and could have been lovely playmates. But the queen loved only her daughter Pasca and made Itr serve the younger. Pasca, she claimed, was the true heiress and would one day wed the High King. When the girls grew older, they set off for the Winter Castle from their own home at the Summer Castle. But on the way, the illegitimate daughter, Itr, usurped her role. She had learned dark magic and used it to make Princess Pasca mute. On reaching the Winter Castle, Pasca could tell no one who she really was. Poor girl, she could not go home to her mother, and her half sister married the king's son and made the true daughter become the king's Goose Girl. But God saw the true daughter and had plans for her."

"Did he now?"

Amis cleared his throat and worked his response into the tale. "Oh, yes, Your Majesty. God saw how poorly they treated her, and you know how he hates sorcery. Don't you know? He alone can wield the supernatural, because he is in control of the supernatural. It's plain to me. He surrounded the Goose Girl with good things. Geese are usually hateful creatures, but these geese were kind. He made it so the true daughter could talk to the geese through her signs. Even the wind listened and did her bidding.

"One day, the king saw her out in the field with her hat off, her long hair carried along by the wind. Somehow, he knew something was wrong. There was something about her . . . . He sent for the Goose Girl, and when she stood before the king, he asked her who she was and what she was about. He clearly saw that she looked like the girl whom he had wed, and he wanted one of them to explain. When the mute Goose Girl could not, Princess Itr made up a story detailing horrible lies of what the Goose Girl had done to become a mute servant. She ended her tale by saying the Goose Girl should die. But the king was wise, and the pretender received the punishment instead. God granted the true daughter her voice back, and she could speak again. They annulled the first marriage and the true daughter wed the king's son, though—" Amis stopped short and stared at the queen openly.

Her mouth pinched together. "Though what?"

"Well, Your Majesty, there are some that say she would have been better off if she hadn't. But that was only the beginning of her adventures."

The queen smacked her lips and clapped her hands even as her eyes narrowed. "It has been ever so long since someone dared to tell me my own tale."

Amis couldn't stop the bounce that came as he spoke. "A wise man would never recount such a story unless he had a purpose."

"And what purpose would that be, I wonder?" The queen leaned in, her mouth now a firm line.

"Oh, I think you know that the mischief done to and in your family is far from over. The creature you keep below is the one who taught the pretender how to make you mute. But would you like to know why she is valuable to you now?"

The queen looked back at the guards and then leaned closer to Amis. "Tell me everything."

GWYNNDOLEN STOOD at the side of the field, restlessly watching, wishing that this was really the year for the true tournament. If it were, then all the warrior monks and the sisters from the convent would have gathered to fight as well. As it was, she knew the monks and sisters would only arrive in time for the christening, and they planned to return home directly. According to their spiritual calendar, though they were ready in season and out of season to give a defense for their faith, they would not take part in some showy exhibition to satisfy the High King. She wished she could go to battle against such worthy opponents, but she would have to settle for those she saw filling up the field before her.

Of course, if Camilla had her way, they might soon be fighting alongside one another to fend off the forces of darkness.

Gwynndolen wondered if it made her a bad person to expect such an eventuality with excitement. It was only right that she, having a warrior's heart, would look forward to crushing those who would try to destroy faith in the true God. Hopefully Camilla wouldn't make her move until Jacob could persuade Father Iohannes of the urgency. Surely they would arrive on time!

If, however, the tournament proceeded as planned, she would fight in the melee with a few weapons of choice. Knowing her strengths and weaknesses as a fighter, she would have to use her nimble feet to keep herself from being crushed by the princes and lords. No one had noted her when she passed by the stables and entered the training grounds. All around, princes, lords, and a few of the younger kings paired off. Some were standing about talking, but most were at work, striking at one another, trying to trip each other up. Only a few seemed in deadly earnest. Most were just warming up to the idea of swinging weapons. Gwynndolen, still dressed in her normal gowns, entered the wooden stands built to accommodate the spectators for the summer's tournament and sat beside

Edmund on a bench. He looked over at her, clearly confused. "Why are you sitting down with me? Aren't you going to go out there and train?"

"Clearly, I can't bear to leave your presence," she said in a ridiculous, breathy voice.

"Ha ha," he returned with a frown. "Really, why are you here? I think it would help if you were out there—"

"No one will expect me to be training, and my best chance is to surprise everyone. I'll sit here this afternoon to better understand my opponents and then go train elsewhere tomorrow. I wish Georgius and Liam—" Her voice cracked, thinking of her lost brothers. "No matter. I'll do them proud." Now she wished she had a weapon in hand, something to beat back the grief that threatened to engulf her in its wave of sorrow. Edmund placed a hand over hers, but she jerked away and blinked rapidly.

"H-hmm." She cleared her throat and prepared to talk through what she was seeing. Edmund would probably chime in if he saw something that slipped by her. His contrary nature wouldn't let him miss the opportunity. "You see that prince with the mace?"

"What about him?"

"He's pretty confident."

"He should be. Look at the size of him!"

"Well, someone that size best be strong, but also learn to move quick or else—ha!" She barely covered her laugh with a cough when a smaller man came up from behind him and whacked him with a blunt sword.

"Or else that?"

"Exactly!"

"I thought that was your trick."

"It's not mine alone—and it's not a trick, Your Highness."

"'Your Highness'? You know, you slip back into formality whenever you're upset with me."

"I don't know what you mean." But Gwynndolen knew what he meant—and she wasn't really upset with him. Still, she didn't want to discuss it. She'd lose focus on the field if she did.

Oh, how she longed to discuss training with Georgius. He was great at strategy and would help her capitalize on her strengths. But that was no use. Missing her brother didn't help. Missing her stallion was a lost cause as well, but her mind went there next. Because if only she had him, she could easily enter one of the tournament's horseback competitions. No one would expect it of her, especially since she used a short sword when on foot. But she never used a short sword on horseback—she used a long sword. It had taken a long time to learn to balance with it on horseback, and she remembered the ache in her forearms when Georgius taught her to wield it. But it was worthwhile. She needed the range it afforded. Besides, if she could take her enemies by surprise, so much the better. She loved turning things upside down and backward. There was a momentary lull as she chewed her lip.

"What are you thinking?"

"Hmm?"

"You stopped talking, so that means you're plotting something."

"Yes, well, if I'm to win the melee, then I must flip things in my favor. You remember, use what others perceive as a weakness—"

"As your strength."

"Right, and do something no one will expect."

He gave her a look. She knew that look, so she turned

back to watching the fighters before her. "What no one will expect?" Edmund said, his tone low.

"Yes, exactly."

"Yes, exactly what?"

"Just something no one will expect."

"Such as?"

"Oh, I haven't decided yet."

She could actually feel him scowling. "Oh! Look at that one!" She pointed, hoping to distract him, but it would not sway him.

"Gwynnie."

"Don't call me that."

"Then, tell me what you're planning."

She shrugged and then stood up. "I've seen enough for now. I'm going to go check on the horses." He put a hand on her arm and she stilled for a moment.

"We can live without the High King's blessing, you know," he murmured.

"Not if you want to retain your crown, Your Highness. He crowns you and me only if I succeed. And so I shall. I always do." She slipped away from his grasp and took off back toward the stables.

# A TALE OF TREASON

"What have you done?" The High Queen's dark eyes glittered with malice, and Katterina didn't like how they narrowed on Rapunzel when they were admitted into the sitting room. Once a strong, tan woman, the queen now looked shriveled.

"I have done nothing."

"You have! Foolish girl, I know you have!" The woman sputtered her poisonous beliefs from her couch where she sat tucked under blankets, even though the room felt to Katterina as hot as an oven. "You have brought to my kingdom the very ones who want to destroy us all. My husband doesn't understand—he never comprehends. But I can see. I know. I've spoken to Amis about that monster we keep below. After all, I did for you, this is how you repay me?"

Rapunzel's mouth opened, but nothing came out. Katterina stepped in front of her daughter, glad they had left the little one with Prince Paul.

"She never did you any harm, Your Majesty. If there was harm done, it was by the sisters of sorcery. They have brought this danger to your home. It was foolish for any of us to think we could escape their ire. You should know that the caged always lash out, don't they?"

The High Queen's eyes flashed, but Katterina stood firm. Was the queen thinking of the vengeance Itr had taken not so long ago, causing mayhem with the queen's daughters? Katterina glanced at Amis, privileged to sit next to the queen on the couch. He seemed unperturbed by the queen's ire. In fact, he lifted his bushy eyebrows at her and then turned his head and smiled at the queen. It took a moment, but the queen finally sat back and addressed her with far less vehemence. "So you were a cat last I saw you."

"I was."

"And you helped me find the troubadour and your daughter"—she held up her finger to point Rapunzel's way —"to solve my mystery."

"That I did."

"And now you come here, as a woman, and expect me to trust you can save us from these sisters."

Katterina scowled. "I don't know that—"

"Then what are you saying?"

She took a deep breath. Why had the queen insisted on seeing them before Jacob was back? If only this could have waited for the monk's return. He would explain things much better than she. "All of us have had our fill of sorcery, have we not, Your Majesty? If we want to be free of this evil, we must convince your husband—"

The queen held up both hands, and Katterina halted. "No one can convince that man of anything."

"But surely, now that Your Majesty has at last granted the man an heir—"

The queen's eyes flashed and Katterina swallowed at her own impudence. "Yes, but he had already taken steps to set me aside, to choose another in place of me. It has only been with careful cunning that I have maintained my hold." The woman licked her lips and glanced again at Amis. "But why are we speaking of this? The matter at hand is grave enough. And my husband, being the fool that he is, will not heed us."

Amis popped up and spun, laughing, as though the discussion were about a grand evening of entertainment. "Your Majesty, it is our duty to convince him of the danger."

"Sit back down, you fool," she said, but her lips turned up. It was a strange look on her otherwise pinched face. "He will only see the danger once it is upon his threshold. Once the forces of darkness come against us, only then will he gather his own forces to fight back. And I'm afraid it will be too late at that point."

"So what can we do to change things? How can we lift his head, help him see what needs to be done?" Rapunzel asked at last with a slight quiver in her voice.

"If I cannot convince him to wrangle the truth out of the monster below by the time the remaining royal families gather, we will get to the truth without him."

"But Your Majesty, if we torture the prisoner without the High King, that would be wrong! That would be an act of—"

"Some would think it treasonous, but would, in fact, be an act of salvation for us all. Come now, are you willing to help me once more—you and your little friends? It is only treason if we lose."

# SEARCHING HEAVEN

Jacob stood in the shadowed courtyard with his brother monks, each spread several body lengths of distance from each other to go through Lauds, their Dawn prayers. As they chanted of the armor that would protect them, the sun broke over the horizon, lighting the sky in a peach haze, the beauty of which made Jacob want to forget the danger they were in. Was this a temptation toward a false sense of security? He pushed away the thought and tried to refocus. He wished Father Iohannes would have joined them, but the older man had declined, Jacob supposed, because of his advanced age. But he missed the man's presence in the spiritual fight. How much more important was it that he practiced this morning? He must be vigilant, ever alert to the schemes of the enemy and the threat of complacency.

Had he already succumbed to the enemy? Is that where his feelings for Lady Katterina originated from? He shook his head as though to clear it. He must concentrate. Only then could he discern what God was trying to say— about the battle ahead and the battle within.

Each line of scripture called for a different defensive or offensive movement with each monk's weapon of choice. The men dressed much as Jacob, chain mail over padded tunics, weapons girded about their waists, legs covered by hosen of sturdy cloth. Jacob now wore the colors of the brethren, having exchanged the Fisher King's royal blue for bright green. He joined his voice to those of his brothers as he gripped his staff and prayed the Lord would use his might through each of them in the coming battle. The momentum built and built, the chanting loud, the humidity in the heavy air making several break out in sweat.

Finally, my brethren, be strong in the Lord, and in the power of his might. Put on the whole armour of God, that ye may be able to stand against the wiles of the devil. For we wrestle not against flesh and blood, but against principalities, against powers, against the rulers of the darkness of this world, against spiritual wickedness in high places. Wherefore take unto you the whole armour of God, that ye may be able to withstand in the evil day, and having done all, to stand. Stand therefore, having your loins girt about with truth, and having on the breastplate of righteousness; And your feet shod with the preparation of the gospel of peace; Above all, taking the shield of faith, wherewith ye shall be able to quench all the fiery darts of the wicked. And take the helmet of salvation, and the sword of the Spirit, which is the word of God. (Eph. 6:10-18)

.  .  .

THE RECITATION ENDED with their weapons striking the enemy they each pictured before them. Jacob pulled his staff in close as the monks broke ranks and began filing back inside the monastery. But Jacob stayed still, waiting for the others to finish going inside. Once they had, he began again, reciting the holy scripture, imagining the enemy even now devising evil plans. His arms moved, his legs lunged and straightened. He pulled, pushed, then spun the staff through the air. His body continued moving, sweating, his lips reciting the holy words, his mind searching. Where was the way ahead? What was God calling him to do? Why was Jacob separated from those he had vowed to fight alongside, those he had vowed to protect?

He finished and began again, finished and began again, the sweat now dripping down his face, soaking his garments. He knew he would need to stop soon. His body cried out for water, for nourishment, but his soul wrestled with the way ahead. *Speak to me, please!* he called to the God of his soul. *Do not withhold your wisdom from us now. We are nothing without you. We will lose this war to the darkness if you do not fight for us. Please use us, fight through us or don't let us fight at all.*

He noted where the sun had risen to. His brother monks would gather soon inside for Prime prayers; he would have just enough time to clean himself and drink some much needed water. But he couldn't eat, not until he had his answer.

# AN UNLIKELY ALLIANCE

"Not like that!" Lady Florese snapped, causing Rapunzel to drop the books off her head. Not only was she not allowed to dine with the nobility of the other kingdoms, she couldn't even mingle with them until she proved to Lady Florese that she had the right composure. Despite Luciana's faith that Rapunzel wouldn't need much instruction toward this end, Lady Florese had been after her all morning, not even allowing Rapunzel to take Helena down to the gardens to play among the flowers.

"When presented to the High King, you must bow with reverence. You must keep your head lifted even as you bend it."

"How can I keep my head lifted while my head is bent? This makes no sense. I've met with the queen on numerous occasions and she has never faulted me for—"

"Then she was being too kind."

Rapunzel was sad that Lady Bazzu had not joined them this morning and wouldn't be here until midday meal. Of the two ladies, Lady Bazzu was the most encouraging and had been the one to say that Rapunzel had enough natural grace to meet with the High Queen yesterday. Why, then, did Lady Florese not think so?

"Now try again, like this—" And Lady Florese bent low to the ground without slouching at all. Somehow, she made it look easy. "The nobility will have all gathered in just a few days' time and you will be presented formally. That is why we must work hard now, to get you ready."

Rapunzel nodded and tried again, fighting the swelling in her throat. This felt like a ludicrous waste of time. She just wanted to go home.

Edmund hobbled over to Paul across the training grounds midway through the morning. Paul paused his work with Dietz and told the young man several stances to work on.

Paul had noticed Prince Edmund out and about the day before, and now he gave the man a smile. Funny how their onetime rivalry for Rapunzel seemed to have melted into a friendly respect—especially now that Paul knew of the betrothal between the prince and the fiery redhead he had fought alongside in capturing Amee.

"Prince Edmund," he said, taking several steps toward the sitting area in order that the prince didn't have to walk as far. The way the man was leaning on his staff, they needed to keep near the benches, just in case. "You're looking much better." His voice was louder than he liked, but he had to speak over the clangs of swords colliding against shields and armor.

As the two clasped hands, Edmund's mouth tipped up into its crooked smile, as though he knew Paul was helping him save face by crossing toward him. "I was hoping to catch you before you began practice this morning, but it seems I took too long."

Paul nodded. It couldn't be easy to go from a self-assured man who could care for himself to a cripple. But surely Prince Edmund was doing some better already. Perhaps the wound would not be long-lasting and he would heal in time. "What can I do for you, Your Highness?"

"Am I that apparent?"

Paul shrugged, his shoulders making a strange creaking sound, with the armor lifting and dropping. "We are on the same side now. I am happy to help the man who used his dying breath to ward off Camilla."

Now it was Edmund's turn to shrug, as though his sacrifice was not to be thought of. As though he had not been willing—and had even tried—to give his own life. "Well, it turned out God granted me more breath to live. Anyway, I did only what you would have done."

Paul could only hope that he would be that selfless in the face of evil. "We may soon see in the coming days."

Edmund's smile slipped from his face. "Yes, danger is coming. If only we could convince the king. Gwynndolen tells me that Jacob stayed behind to convince Father Iohannes to come and speak with him."

Paul nodded.

"I had hoped—" But something broke the prince's concentration. Paul turned to see the redheaded lady coming out onto the training grounds from the direction of the stables. "But I must ask you something else entirely. You may have heard that my betrothed must fight in my stead during the tournament."

Paul kept his face straight. He wouldn't demoralize the prince by showing his feelings about such a matter. If keeping Rona's throne safe was on the shoulders of the Lady Gwynndolen, perhaps Edmund had sacrificed too much.

"Can you help prepare her? I know there is precious little time, but her brothers have trained her well until now. She's—" He lowered his voice, and Paul saw she had spotted them and was coming straightaway. "She's all I have left in this world. I'd give up my throne to keep her safe, but she convinced me we must try to save it. I don't know that she's ready to face—" He gestured to the princes and lords on the training grounds, crashing into one another repeatedly.

Paul put a hand on the man's shoulder. What if he were wounded and only Rapunzel could save their kingdom from the greedy High King? They would sorely lose, and Rapunzel would forfeit her life. "I will do all I can to help Lady Gwynndolen."

"Thank you, I owe you—"

"Don't think on it. We all owe you for what you did in the marsh. My prayer is that you will heal and that you won't lose your throne while you recover."

Edmund nodded, his eyes on the approaching lady. He lowered his voice further still as she drew nearer, and Paul could barely hear him over the ruckus being made. "But her pride won't accept your help, I fear. She told me yesterday she would go off and train by herself. Somehow, you must keep her from guessing—"

"Here you are!" she stated, and looked up at Paul. "I see you two are getting along. What was it you needed?" She shifted as though wanting to get away quickly.

Edmund spoke up. "Paul and I were talking about his ward, Dietz. It seems the boy has some natural talent with a staff, but has a way to go. Would you be willing to help Paul in training him?"

Gwynndolen arched an eyebrow, her eyes looking between the two princes. "But I was going to—" She looked at Paul and then Edmund, lifting one brow. "I need to work on my training, and I'd rather do it without an audience."

Paul nodded. "I understand that."

She huffed a breath, looking at Edmund. "I can try to help a bit."

Paul noticed Edmund's wide smile, but kept his own in check. He held out his staff. "Are you much good at working with a staff?"

"I much prefer my short sword, but my brothers insisted I learn multiple weapons." She exchanged her short sword with his proffered staff and took its balance.

Paul frowned slightly at the mention of her deceased brothers. He never knew what to do with such fresh grief. It was probably best if they used the emotion to help them train harder. There were only a few days until the tournament. He needed to see the lady fight so he could take her measure. Edmund was right. Best to put her up against Dietz first, to see how she would respond to a less experienced fighter.

He motioned for the lad to come over, which he did at once.

Dietz stepped forward, brandishing his staff. He bowed in deference to the maid and straightened with only a slight wobble. He was still getting used to the armor Paul had insisted he wear for their training sessions. Gwynndolen bowed her head, wearing leather hosen and chain mail over her tunic as her only protection. She waited, eyes alight, and Paul could see her waiting was a game. Dietz looked unsure what to do, but when he glanced at Paul, he nodded him forward. The young man took a step to engage, and she had been waiting for it. Though she didn't smile with her lips, her eyes glinted in merriment. Each step that Dietz took, she quickly countered, but Paul saw that there were several openings she didn't take. Was she missing them?

But then he caught sight of her pulling back. She was so quick he nearly missed it. The lad had her on range, and she was making up for it with the weapon's reach. But she was refusing an easy win. Her movements kept up the façade that the young man was causing her more difficulty than he was. Paul noticed the lad's eyes light up at the challenge she was presenting. In fact, though she let the chance go by twice, on the third time that Dietz left himself open, Gwynndolen tripped him and then aimed her hands over his throat as though she would drive the staff into it. As one of the most vulnerable areas of an armored man, Paul admired not only her cunning, but her restraint as she held the staff still, panting. Dietz didn't move, and then finally, when he realized she would not strike, he lifted his visor and Paul could see a wide grin spread across his face. Finally, an opponent who could call the young man out but not leave him humiliated, as seemed to be the case with Paul. Surprising that he didn't find defeat at the hands of a lady humiliating.

Gwynndolen held out her hand, and Dietz grabbed hold of it, jerking up to his feet with a smile. "M-my lady, you are qu-quite good."

"Thank you, but you impressed me as well. Will you be fighting in the tournament?"

"No, I'm not the son of a king or a lord."

"I'm not the son of anyone," she laughed.

Dietz shook his head, but chuckled.

Paul clapped his hands together twice. "Dietz, well done! Do you think we should fight her together?" The young man nodded, but after several more rounds, he looked done for. "Perhaps we need a good meal before we keep going?"

Dietz laughed and nodded.

Paul stepped forward. "We'll meet back here after the midday meal and work some more. I've heard of the warrior women in the Eastern Ports, and I think they would be wise to fear you, Lady Gwynndolen."

The young woman blinked in surprise, but he could tell it pleased her.

# NIGHT MEETINGS

$\mathcal{N}$ofra moved in the dim light of her shared room over to the table next to the dressing screen. Night was the only time that she could properly speak with Camilla without the other maidservants overhearing. She took out her scrying bowl and filled it quietly with water from their washing bowl and lit the candle. Nofra's dark eyes stared into the water in the bowl. Scrying was a difficult thing for many, but it came naturally to her. She remembered how Amee had first taught her the art, though she had kept Nofra from being seen by Eufemia and Katterina when they had spoken to her through the bowl.

"What have you learned, my child?" Camilla's voice was low, and shouldn't wake her roommates, but she wanted to keep the conversation short, just in case.

Nofra herself was cloaked in a spell to befuddle those who might be trying to sniff out her true purpose, but that wasn't enough to accomplish all that Camilla had sent her to do. The sorceress had showed the young witch how to prepare several pouches, sachets really, of potent herbs.

When Nofra wove the web of enchanted words over the herbs, the sleeper became malleable. For the maids who shared Nofra's room, that meant access to the bedchambers of other noble families.

Poor, ignorant maids! They only woke when Nofra would speak their names, or when she jostled them awake the next morning. She needed time each evening for scrying with Camilla. For time to learn how to use the other pouches she would put beneath Rapunzel's pillows and the pillows of those the princess loved.

"Mother." Her lips fumbled with the word. It still felt strange to call Camilla *mother*, but she fought through the awkwardness. Her heart longed to race down below to Amee, to beg Amee to be the mother that Nofra had once thought she was. The mother Nofra still wanted her to be. But that was not what needed to happen. Amee had betrayed them, and Camilla was here to lead them to victory so that sorcery was free of tyranny. So that her people could live without fear of being burned by the Church. "Mother," she repeated, "the High King is exactly as you said. He fears nothing, except maybe his wife."

"And what of her? Will she be a hindrance?"

"I'm uncertain. There is something she is planning, but I haven't been able to——"

"Then, you must find out." Her voice growled. "There is no excuse for not knowing when you lie so close to those who wield the strongest power against us."

Nofra cleared her face of expression. "Yes, of course."

"My sister didn't trust you to find your way and help the cause, but I do. I know you can learn more than she ever taught you."

"What will you teach me tonight?"

"How to hold someone in submission to your will."

Camilla's rough voice smacked over the word *submission* as though it were a delectable treat. "Are the maids in your room sound asleep?"

"Of course." Nofra leaned over the bowl. "It was even easier than you said."

"Choose one and point at her. Make her come to you without waking."

The witch looked at the three maids tucked into their beds. The narrow cots crammed close together, as all the servants' quarters had doubled up occupancy with all the visiting nobles. She would have to take care not to lose her concentration, or she might disturb and wake them all.

Nofra inhaled, reaching for the source of her power down beneath the dungeons where Amee languished. The power tingled in her pointed finger as she lifted and directed it at the youngest maid. This was what Amee had been teaching her long ago. It was as easy as breathing for Nofra, except that her breath hitched and she dropped her hand.

The girl shifted in her sleep, but did not sit up. Nofra blinked.

"What were you thinking of?" Camilla's voice echoed out of the water, the bowl vibrating slightly.

"Nothing. I'll try again." She pointed and refocused. This time she envisioned the swamp, and Mauro coming across the waters, his oar dipping in and out. Beneath the waters, she could feel something, something calling her. The tips of the roots of the trees drank the waters, and she also drank of its power.

The maid sprang out of the bed, but got caught in the tangle of her blanket and fell over.

"Don't let her wake up!" Camilla barked. Had the sorceress heard the maid's thud?

Nofra held tight in her mind to the maid. A vise around her head slowly squeezed, but she ignored the pain. Carefully, like a puppeteer maneuvering the strings of a twisted marionette, she repositioned the girl to get her untangled. Then, she had the girl remake her bed.

"Good, I can feel her will bending to yours," Camilla's voice rasped, sending a thrill down Nofra's spine. "Now, have her dance."

Nofra didn't hold back a giggle as she did so. Amee had never let her play with this much power! She could feel a hunger growing in her belly, but it wasn't food she was craving. It was power.

"Send her back to bed. You've done enough for tonight."

"No—" Her voice surprised herself and Camilla. "I want to do more."

"You're not ready yet."

"I can do it. Just tell me what."

Camilla didn't answer at first. Nofra held her breath. "All right, we'll try. Hold on to the maid dancing and choose another one to climb out of bed. Don't let either wake up."

Nofra moistened her lips and breathed deeply. The rhythm of the young maid's dance continued as she reached into the mind of the older maid in the next bed. She shifted the new maid to sit, but a sharp pain shot through Nofra's head and her mind darted back to Amee. Both maids fell, one back on her pillow and the other sprawled on the floor, head down.

Before the maid scrambled off the floor, Nofra snuffed out the candle and poured the scrying bowl water behind the screen into the chamber pot. She poured slowly, creating a noise as though she were relieving herself.

"Oww," the maid moaned.

"Are you all right?" Nofra called back, as though in alarm.

"I—I don't know how I got here."

Nofra's eyes adjusted to the dark quickly. She could see the maid was trying to find her way back to bed. "I hope I didn't wake you. I had to use the chamber pot."

"No, I don't think you woke me. Don't know what did." She sounded befuddled as she climbed back under the covers. "Let's just go back to sleep."

Nofra got back into bed. She'd have to explain what had happened to Camilla tomorrow night. Her chest burned and her eyes smarted. Camilla probably already knew.

# AMONG THE PRINCES

Rapunzel wanted to cheer. She was out of her chambers at last! Usually she preferred a bit of solitude or gathering with only a few friends, but today her heart lifted at the thought of gathering with the entire court.

She hugged little Helena, who jabbered back, incoherently but with glee, as they followed Paul in line. Though her ladies-in-waiting were watching just behind her, Rapunzel tried not to think about them. Instead, she tried to peer around the ladies-in-waiting just ahead of her. Could that be Prince Roland's family? It would make sense for them to be introduced right before Paul, since he was the younger brother.

The herald was droning on just inside the door, speaking loudly in Latin. The line moved up slightly and time seemed to stretch on. Rapunzel caught a glimpse of a rotund man and realized it was indeed Roland! She leaned forward, as though wishing away those between Paul and his brother. The two were great friends and she wanted them to have a chance to spend time together. Finally, the herald announced Prince Roland, along with his wife, Princess Aalis, who was holding their son, and his widowed mother, Queen Gila. Because the herald waved their attendants ahead, Rapunzel could advance in line far enough to see inside the vast throne room.

How wonderful! Roland looked like his same jolly self, but even better, little Eng had filled out, much like Helena. He wasn't exactly chubby, but he no longer looked emaciated, and his once sallow cheeks had a pink color to them now. She saw Princess Aalis hand off Eng to a woman who appeared to be a nursemaid.

Rapunzel's gaze watched as the noble women strode forth to curtsy deeply before the throne. Queen Gila and Princess Aalis were looking well, able to smile again. The death of the manipulative King Onfroi, Paul's father, had freed them. She remembered what they had been like when they first met—the queen stiff and almost silent, the princess unable to leave her bed most days. But here they were, no longer under the rule of the man who had orchestrated the kidnapping of Eng, the king who had sought power from the sorceress Ute.

"Don't forget to lower your eyes when you give your curtsy, Princess." Lady Florese's reminder snapped Rapunzel back to attention as they were waved into the throne room.

"Announcing Prince Paul, heir to King Guiscard, the Fisher King, and also his wife, the Princess Rapunzel, with their adopted daughter, Princess Helena, and Princess Rapunzel's mother, the Lady Katterina."

Rapunzel followed Paul's lead and then curtseyed, her deep blue gowns fanning out as she bent her knees and lowered her eyes. Helena clapped her fat little hands in amusement, as though Rapunzel were playing a dancing game with her. When she straightened, she glanced up at the long purple carpet that climbed up the stairs to rest beneath the feet of the king and queen. High King Zakarriyya and High Queen Pasca sat with stiff backs in their ornate, purple-cushioned thrones, bright purple banners with their silver crest behind them. The queen's eyes flashed as she held her infant son close to her chest. It made Rapunzel feel better about not having someone holding Helena for her.

They were then escorted to the Great Hall where all the kingdoms' representatives would dine. Rows and rows of long tables spaced far apart were set with silver trenchers and goblets. Bowls overflowing with fruit rested between lit candelabras. It was awkward standing and waiting for everyone to gather, but at least Rapunzel was able to occupy her thoughts with Helena as the little girl giggled. She smiled gratefully across the table at Prince Roland, who was making funny faces.

At long last, the final noble family was walked to their table and the herald indicated that everyone sit, breaking the silence. Roland didn't sit right away, but took the time to come around the table. He grabbed hold of Paul and pulled him tight while pounding on his brother's back. Rapunzel heard Lady Florese, standing behind her, "tsk" at the breach in etiquette.

"It's that good to see you again, brother."

Paul laughed at his brother's exuberance. "Yes, it is a blessing to see you smile. Your family looks much improved."

"Yes, we traveled by sea from the Northlands and had quite an easy go of it. Only arrived yesterday, but I'm not tired, though Prince Eng was feeling cramped by the end of the trip." Roland returned to his seat.

"I understand. Our Helena tired of being inside the carriage. On the way home, I think I will take her on my saddle if her mother will allow it." Paul gave a wink to Rapunzel.

Rapunzel grinned back at his teasing before looking across the table at Princess Aalis and Queen Gila. She adjusted Helena on her lap and wondered what to say. Though she had spent time with them last winter after King Onfroi's death, she barely knew them.

Helena reached for a strange, thorny-looking fruit. Would it hurt her? Rapunzel swatted her hand away, saying, "Wait, little one." She pressed her lips together when she heard Lady Florese "tsk" again.

Helena fussed, and Rapunzel looked up apologetically at Gila and Aalis, but Aalis laughed. "That's why I handed Eng over to our nursemaid, Confortata. So much easier at affairs like these, don't you agree?"

Rapunzel couldn't help glancing over her shoulder, even though she knew that Lady Florese would be shaking her head. The woman had tried in vain to convince Rapunzel that she should allow Nofra to act the part of a nursemaid while they were at official dinners and such.

"Princess Rapunzel"—Lady Florese's had eyes narrowed when she spoke to Rapunzel before they left the bedchambers—"why must you be so stubborn? You can be an exemplary mother *and* get the help you need in order to care for the duties of your station."

But there at the table, Katterina interceded. "Silly me! I should know better than to insist our spirited Helena come with us to meals, but we have shut her in so much lately, she needed out." Katterina took her off Rapunzel's lap. "Here, let me have her so that you can eat, and then you can allow me to have a turn. Next time, we'll know better, won't we?"

Rapunzel felt herself nod while her cheeks burned. She should have known better now. Princess Aalis smiled in understanding, and the smile lit her face. "You look much improved, Princess Aalis."

"Yes, well, having my child back has helped a great deal. But, it turns out, children are a handful! Did you know that little ones could be such wonderful trouble?"

Had some of her husband's sunny attitude infected the princess? Rapunzel smiled back, and searched for more words. "Will the High King be crowning Prince Roland when he crowns Paul after the tournament?"

Princess Aalis nodded, her eyes moist. "I think there are several who will receive that honor, mostly from the Northlands."

Katterina had scooted her chair back far enough that Helena sat with her back against the table, playing a clapping game with her. Rapunzel swallowed her bite and responded. "Paul said there were eight kings lost in total last winter, but even more who have abdicated their thrones since the curse."

"One might wonder what will become of the Northlands with such young rulers in charge."

Katterina shifted in her seat, her face snapping away from Helena.

"What is it, Mother?"

"Perhaps with such young blood, it would be wise to keep older counsel, but only if that older counsel sees the current threat."

Princess Aalis's face drained of color at this, and Prince Roland frowned. "What is wrong, Aalis?"

"What threat? We haven't heard of any—"

Rapunzel wanted to stop her mother from speaking. This did not seem like the time or place, but Katterina plunged ahead. "We who have seen and heard what happened in the Northlands must speak sense to the High King. We have already convinced the queen, but the king is stubborn. He thinks the threat over, but the sisters of sorcery keep reuniting."

Prince Roland lowered his brow. "But Ute is dead. You saw this yourself last winter!"

Helena clapped her hands, but Katterina paid her no heed. "Yes, but the two remaining sisters reunited this spring. We helped capture Amee, but Camilla is at large. She is no longer bound to the western Illyan Sea and has threatened war."

Paul spoke up at last. "Lady Katterina speaks the truth. We have been trying to find a way to help the king understand how perilous the future is."

Aalis stared at Rapunzel, from one mother to another. "But we've just come from one problem. How can we head into a war? How will we protect our children?"

Queen Gila, silent up till now, put her fork down and touched her daughter-in-law gently. "Wait, Aalis—I'm certain we can trust that there is a plan. Paul, I don't imagine that Brother Jacob has been silent about this. What does he think needs doing?" Rapunzel remembered that the monk had lived most of his life serving Queen Gila's father before her brother became the Fisher King. When Paul had come of age, she had trusted Jacob to train Paul. The woman obviously held the monk in high regard.

Paul nodded. "Jacob is even now with Father Iohannes, fasting and praying as they seek to discern the right course of action."

The queen took in a deep breath and smiled at both

Aalis and then Rapunzel. "You'll see, Aalis, Jacob will see it right. Until then, we must put on brave faces."

AMIS RAN inside the Great Hall where the court was feasting. He began a series of handsprings that ended with one double flip up onto the dais where King Zakarriyya supped with Queen Pasca. The fool threw his hands up in the hair, then reached into the centerpiece before the king and pulled away two apples and a pear. He juggled them, hopping down to dance in front of the tables where the nobility were enjoying their food. He knew, soon, other jesters would take their turns entertaining and showing off their talents. But he would shine! His eyes roamed until he found Prince Paul. Flashing him a grin, Amis tossed Paul one fruit after another, and they began juggling across the table, to the astonished gasps of all around them. Raising his eyebrows twice, he managed a backward flip into the air while Paul took over the juggling. Then Amis landed, allowing Paul to pass him back all three pieces of fruit. Hazarding a quick glance at the king, he saw his sovereign was paying him no heed as he held out his goblet for more wine.

Aha!

Quick, before the waiting staff had filled every goblet, Amis tossed back the fruit to Paul and then grabbed four empty goblets to juggle. They were clunky, and he wasn't quite certain he could handle their odd mass, but he proceeded to balance one on the end of his chin and one on the toe of his raised foot, all while juggling two in the air. Yes, he could manage this. If only he could sing at the same time! But that was a feat even he could not do while balancing the goblet.

Out of the corner of his eye, he saw another jester dashing in from the hallway the servants were using. He was small and lithe, dressed in a bright yellow tunic and matching hosen, possibly still a youth. Amis resisted frowning so as not to upset the goblet. But it was his turn to entertain! No one else's! Missing one goblet, it pinged across the floor. Amis faltered and crashed into the other jester, right in front of the king, where they tumbled, tangled in a heap of elbows.

Amis untwisted himself and tried to help the youth, discovering to his surprise a young woman with olive skin and a mass of thin black braids released from her cap. Clapping erupted from the dais and the High King stood swaying as he guffawed.

The fool felt something he was unsure he had ever felt before. His cheeks were burning. Sure, he had fallen; he had tripped; he had lost his hold on his objects before, but only in practice. Never before a crowd and certainly not before the High King. This was why Amis practiced. Not that he had been feeling well lately, and his practices had been a bit off . . .

But, as his mind's eye conjured up the image everyone else must have seen, a chuckle burst out. It was all too funny. What had happened? Who had sent this other jester to entertain the king at the same time as he? Amis bowed to the maid in question with deference, though her station didn't deserve such honor. "Have I come on the wrong day? Was I to entertain tomorrow night?" Always better to accept the blame himself.

Her deep-set brown eyes looked on, bewildered, at the

High King, who was slapping his knee. "I-I don't know. I was told—" But she broke off as the king interrupted.

"Ah! What great fun to see you two muck it up! What a grand time this has been for Us! We know, it isn't kind to mislead you, but We were genuinely curious to see what might happen if We employed two jesters on the same night."

Amis bowed with a flourish while the maid continued to stare slack-jawed. "Your Majesty, accommodating your every whim is a delight! If we had known beforehand, we could have coordinated an even greater kerfuffle. Would that have been to your liking?" He noted that the High Queen rolled her eyes at this.

"We would have known you had set it up, and that might have ruined Our enjoyment."

"Do you not trust we could entertain you that way?"

The king stroked his chin and the scruff of a beard that grew there. "If you think you can do better, then We urge you to try it next week, the night before the tournament."

"So soon, Your Majesty?"

"Yes, speak with my steward and he shall reschedule the entertainment so that We may be amused—or not—by you again."

# THE ART OF DIPLOMACY

*P*rince Edmund grimaced, sucking in a jarring breath at the pain that shot through his side. How long would these cracked ribs hurt? He looked over at his source of concern. He could clearly see the Northland kings and princes a few tables over from where he sat in the Great Hall. The burly man across the table from Paul must be the prince's brother. Edmund had noticed the animated greeting with the garrulous man, but right before the jesters came in, something was said that soured the expressions at the table. He could not concentrate on what was happening next to him as he wondered what was going on with the Northlanders. Nodding as people spoke, he kept his face neutral but didn't add much to the conversation.

Gwynndolen said something to him at the end of the meal, and chairs scraped back as the ladies retreated to do whatever ladies did. Curiosity burning, he limped his way across the hall to follow the High King to the throne room to discuss politics.

Seeing Edmund approach, Paul gave him an amiable

smile, placing a hand on his shoulder and introducing him to the large man who was, indeed, Paul's brother. Paul's voice lowered, as though they were conspiring. But in reality, the prince simply confirmed what Edmund had suspected for the last week. "I know the names of many of these rulers, but I hadn't planned on having to deal with them on this level till a few years ago when my aunt died without producing an heir. I'm a second son—I'm supposed to be off fighting wars. This politicking was Roland's job."

Prince Roland gave a hearty laugh. "Welcome to my world, little brother!"

Paul shook his head, turning away a goblet offered by a passing servant. "I'm more comfortable with a sword in my hand than—" His left hand jerked slightly toward the approaching kings.

Edmund nodded along to Paul's concerns. He understood what Paul was saying, but he had learned to serve lords and ladies, princes and kings by knowing just which tale to sing them. Playing at court was much the same. If he could learn the art, surely Paul could as well.

As soon as he thought this, though, Edmund noticed King Tasufin approaching. The prince resisted rolling his eyes. He had just spent time on the king's island as the man pandered to Edmund's father, hoping for Edward to wed his daughter. There was nothing wrong with the girl, but there was something very distasteful about the smarmy little king. The man stroked his crooked beard as he attempted what looked to Edmund like a sympathetic smile. That is, if Edmund didn't know better. The king placed his small hands on each of Edmund's shoulders and, for a moment, the younger man was afraid that he would hug him. "Your father was a good man, a wise king.

He looked ahead for the good of his people, always finding alliances and trade agreements that built up the Ronan throne. You must be devastated."

Edmund lowered his eyes, unsure of what, exactly, he was. His complicated relationship with his father had been difficult. He had never pleased his father, but he would stand firm before this man. And what better way to do that than to redirect the man into giving Edmund the support their little group needed? "My father's death was needless. There are dangers in the sea that we must make the High King aware of."

"Yes, the pirates—"

"It is far worse than pirates, King Tasufin. It was Camilla who brought about my loss."

The king's eyebrows drew together. "The High King doesn't share your view. He blames the storm and the pirates. He can't credit a sorceress with being stronger than himself, my son."

Prince Roland had caught the tension between them and now coughed at the term of endearment. Edmund simply endured the odious man, who now leaned in, his breath stinking of garlic and wine.

"Let me advise you, as your own father would if he were here. You must stay on the good side of the king, anticipate his moods and provide for his desires. The man is ecstatic over having produced an heir. It thrills him to have gathered everyone here to celebrate and clash swords a year early. What man, much less king, would want to quibble about sisters who practice sorcery? He has decided that threat is behind us. Do your father's memory proud—serve the king well, fight in his tournament, stroke his ego, send him more horses once you return home. Wed soon and produce an heir loyal to the

High King. This, my son, you will do to honor your father."

Edmund gave a self-deprecating laugh, but shrugged the man off as he answered honestly, "I cannot fight this year because of my injuries."

The king's greedy little eyes lit up and he gazed at Edmund's staff. "I had heard something about this, but supposed it was mere rumor. Are you really so badly injured?"

Edmund feigned nonchalance while the man continued to crowd him. He refused to cringe. "But I think the heir I have chosen will surprise you all."

The man stepped back, a hand to his chest. "Oh, really, there was another survivor?"

"Yes, and she is quite a good fighter."

"A lady is fighting in your stead?"

"Indeed, my betrothed will marry me and then fight for our kingdom's honor." The little king spluttered, causing Edmund's mouth to quirk into his lopsided smile. He grabbed a goblet from a passing servant. Why not? "To the women we depend upon. From the cradle to the grave, they keep us in line."

"Hear, hear!" Prince Paul's and Prince Roland's voices lifted as they, too, snatched up goblets of dry red wine.

After finishing the drink, Paul put a gentle hand on Edmund's shoulders. "King Tasufin, I hope you don't mind. I have something I wish to ask the prince in private."

Prince Roland smiled broadly and turned to the weasel-like man. "So much the better, for I want to discuss the potential of this coffy bean you have been bringing the High King. Perhaps we can work something out between your kingdom and mine?"

Edmund hid a smile at the way the excited king

excused himself to discuss the trade agreement. "Thank you," he finally voiced once the other two were away. He noticed neither he nor Paul had finished the wine in their goblets, but still they gave them to a passing servant.

"You are welcome." Paul dropped his hand from Edmund's shoulder. "Though I must say, you managed him well. I should be happy to do half so well."

"Yes?" Edmund shifted his weight, surprised at how wobbly his legs felt. He glanced about for a bench.

"I wanted to tell you how Lady Gwynndolen is coming along." Paul paused, his gaze dropping to the floor momentarily. "Her brothers trained her well, as you said. But I am concerned that she is unprepared to face what is ahead of her. If it were only the melee, I would not worry, but we know that the forces of darkness are mounting."

Edmund's shoulders slumped, but Paul put his powerful hands on his arms, as though to bear him up. Edmund shuddered as pain pierced his ribs.

Paul dropped both hands and stepped back. "Oh, sorry. But I don't say this to frighten you—or her. Believe me, I only want you aware. I am likewise concerned for Dietz, but as they are practicing together, I think they will get stronger."

"But is there enough time?"

Paul hazel eyes clouded and he rubbed a hand on the back of his neck. "God only knows. I'd feel better if Jacob had returned, but I've now heard there's a delay with the warrior women's arrival. They, too, are waiting on word from Father Iohannes."

"Will Camilla wait much longer?"

"I don't know why she doesn't come now. We are ripe for her mischief."

"She must be waiting for something, but what?"

Both men shook their heads. Paul broke the silence. "I trust you are praying?"

"I am, though I think others are better at it than I."

"It's funny, I would have thought—" But Paul broke off.

"Thought what?"

"Nothing, just thinking that Amis and Rapunzel have both had signs from God before." Paul shrugged. "But I've not spoken to either of them of such things, we're all so busy with the affairs of the kingdoms right now."

"I'd say our whole company has our hands full. We'll keep praying and trust that God hears us." Edmund hoped that was the right thing to say.

Fortunately, Paul nodded and took his leave with a small bow. Edmund heaved a great sigh, but winced at the sharp pain that pierced his side. He gingerly sat down, grateful for the bench just outside the throne room where he could catch his breath before heading back to his chambers to rest for the night. He would have to retreat for now; his energy was spent.

# DISTURBING STRUGGLES

The next morning, Gwynndolen tripped and hit her backside with an "oof!" She bounced back up, causing Paul to jerk back in surprise. He advanced with a quick stride, but she circled back around him. He didn't smile as he countered, sending her retreating once more. Backward he went again as they advanced, retreated, all the while clanging their swords, one against the other. Drenched in sweat, she fell once more. But this time, Paul stepped in and pointed his sword at her chest. She couldn't believe how vulnerable she had left herself. If he were a true enemy, he could have killed her, but he held out a hand to help her up.

Chivalry? No, she wouldn't have it! Gwynndolen slapped his hand away and stood to her feet. She shot a look over at Edmund and saw that was exactly the wrong thing to do, and she couldn't calm the shame that flamed her cheeks. It was happening again. She couldn't focus. Flashes of her brothers filled her vision, memories of their training, how they had taught her each move, each stance. Without them, she would have died—well, she *had* died.

And then they had died. Now, she couldn't think straight while fighting.

Gwynndolen looked back at the prince. Bested by Rapunzel's husband? She would never win the melee this way. If only Edmund hadn't been watching! What if he decided she was a lost cause and tried to take his place in the tournament back? He could barely hold himself up, much less wield a sword.

She noticed the downward cast of his face and she wanted to skulk away, to fume in private. But if she could take the applause when she won, she needed to learn to take defeat as a good swordsman. Oh, how she hated it. She brushed herself off and walked over to Paul, who eyed her with a neutral expression. This man was good at keeping his own counsel. "Thank you for your help, Your Highness. I am sorry for my flashes of temper. I will try to rein them in."

He jarred her with a hard pat on the back, revealing a friendly smile. "You will do better next time. I think that to stand a chance in the tournament, you must practice something new. Are you up to the challenge?"

Her brow furrowed. "Of course, Your Highness."

"I thought you would be—trust me and I will help you in tomorrow's practice. You are very good, my lady—I just got the better of your temper today."

She gave a sharp nod and went to go clean up. It had been another long, grueling day. Her throat tightened at the thought that she hadn't worked this hard since training with her brothers. And for a moment, she missed her sister Beatrix. How Beatrix would wrinkle her nose at Gwynndolen, claiming she stank and needed a good bathing. Gwynndolen blinked back a tear, even as laughter bubbled up beneath the sorrow. She was glad that before she lost her sister they had learned to tease and laugh, no longer giving and taking offense.

Clearing her throat, Gwynndolen entered her chambers and allowed her court-assigned maidservant to help clean her up. It took scrubbing and fresh clothing and many tugs of a comb through her sweaty hair before her maid could rebraid it, working in ribbons that gleamed among her copper locks.

What a study in contrasts was her life. One moment fighting with men, and the next, she'd be off to gossip with women. Still, if she was to be queen, things would have to change within her to balance the tension between her roles. She wasn't sure that she was up to another challenge. Had she been wrong to accept Edmund's proposal of marriage?

A knock on her door sent her maidservant scurrying to open it, while Gwynndolen tucked a wayward lock into her braid. It would probably never stay put, would it? She stood to greet Rapunzel, who entered with her toddler on her hip.

"Rapunzel!" Gwynndolen smiled and reached for Helena, who instead grunted and wiggled to be released. Both the women laughed as the little girl got down and practiced her walking, which was getting faster and faster.

"I wanted to come and see how you were doing. There was no time to speak to you last night since I had to get this one off to sleep. Is everything going well?"

"By *everything*, do you mean, how am I getting along with Edmund?"

Rapunzel laughed. "Well, it's less than a week till you wed."

"I know." Gwynndolen realized she had a hand on her heart like some simpering maid. She made a fist and thumped her chest, a sign that a warrior was ready for a challenge. Wanting to change the subject, she looked closer at the princess. "What about you? You seem to have survived the High Queen's meeting."

"Yes, so far. Now that all the kingdom representatives have arrived, she has agreed to meet with all of us."

"That should prove interesting, if nothing else. Tell me, does she always look so—"

"So what?"

"Predatory?"

"Mmm, that's an apt way to say it. Yes, she does, in my experience, although it seems worse now."

"Well, maybe I should decline. I have the tournament coming and the wedding—"

"Don't try to get out of it. We need you there. It took convincing to get her to agree to see all of us at once. I would rather we didn't have to, but if we are to defeat Camilla—"

Gwynndolen made a face. "What wonderful queens we will make, always fighting sorcery and other plots of intrigue."

"Perhaps we will define a new standard for queens!" Rapunzel laughed.

"That's not a bad idea, Rapunzel."

"I only said it in jest."

"Edmund said something like that, that I should decide for myself what kind of queen I wanted to be. Have you thought about it much?"

"I think on it all the time, especially anytime Lady Florese is correcting me."

Gwynndolen grunted. Rapunzel had informed her friend all about the type of training that the princess was undergoing while Gwynndolen was swinging swords. "I don't know how you can stand it."

"I don't have a choice, now, do I? Sometimes you have to ask for and receive help. If I want to make my husband and kingdom proud—"

"That's nonsense. One only has to look at your husband to see he is quite proud of you. And look at your child. She adores you! If you satisfy the High Queen in your meeting, then I think you are well on your way to becoming the queen God has predestined you to become."

"And you?"

"And me?"

"You're working so hard—you are becoming exactly the queen Edmund needs, the one God desires for him."

Gwynndolen walked over to the dressing table, but Rapunzel followed behind and looked at her in the silver glass.

"What's wrong?"

"Your husband bested me. If I can't win the melee, the king won't give us his blessing, and Edmund will lose his island. Prince Paul said he was just having a good day, and I was having a bad one, but I don't know that I can improve. And if Edmund sees me fight that poorly again, I don't know that I can keep him from jumping in."

"Gwynndolen, Paul's there to help you. You know that, don't you? I think God has brought us all together so that we can receive the help we need."

She gripped the back of the chair. "Queens who ask for help?"

"I have to ask God for help all the time," she admitted —but even as she spoke, Rapunzel's gaze dropped.

"I hate asking for help, but I really don't know what I'm doing."

"Nor do I!" Gently, Rapunzel turned her friend to face her so they could see each other clearly. "I'm unsure of what I should do to be a queen, a mother, a wife, a courtier . . . I think that is why we make such great friends."

"After luncheon, we will go for a ride!" Gwynndolen laughed. "It will be the best fun! Don't you think so?"

Rapunzel's eyes brightened at the thought. "Do you think it will be safe with Helena?"

"My mother never let a babe in arms stop her from riding. I'll help you select a gentle horse and find a snug sling so that Helena can ride tucked against you. I think she'll love it." She took a deep breath. "We shall find our own way, princess. Nothing will stop us."

# DESCENDING WITH THE QUEEN

*A*s Rapunzel entered the High Queen's sitting room for the second time, she was struck again by how frail the queen looked. The woman's once-vibrant brown skin now looked waxen, and her unbraided hair revealed vast streaks of white among the coarse locks. Nearby sat her eldest daughter, Princess Qasmuna, prim and pinched as before. The queen nodded, and the daughter left, though she looked at Rapunzel with something akin to hatred.

No one in their group had missed the look. Paul turned to Rapunzel with raised eyebrows, but Rapunzel simply shook her head. They didn't need to worry over the daughter, only the queen, who was bent on defeating the darkness at any cost.

The queen now sat alone, once again engulfed by yards of fabric. She looked as though she was hiding inside the fur-lined collar despite the warmth of summer. Of course, the castle was cooler than the outdoors, but not enough to warrant the heat of the flames in the fireplace. If they stayed in the room much longer, they'd all be sweating.

Rapunzel swallowed as the silence mounted. She had nothing to do with her hands. She tried grasping them behind her and then folding them in front of her. Was Gwynndolen feeling as unsure as she was? A glance at her over at Gwynndolen and then at her mother revealed their discomfort as well. Paul and Edmund seemed to hold their own, though, not shifting their weight from foot to foot like the ladies.

If she had Helena with her, the weight of the squirmy toddler would be a pleasant distraction from the oppressive silence. But she knew it was best to leave her child safe with Nofra. What vitriol would the queen spout? If only Rapunzel could protect her child always.

"Why do you think you are here?" the queen asked, her dry lips smacking, her brown eyes reminding Rapunzel of the coffy she had drunk. There was a fever behind them that Rapunzel couldn't understand, couldn't fathom.

"My health," the woman said as she gestured to herself and looked at them in derision, "after birthing the king's heir, has suffered. But my mind is still sharp. I have had enough of gossip. I long for action. Now that all the royal families have gathered, my attempts to help my husband see we must act have gone unheeded. Prince Edmund, I thank you for your help in convincing Obertus to *lose* a few ships, but I believe it will take all of us to plan what we shall do next. Come, we will determine how to proceed. And to do so, we must descend."

Rapunzel followed as the queen led the way, her slippered feet padding over the clean-swept grey stone floors. Paul, Rapunzel, and Katterina followed behind her, with Edmund and Gwynndolen next, and Amis last of all. Rapunzel was glad for Paul's presence. She tucked her hand in the crook of his elbow as they walked. Should they be speaking? Rapunzel did not know where they were going or how a conversation with the queen should go.

As if reading her thoughts, the woman broke out in a giggle that defied Rapunzel's image of the woman. For a moment, the last glimpse she remembered of the queen in the Winter Castle flashed through her mind, the night Rapunzel had solved the mystery of the tattered shoes. The self-assured woman had been swept up into the arms of the High King while they danced. He harbored an adoration for her, after a fashion, but it wasn't a love that Rapunzel would ever want to experience. It was self-serving and short-sighted. The princess didn't mean to think about it, but her thoughts strayed. Where was the king keeping his mistress and illegitimate son? Though the king had been wrong to take a mistress, Rapunzel still hoped they would be safe from the queen's venom.

The group stopped before a guard, who nodded at the queen. They followed the stairs down into the castle's dungeon.

Amee shook and trembled. Why could she not rid herself of the weakness that invaded her limbs, that malformed them into different shapes? Where was her control?

She heard footsteps slapping against the wet stones in the dank dungeon. And there was some sort of clacking sound, a staff perhaps? As the sounds descended the winding steps, she could see light pushing aside the shadows. Her eyes adjusted to the torch's amber light, and she could see the High Queen advancing with a small group. Here were Amee's captors—most of them, anyway. One of the princes held the torch as he walked next to the queen, followed by the rest, with the fool who gaped at her last of all. Was she a spectacle for them to come and look at?

But it was Katterina's gaze that pricked her heart unexpectedly. Katterina's eyes, filled with pity. No—it was compassion. Was it true that because they were both mothers who had chosen poorly, they were bound together? For a moment, Amee's mind wandered as she thought of the cat who had fetched and carried messages back and forth between herself and Ute. What had it been like for the woman to become a cat, one who was never in charge of where she went?

Amee's body jerked again, this time morphing into a dragon. Scales of black and wings of purple. So like Ute that she wanted to cry. She was grateful for the humongous dimensions of the dungeon, but she had transformed so quickly that now she was backed up into the corner, both wings crimped up into the walls.

"Well, that can't be comfortable." Lady Katterina said.

"No, indeed," agreed the High Queen.

Amee stepped forward, unfurling her massive wings. "What do you want?"

The High Queen smiled, a flash of white in a shadowed face. "I think you know. Tell us what your sister desires and what she is planning in order to get it."

Amee laughed. But it was hollow. She took one more step forward, careful not to get too close to the invisible barrier. "You know what she wants. The same thing both my sisters wanted. Power. And she'll do anything to get it."

The queen waved a bony hand in front of her face. "Yes, yes, but what specifically will she do?"

Amee writhed, stepping back with her clawed feet. "Why would I tell you that?"

"Because you want something from us. You need something that only we can give."

Amee's lids drooped, and her head hung. "I only want to die, to be done with this miserable life."

Katterina couldn't help asking, "Really? You want to die with Dietz hating you?"

Amee startled at his name. Not that anyone could probably tell the difference. She was so often jerking to shift and change shapes. "Of course I don't want that. No one would want that."

The High Queen seemed to smile at her discomfort. "I'm told you betrayed everything you worked for to save his life, but do you really think he is safe? I, like you, know power. How it corrupts, how it wins. Your son is not safe as he is. He needs to spend time with you, his mother, to comprehend how to safeguard himself from your sister. She would kill him for what he has inside, wouldn't she?"

"And why would you help me, Your Majesty?"

"Because you are going to help me."

"Oh, and how can I do that from this cell while I can't even—I can't even control what shape I take?" A loud growl ripped from her throat as she shrank down to the floor, her body becoming covered in a cow's hide as she moaned and kicked her hooves.

"You are going to share with me all that you know of the plans to destroy the kingdoms. Everything you tell me will grant you more time with your son."

"How will you know I am telling the truth?"

"Because the monk bound you in the name of Jesu , you will not lie. And I think you are tired of lying, aren't you?"

Amee felt her head bow in resignation. To see Dietz again, to spend time with him, she would give anything. She would do everything.

~

KATTERINA WAS unsurprised by Amee's knowledge. She seemed to know everything that would happen in the days ahead. How Camilla and the covens would lay siege to the Summer Castle, how the pirates would hold off any vessel that would come to aid them. And all this while the foolish king insisted on holding the tournament, as though that would matter if they all died.

No, their only hope was in the God they worshipped, the God Camilla thought was weak. If only Jacob had returned with Father Iohannes already. If only he were here now, he would know what to do against the plans of this sorceress.

The queen turned around to look at Paul and Edmund, her prominent forehead wrinkled in question. "Well, princes, what do you say? Your High King doesn't see the threat ahead, but if we do nothing, we will all die a slow death of starvation during a long, drawn-out siege. Our storehouses would fail quickly with as many guests as we have now from all the visiting nobility."

Edmund grimaced. "Your Majesty is most astute. The ships that are 'misplaced' will only be able to help us a little. What lies ahead is calamity unless we convince the king that we must gather the armies of the kingdoms and—"

"As I have explained, there is no convincing the man. He does not see the threat—will not see it! It is up to us to act."

A squawk turned their attention back to the newest transformation of Amee. She was now a strange sort of rabbit crossed with a lizard. *Grotesque* was too kind a description, to Katterina's way of thinking.

Edmund stepped forward, leaning heavily on his staff, Katterina noticed. "Your Majesty has stated that the name of Jesu has bound this creature."

"Yes?"

"Can't his name bind the other sister?"

"Of course," the queen snorted, "but we must locate her first, and you know as well as I do she will not come until she is ready to strike."

Paul shook his head slowly, and the torch in his hand wavered. "Then we must prepare ourselves how our warrior monks and the warrior women prepare themselves, with prayer and fasting."

The queen divided their little group by walking back to the stairs, and then shot over her shoulder, "Fine. Choose to pray if you must, but I am not on speaking terms with God. You will have to pray for me."

Katterina blinked. Was that all they could do? Pray and stop eating food? Surely there was more to do than that! But voicing such a thought showed her impatience, her lack of spiritual maturity. *God, is this from you?* Her spirit reached out, but she heard nothing audible, simply felt a void where her peace had been. They needed Jacob. If only he were here now.

Rapunzel was watching her. "Mother? Do you think there is something else we should do?"

The queen, having climbed a couple of steps, turned around to regard them.

Katterina looked at Paul. She shook her head. "No,

Paul knows what he's talking about. We should fast and pray."

"Pray, by all means, but do not fast, at least not now," the queen's voice warned. "My husband will not abide fasting at his feast. If he is to sanction the union of Prince Edmund and the Lady Gwynndolen and the upcoming christening, we must celebrate."

Had the mood not been so dire, Katterina might have smiled at the color that rose to Gwynndolen's face. "What's wrong, Lady Gwynndolen?" she couldn't help asking.

"Nothing. Just . . . so much. The High Queen's seamstress has been so helpful—my wedding gown is nearly done. But still, it's all happening at once, isn't it? A wedding at daybreak, then the christening, and the following day begins the tournament—" Her eyes darted to Edmund, who gave a sideways smile, and for a moment, Katterina felt a pang of jealousy bite her. To be free to love. She tried to remember what that had been like. If Jacob was free— But she shouldn't be worrying over that. Not now, not with all that was going on. With one last look at the shaking Amee, she followed the group back out of the dungeon and toward the light.

# A STILL, SMALL VOICE

Jacob was close to the end of the Scriptures when he heard it, that still, inaudible voice speaking, confirming what he knew to be true. Birds were calling overhead as the sun broke through the horizon, with rays of bright orange spilling into the morning sky. His hands froze on the staff mid-swing, his movements stopped still by the answer burning in his chest. God had revealed himself. Jacob had to tell Father Iohannes. Not wanting to disrupt the worship of his brothers, he compelled himself to finish Lauds. Taking in a deep breath of the salty air, he focused on the last few movements. He waited till all the brothers had preceded him and then hurried to intercept Father Iohannes, who was alone in the chapel.

The man was kneeling before the altar, his head so low it touched the stone step. Jacob knelt beside him. The sweat on his brow cooled as he waited. He had learned patience at an early age, and it had served him well. His breathing slowed, his mind and spirit reaching out to the God of his youth, the God of his present, the God of his future. *Guide us, O Lord, and lead us not into temptation, but deliver us from evil.*

"Amen." the older man's head lifted, and he smiled, as though he could hear the words that Jacob had silently prayed. "You have heard from our Lord, Brother Jacob? Seen a vision?"

"I have." He crossed himself and looked at his mentor. "And I think you have as well."

"Indeed." Jacob stood, but the older man touched his shoulder, prompting him to sit down. "Before we discuss what we have seen, I must ask. Has the Lord revealed himself to you about your feelings for Lady Katterina?"

Jacob lowered his head. "I will honor my vow to love the Lord my God with all my heart, mind, and strength. I will love my neighbor as myself."

Father Iohannes nodded his head, waiting.

"But I cannot purge my feelings for the lady."

"Would you jeopardize your soul for her?"

"I have prayed and feel the Spirit of the Lord confirming within me. I do not put my soul in jeopardy by loving her."

Silence descended for several moments as they stared at one another. "Would you jeopardize her soul?"

"I don't understand."

"You say you will honor your vow to love the Lord your God with all that you are. But how can you if you take this woman, this woman marked by sorcery, as your wife? If you make an idol of her?"

Jacob shook his head. "I know it will take much focus to always put God above her, but I will do so. She will not become an idol."

Father Iohannes's face twisted into an uncharacteristic

scowl. "You should purge these feelings and return to the Lord."

"I have never left him. I have never abandoned my calling. Would the Lord have blessed me with the vision if I had? I have not. I will not. My vow was to serve him with all my soul. My pledge was to live a chaste life as long as he called me to it. I can see nothing evil in taking her as my wife if she agrees."

Father Iohannes held up both hands. His voice lowered. "I think we must put aside this disagreement for now. Though I would rather be united in all things, now is the time to gather the council together. We must make plans."

Jacob took a breath and shared what he had seen, and Father Iohannes, true to his word, did not bring up Lady Katterina again. When they rose, Jacob noticed how stiff the older man was in his movements. He envied the man's wisdom, but not the aches that evidently came from aging. The monk had to stop himself from offering the man his hand, not wishing to offend. Father Iohannes had never been a fragile man, and he did sing and beat the floor with his staff at their indoor prayer times. It was his absence from Lauds that worried Jacob, but he pushed the concern from his mind and concentrated on the task at hand.

Following Father Iohannes into the study, the dark wood which smelled of the linseed oil and beeswax that had polished it for centuries comforted Jacob. He stood straight and tall, smiling at the council members as they arrived. The men came in, wearing their bright green robes and hosen, having taken off the chain mail and padding from the morning's exercise in the courtyard. They had their weapons belted around their waists, but that was to be expected unless they were meeting in the chapel. No warrior monk was otherwise without his weapon.

Father Iohannes crossed himself and prayed for guidance, his prayer simple and swift. It was no time to belabor words; these were now times for action. "We must rally the brothers together and ride to see the warrior women. Jacob has spoken with us. Brother Jacob?"

Jacob tipped his chin and then looked each brother in the eye. These were faithful, strong men. Men who would give their lives. They would stand fast till the end. "The High King fears the sorceress, but will not admit it, even to himself. He cowers in his castle, hiding behind the ceremonies and celebrations he has planned. He inherited the loyalty of the kingdoms, but if he does not defend them, he will lose them.

"We will march through the day and night until we reach the convent, and God will meet us there. God will give us word of what has been happening among the scattered following of the sisters of sorcery, and with this proof, we will march on the Summer Castle and demand the king either do right by the kingdoms or relinquish the crown."

Jacob glanced around. Several members' mouths hung open.

"We will ride out at dawn tomorrow. We will take the holy Scripture and our weapons with us. Brothers, are you prepared to fight the forces of evil?"

"Of course!" The voice of Brother Thomas rang out. He was a tall, dark man whose enthusiasm lifted the spirits of those gathered. "And will we proceed to the Summer Castle at last and face the High King?"

Father Iohannes stared at Jacob. "Brother Jacob now knows what to say to the High King. But as I have said, first we will strategize with the warrior women."

Another, Brother Philip, clapped his hands. "This is good news! Do you know what the king will say?"

Father Iohannes nodded. "But I will not be the one to speak of it. That must fall on Brother Jacob." Father Iohannes turned to look Jacob in the eye. "Wherefore you have taken your vows to serve and protect, now you shall see to it."

Jacob nodded. His vows. Was he chosen because he had taken his vows? The image of Lady Katterina flashed before his eyes. Was it best if he never thought of her again? There was too much at stake now. He had chosen God long ago, chose him even now. Could he be wrong about Lady Katterina?

# THE PULL OF MAGIC

*D*ietz gathered his courage and deepened his stance as he saw Gwynndolen getting ready to charge him. He was glad he hadn't eaten that morning and that Paul was allowing him to practice without armor. He knew the girl was better than he was, but an unfamiliar feeling of optimism lit up inside him. Paul thought he belonged here, with them, that Dietz was worth training.

A goofy grin filled his face before he remembered to lunge at her with his staff held in both hands. Dietz quickly adjusted, and they crashed into each other, his grin now wiped off as his lips whitened in determination. He wouldn't allow her—or anyone!—to stop him. With each practice, he was growing stronger, better. When Gwynndolen spun away, he nearly fell, but kept his balance. The next time she charged, his lunge was so deep, it was easy to spring forward, pushing her off-balance. She regained her composure and then came at him again, but he held her off a little longer this time, refusing to let her in his circle.

Oh! Her face! Why was it so flushed? He was a little afraid, but he tried to not let it show. He didn't want to be afraid; he wanted to inspire fear in his "enemy," even if this was just practice. Again, the urge to use the magic he had learned as a tiny child was strong, but he pushed it away. Hadn't he chosen to serve a new God? He would learn without the old ways, and he would add these hard-won lessons so that one day he might win. But it was hard to remember that when her beet-red face was rushing at him. Was she that determined to prove herself?

Suddenly, the sound of his brothers mocking him clanged about in his head. Only a fool would allow a woman to best him when he had powers he could summon. But no—that wasn't his life anymore. Instead, he pushed harder, faster, stronger. He surprised even himself, and he could see the shock in the flash of her eyes. In the last moment, she got inside his range and swept his leg out from under him. He fell to the ground, panting, but then he heard clapping. He looked up. Lady Gwynndolen stopped clapping and held out her hand for him to take, shaking her head. "Dietz, you're getting harder and harder to beat. Shaking my confidence!"

He took this as a compliment and smiled.

"Well done, both of you!" Paul reached out to grip both their shoulders. "Gwynndolen, you have a surprising bit of speed and your nimble spins and kicks will take you far. Dietz, I think you shocked yourself. You let her push you into a corner for a moment, but then you worked your way out of it. Well done!"

Dietz wished he could win outright, but for now, he would take the progress he'd made and content himself with that.

CAMILLA WAS HUNGRY AGAIN. She needed a feast, not the meager sampling of power she could pull from the weak men in the ship's belly. The plague that had devastated the Land of Midnight two centuries earlier had cut off the continent from the rest of the known world. The men were the most vulnerable to it, but it had killed thousands of women as well. As their civilization had dwindled and shrunk, generation after generation, a ship full of brave women who had been immune to the plague had set off to find help. But of course, no port in the Kabir islands would allow them to take harbor. The Midnight people had been ostracized for too long. That's when Camilla had found them: lost, alone, uncertain.

Her family's book of magic told of how they had caused the plague in the first place to stop the spread of faith in the weak god. She remembered studying it as a little girl before the first War of Sorcery. Her mother had read to her until she and Ute could read to themselves, Amee joining in their learning after she was born. She still remembered large chunks of the book by heart, but the book itself was lost somewhere in Ute's lair. If she could find it again one day . . . But there was no time for such thinking now.

It was from her family's book that Camilla had remembered the olio plant that grew in the Illyan Sea. She had taught the pirate women how to use it to treat the plague victims. For the last ten years, she had aided the pirates and the Midnight people, taught them to disdain the weak god who hadn't, who wouldn't, save them. They had learned a healthy respect for her sorcery and had begun doing her bidding out on the seas. She nurtured them, and when she had tapped back into her power source, it had been a simple thing to direct them to join her in destroying the High King and bringing down the Church.

The pirate ships now weighed anchor at the islands of Lamir, nearly ready to begin the blockade at the mouth of the Gulf of Alleria. Only a few more ships, and it would be time. But Camilla was weary of traveling between the pirates and Amee's covens, and gathering information from the spies she had set in the Summer Castle. She shouldn't have to do this alone. If only Amee had not— But it was no use. She would simply need more fuel to continue to coordinate the plan and see it to completion.

The sorceress followed Hadijah's first officer belowdecks, the creaking of the ship emphasizing each step. She had to duck farther the lower they went, as though the ship had been built for mythical dwarves. The lantern's light barely penetrated the darkness, but that didn't bother Camilla, whose leviathan eyes could see no matter how little light there was.

It was the smell that bothered her. The pirates bathed and kept fresh clothes on the men, but the disease caused horrible gas and body odor like rotting garlic. It was less than appetizing. But Camilla knew why the pirates kept them around. They considered these survivors of the plague to be vital to a safe journey through the waters, a strange good fortune charm.

She looked at this morning's victim before she began feeding, wrapping her tentacles around him, squeezing him and letting the suckers on her tentacles leech away some of his energy. Emaciated, brown eyes blank, his ribs were all too easy to count beneath his dark skin. His belly was round, protruding, testifying to his malnourishment. The olio plant had saved many men from plague in the last ten years, but victims like this were too far gone to improve.

Instead, they languished, dependent on the drug for their life, but unable to get better. The Midnight women decided it was part of their duty to keep them alive as testimony to the drug's power. Some had even sung songs of worship to Camilla's name while they kept the poor men alive. Of course, there was now a young generation growing up healthy, but they were too young to have positions of power yet. They were growing up beneath the instruction of the pirate women, who taught them that men were weak and women must rule over them.

Camilla loved the thought of that. She relished the thrill of knowing that this people, her people, worshipped her and would serve her as she asked. And now that she was free to roam, she only needed power to visit the rest of her people. Once the High King was overthrown, she could rule all the known world, including the Land of Midnight. There was nothing, no one, who would dare stop her.

The man before her groaned and then flopped over, lifeless. She had drained him too thoroughly. The short but powerful pirate behind her spit to the side, warding off evil. Camilla turned to glare at the woman. "If I need all of his energy, then he will serve my purpose. I keep you safe—I grant you passage through the waters, don't I? You don't need these men unless I decide you do. Understand? Throw his body overboard!" She hated having to explain herself, but it was necessary if she was to remain in control of how their theology was being built around her.

There were times she wished she could conquer all by herself. But until she was stronger, until she had the throne herself, she would still need help. From Amee's covens. From her own pirates. And soon, from Amee herself.

# THE MAIDSERVANT

Nofra stared into the glass at the princess. Every morning she would unbraid and comb through the tangles in Rapunzel's hair, working in a little water and olive oil as needed. Combing the thick mass and then braiding it into a crown around Rapunzel's head gave the princess a regal look. Her hair was much softer now that Nofra was caring for it, and though it was coarse, Rapunzel's curls were not as tight as Nofra's spirals and were a little easier to handle.

Little Helena cooed and laughed, toddling about the chamber as Nofra worked, smiling to herself. "What will you be doing today?" she asked, weaving ribbons of dark blue among the golden tresses. Amazing how the dark color stood out in such light hair!

"I'm uncertain." The princess was trying not to fidget. It was obvious she still wasn't comfortable being tended to. "I think the High Queen wants to see me again, and my friends as well. Of course, it will have to wait awhile—the contestants are still preparing for the tournament."

"Including your husband?"

"Yes."

"Do you train with him?"

"No, not I! I leave that to Lady Gwynndolen!" Their honest laughs filled the chamber and little Helena joined in the giggling, crawling over to the chair and pulling up. Though she could walk, Nofra had noticed that the little one still went back and forth from scooting and bear-crawling to pulling herself up and walking. She tugged on Nofra's dress, making the women laugh more.

"Does she want me to hold her?" Nofra asked, hoping the princess would not take offense.

Rapunzel nodded. "I think she does."

Nofra bent down and lifted her up. Immediately Helena reached for a blue ribbon resting on the vanity table. "Ha!" Nofra laughed and lifted the ribbon to the child, who promptly shoved it in her mouth. "So I was just a means to an end!"

Rapunzel smiled. Nofra was at last making progress, gaining her trust.

A knock on the door sounded before Lady Katterina entered, and Nofra's chest tightened.

"Mother, you're smiling!"

"Is that such a surprise? My daughter looks lovely and her maidservant is helping with my energetic granddaughter."

Rapunzel nodded. "All is well as long as Helena doesn't swallow the ribbon."

Katterina came over and kissed the little girl's forehead, then looked at Nofra a moment longer than was comfortable. "She likes you."

Nofra didn't know what to say to that, so she just nodded.

"Now, there must be some other reason for your smile,

Mother. You haven't really smiled since—I mean, I just haven't seen you smile for a while."

Katterina dismissed this with a lift of her shoulder and knelt on the rug as Nofra placed the squirmy toddler down. "Well, that's about to change. I don't have to follow you around like a lost pup."

"That wouldn't suit you at all."

"Nor any who had been a cat! No, I have discovered what to do with myself while you spend your hours continuing your training. The court apothecary has agreed to let me accompany some of his servants as they go gather herbs."

"But, Mother, we are to meet with the High Queen today. Please, be there."

"We aren't going out today, though I have to talk with the apothecary before our meeting. I'm so excited! They have exotic plants and herbs we don't have in the Northlands, and if I'm very careful, I can preserve them so that they travel well with us. I can create new poultices and tinctures to care for those who are suffering."

Rapunzel smiled, but Nofra noticed the way her eyes dropped.

"I'll still be back in plenty of time to attend the evening meal. And never fear, I'll sit by your side once the tournament begins in a week's time."

"Yes, of course, don't mind me. I just shudder to think of all that I have ahead of me."

"Learning to be a queen is no simple task."

"Neither is treating the ill. Go and do well. I'll see you soon."

Katterina kissed Helena with a smile and left. As soon as she left, Rapunzel frowned. Finishing up, Nofra rested a hand on the princess's shoulders. "Is there anything else I can do?"

Rapunzel caught her eye in the looking glass, before Nofra looked down. "No, there's nothing you can do. I must learn to be a queen and—" The princess was struggling with something. Her eyes looked moist for a moment, but she cleared her throat and gave a weak smile. "Instead of accompanying me, could you occupy Helena? I'd rather not take her with me for this morning's instruction."

Nofra smiled. This was working better than she had hoped. She didn't feel the least guilty as she hefted the little one. Helena laughed and clapped her hands, anticipating more fun with Nofra.

DIETZ RAISED his fist to knock on the Princess Rapunzel's chambers when the door opened, revealing a young woman holding Helena. She frowned as she looked at him, probably mirroring his own expression. He had seen her trailing behind Princess Rapunzel the day before, but thus far had no interaction with her. "May I help you?"

And now he would have to speak with her. "I have a m-message from P-Prince P-Paul for his wife."

"Are you his messenger?" Something about the tilt of her chin and how she narrowed her eyes set him ill at ease.

*No, I am his ward, and when he asks me to bring a message, I do it.* But his thoughts wouldn't come out of his mouth so clearly, so he spoke the one word he knew he wouldn't mess up. "No."

"Well, the princess is receiving instruction and has left me to tend to the child." She held out her hand expectantly.

Dietz stared at her hand and shrugged. "The p-prince d-didn't write it d-down."

The maidservant gave a dramatic sigh as she replied, "Then I suppose you had best say it and I will give the message to the princess as soon as I see her."

Dietz swallowed. "He wants—could she—he'll be w-waiting for her at the m-midday m-meal." There was more than that, but he couldn't manage the words. They were so clear in his mind, but his stupid tongue struggled to keep up.

The young woman nodded and closed the door, but then stopped. "You're Dietz?"

He nodded.

"I thought—" But she stopped, staring him straight in the eye. He felt something shift inside him. She looked as though she shimmered, just slightly.

"Wha—?" But she closed the door, and he stepped back, confused. Who was she? And what was she doing here?

# AN ODD STILLNESS

*J*acob should have felt exhausted as they continued their march, having traveled on foot from dawn till dusk. Their chanting prayers kept track of the hours as they made their way along the coastline. At Lauds, the sun peeked up over the waters, and they started off, chanting their armor.

Jacob, one of the first to help carry the litter that held Father Iohannes, found his mind was practicing the motions even though he wasn't physically able to go through the whole practice. At Prime they took turns praying aloud, and then at Terce, their feet beat the sand as though they were beating their staffs in rhythm. Barely stopping at midday to refresh themselves, they had pushed forward, marching in formation, their feet churning the sand beneath them. The midafternoon prayer of None had them chanting the beatitudes, and Jacob was grateful to take his place among those marching and not carrying. He felt every year of his age and looked at the younger monks with humor. They would feel the same as he one day.

By Vespers, they were approaching the convent. The sun was setting, its blazing goodbye burning a coral streak of pink across the sky and reflecting in the waves as the tide let out. He saw lamps being lit in an outer courtyard that led to the sea. There the warrior women were finishing their evening prayers of gratitude, and solo voices called out for healing for different ailments.

They must have heard the warrior monks approaching. The sand did little to muffle the sounds of so many monks' marching feet, but it did not alter their prayers. The women finished when they had chanted the last of the scripture, "Hallelujah to the Lord of heaven and earth," and not a moment before.

A tall, dark warrior stood facing the women with her back to the sea, a sword sheathed in her belt. Rows and rows of women bowed to her. They were of different heights, shapes, and coloring, all wearing bright green padded tunics with glittering chain mail on top, and hosen covering their legs. It had been a long time since Jacob had met a warrior woman. They mostly kept to the Eastern Ports. Though they had sent out missionaries once to carry the gospel throughout the kingdoms, the sisters who spread out, like many of the monks, did not keep up the warrior mentality once they left behind the Eastern Ports. No one had seen the need for it in the lull that had followed the end of the War of Sorcery. None, till now.

The woman turned and greeted Father Iohannes as he stepped out of the cushioned litter. "We were expecting you well before this, Father." The abbess spoke in Latin, an unusual soft lilt on her r's. "But when we received your message to delay our departure for the Summer Castle, we committed to praying longer and harder. We have prepared to hear what you have to say so that we can know what part we will play."

"You honor the Lord with your diligence," Father Iohannes said, bowing a slight nod. The woman beckoned them to follow the women up into the buildings that were raised on sturdy columns. Jacob hid his surprise. He would have thought she would ask Father Iohannes to lead the way, but Father Iohannes did not seem off-put, and it relieved him. Perhaps things had changed slightly; perhaps with Father Iohannes in charge now, women would receive more honor because of their station. After all, God had made them in his image. Though the man was the head of his house, women were an essential part of creation, and man was not whole without her.

Jacob realized with a start that he was thinking of himself and Katterina. She was never far from his mind. Was she well? Would she survive what was ahead? If he were to ask, would she join herself to him, share his life? There was so much he did not know of her. He was still uncertain of her age. Her daughter was a young woman, not over two decades, with a child of her own. And he knew Katterina had been just a girl, barely a mother, when she transformed into Cat. Was she even six and thirty? He couldn't help wondering if Katterina would want another child, one she could actually watch grow up. She had missed Rapunzel's upbringing. Could God use him to redeem that part of her life? Would she even want to have children with him? He furrowed his brow as he followed the warrior women inside the convent. What a strange thought to be thinking while he walked into a nunnery. Indeed, it was too easy to be swayed to think of earthly things when there were more pressing issues at hand.

~

THE MORNING LIGHT hit Amis in the face as the door flap lifted in the wind. That was odd. When was the last time that he had slept until morning? Amis sat up on his bedding and rubbed his bleary eyes. He was alone. All the other servants had rolled up their bedding and placed it in neat rolls in each of the corners of the tent. He groggily realized the noises that had reached his sleepy brain must have been the other servants rising earlier.

Like most of those who served the royals gathered to the Summer Castle for the celebrations, Amis had made his temporary home in a tent outside the castle with other servants. Amis had tried to make friends with the three of them, but they weren't the jovial sort. Each evening they returned to the tent from their duties, exhausted and disgusted with humidity and rain. Though the tent kept out some of it, each morning they still woke up damp. There was a moldy sort of smell growing that worsened as the unwashed servants bedded down each night. It was difficult even for Amis to see the bright side of being soggy and smelly.

But it wasn't this that Amis felt was strange. This was a mere inconvenience of life. No, it was that something felt off somehow. Like a joint out of socket. He clasped his hands between his knees and tried to piece his thoughts together. Was it because he had stumbled during a performance? That had been distressing, but laughable. No, it was more than that. There was a feeling of disconnection.

He missed their little group; he missed the pattern of rising and going somewhere together. Rapunzel might be the one who had said she had itchy feet, but Amis could relate. Spending more than a week in a tent with strangers that didn't wish to make friends was hard on him. The fool had unspent words and energy, but as time went on, the melancholy of disconnection dragged at him. Shouldn't he be using his time with greater care, preparing for what was ahead—but it was hard to focus. Amis had been trying for days without success to find the fool he would need to perform with. He sighed. This shouldn't be so hard.

When he was young, his father had taught him to use all of his time to sort through the stories and songs he knew. He could put new ones together out of the pieces of the old, or he could weave them into something different altogether. There was a way to measure an audience, to note its likes and dislikes and be able to serve them what they wanted. He wasn't always able to spend time with the lord or king he served, but if he did, it was easy to see how to stroke their ego.

Of course, once his father brought him before the Fisher King, he learned there was a different sort of nobility. The kind of king who wanted to hear the truth, wanted to know what was what. Even though Amis served other lords and kings, he always returned to the Fisher King for this reason. He didn't need to hide the truth of his stories; he could share what God placed on his heart without subterfuge.

But that would not be the case here with the High King. This man—Amis smiled to himself, for the monarch was really only a man—was one who wanted to hear his own praise. He wanted to hear that all was well when clearly it was not. A frown overtook his mouth, his thick eyebrows crowding his scrunched forehead. How could he cut through the lies that the stubborn king clenched his fists around? Amis didn't want to be the prying sort; he would much rather serve a king and a people who wanted to know how to change.

No. This was more of a job for the warrior monk. Amis sighed again. The answers he was searching for were just out of reach. Where were they? Why couldn't he think of them right away? The stories he liked to think on, the tunes that he would weave together in his mind, would often come humming through his chest. It would fill his mouth with a melody. He would likely do some odd task, like juggling different balls he kept tucked inside his tunic to keep his skills sharp and his hands busy.

But, he realized all at once, he was just sitting still on his bed. His hands were passively holding each other, doing nothing. Where had his energy gone, the determination to take the story of their misadventures and set it before the High King? This wasn't like himself at all! Let the High King flout it at his own risk. Wasn't it Amis's duty to rise and tell the tale?

With more difficulty than he ever remembered, he stood up. The fool took a moment to stretch and then roll up his bedding. Now to find the prince, or maybe the princess. He needed to be back in the company of others who shared his purpose to help him shake off his lethargy.

# THE SONG OF WAR

Gwynndolen readied herself for another day of practice. Oh, her arms were sore! Practicing with the length of the staff had altered her grip since she needed two hands to hold it. Today they were to practice with the long sword, which would also require two hands, and the weight would increase as she swung. But she knew she could do it, if she just decided to.

The morning was already humid, as though a heated vapor were being held over her skin. If only she didn't have to wear the padded tunic and chain mail. But if she didn't, the weight of the chain mail would alter her strikes and stances when it counted most. A trickle of sweat dripped down her back. Yes, she would need another bath before the day was over.

Crossing the green field over to Paul, she nodded to the jester, who had surprised them in joining their practice. Though it still made her nervous to be out with so many other competitors, she wanted to trust Paul's counsel. Dietz was with them again, and he gave Gwynndolen a cautious nod. The young man was not one for much smiling.

Paul motioned for them to come closer to him, and like corners of a map, they folded together. "Lady Gwynndolen, you and Prince Edmund will marry at dawn in a few days. Then, there will be a day-long feast to celebrate the christening and, God willing, Father Iohannes will have arrived by then. Only after the christening will the High King start the tournament."

Gwynndolen nodded, eager to get started and prove herself better than the last time. Edmund had already given her this information. Why was Paul intent on repeating it?

"But I don't think what the king has planned will happen the way he thinks it will. We know that there are darker forces at work, forces that will come against us, and we'd best prepare for them. Don't forget, the High Queen is at work, trying to dissuade her husband from holding the tournament and ready us instead for what's coming."

Gwynndolen wiped her sweaty hands off on her hosen. "I'm not sure this helps, Prince Paul. I already feel wary, knowing Amee is in the dungeons planning who knows what with Camilla."

"God."

Everyone turned and stared at Amis, who had apparently grown bored and was walking on his hands. How on earth did he keep his hat on while upside down? He flipped upright. "You asked who knew what the sisters of sorcery were planning together, didn't you?"

"It was a rhetorical question." Gwynndolen turned her head to stare as he went back to walking on his hands. How could he talk from that position? Her head would feel as though it were going to pop off if she tried such a thing.

"Perhaps you meant it rhetorically, but Brother Jacob's not here to remind you, so I will. God knows. You all seem quite worried about what they are planning or who might be in league with Camilla or what will happen during the tournament itself or when Jacob and Father Iohannes will arrive. I admit, I've even felt a little down. But God knows, and we can trust he is at work. We only have to trust and try our best." The jester then flipped upright again and gave an extravagant bow. "My lady, you especially need to trust."

"Why is that?" Gwynndolen wasn't sure she liked the way he was looking at her.

He stared intently for just a moment longer and then shook his head and waved his hands out as though to regain balance. Perhaps all that walking on his hands wasn't great for his head after all. "You know, I'm not really sure."

Gwynndolen fought the strange quickening in her spirit. She didn't want to look at the feeling too closely—it might cause her to doubt. What if she tried to back away from the tournament, becoming the coward she was afraid she actually was? "I don't know what you mean. Come now, enough of this chatter. I have a tournament to prepare for, as do you, Your Highness!" She tried to give a bright smile to cover the niggling fear making her hands sweat again as she reached to unsheathe her long sword.

Before she had taken a breath, Paul was on her. He advanced, and she aimed for his shoulder, but his reach kept her sword out of range as he blocked every one of her strikes. He lunged at her and she spun outside his radius— just barely, but found that Dietz had come at her from that side. They were both coming at her? Fine, that was something her brothers used to do. She almost laughed as she backed up, and then drove in, hitting Dietz hard in the chest with the broad side of the sword. She pulled back when he fell to his knees, readying her sword for the last strike.

Gwynndolen gulped, the image of her brothers now before her. She imagined she could hear their screams as they fell beneath the waves with the pirates who had fought them. Pirates she had helped slay, their bodies destroyed by her sword. Dietz was back on his feet, coming at her before she could blink. He struck her hand, and she dropped her sword. When had he learned to move like that?

Paul leaned in. "Why do you pull back here? This is where you should push forward. This is when you drive in, put him on his knees, and finish things."

"Kill him?" Gwynndolen sputtered. Why would Paul speak like this to her? "I've only ever killed people one time. Pirates. And it didn't save—I don't-don't think I can—"

"Not now, but you must prepare as if it is war. Lady Gwynndolen, we aren't just preparing for a simple tournament—you know what is at stake. If you regret having had to kill before, regret all those you have lost, you must still drive forward or you will lose and your husband's kingdom along with you. You know what I say is true."

Gwynndolen swallowed hard, her eyes filling with burning tears, her throat tight. An instinct to scream and strike at Paul filled her—but why? He was speaking the truth. She knew it. He knew it.

Could she do what needed doing? Did everyone suspect how weak she actually was?

She tossed her head and re-sheathed her sword. "I—I need a drink." She choked on the words. Stumbling over to where she had dropped her pouch of water, she blinked. Why was her mind in the past? Why couldn't she focus as she fought? Edmund was depending on her, and the High

King would be watching. But the death of those she loved clung to her, and she felt stained, tainted by her own guilt.

PAUL COULD SEE the war battling in the face of Gwynndolen. A sideways glance revealed the same struggle must wage within Dietz. Amis seemed fine, but was he? Paul waited while they all got a drink and then called them back to him. How could he help them?

He turned his gaze on Gwynndolen. Her face was flushed, her eyes too wide for the panic that lived there. "Do you think I fault you for what trials you have faced? I do not." He then patted Dietz's shoulder, but didn't speak until the young man lifted his eyes to him. "Do you think I fault you for the way you have survived until now? Of course not." He stepped back, now including Amis, as he looked at each of them. "But I caution you, renew your mind. God will transform you so that when the battle comes, as it surely will, you will have right thinking. This is just as important as the weapons you grip in your hands. There is a song that Jacob taught me when I was just a lad and first trained with weapons. You've seen him, Dietz, is he not a true warrior of God?"

Dietz gave a faint nod.

"Of course he is. He puts on his armor every day, and he begins with right thinking. We live in a fallen world, so we must take care to shore up our weak areas, or we will succumb to the enemy."

Paul cleared his throat and began singing, his voice low and wavering on several notes. Singing was something others were good at, not he. He let his voice become more of a chant and he went through the motions, practicing several stances while he chanted. Out of the corner of his eye, he could see a few on the field halt and look over at their little group, but he ignored the attention. He could suffer a little humiliation to help these young warriors.

THOUGH WE WALK in the flesh,
    We do not war in the flesh;
    Though we walk in the flesh,
    We trust in the Lord's armor.

DIETZ HAD PICKED up the tune before Paul had dropped it, and he came over to stand by his mentor. He followed along with the movements, singing out in a commanding tenor. His stammer did not follow him into music, and his concentration seemed to solidify the longer they sang and practiced. Amis laughed and hopped in while wielding his own long sword.

THOUGH WE WALK in the flesh,
    Our weapons are not carnal;
    Though we walk in the flesh,
    We pull down strongholds now.

GWYNNDOLEN at last joined them when they were singing and chanting through for the second time. Her movements were unsure. Paul stepped over to her and began the counter movements so that she would know that each strike she made was to defend herself or advance against an enemy, whose part he now played. A saucy grin took over her mouth, and she thrust back, her alto singing out, as though the words were being written on her heart.

Though we walk in the flesh,
    We cast down errant thinking;
    Though we walk in the flesh,
    We exalt the Lord alone.

Now that Gwynndolen knew what she was doing, Paul began walking between them, adjusting their stances, helping their blocks and strikes. Mind and bodies now fully engaged, their training kept them moving repeatedly. Their lunges deepened, their thrusts sharpened, and their cries became louder. Even when they had finished and returned to sparring one another, Paul could hear the song lifting them up, raising their minds beyond what they were doing in the present to what God had for them in the days ahead.

Though we walk in the flesh,
    We take captive every thought;
    Though we walk in the flesh,
    Every thought bows low to Christ.

They were the hope of the kingdoms, as long as God used them. And so long as their minds stayed on him, they had a chance.

～

Edmund hated seeing Gwynndolen struggle. Everything in him wanted to cast aside his walking staff and join her on the field, but he remained sitting, watching, feeling useless as he twisted his staff in his hand.

"Hard to watch, isn't it?" A baritone voice came from behind Edmund. He turned to regard a weathered nobleman and tried to stand. "Don't get up on my account. I'm only here at the High King's request. Rarely get to see the tournaments, I'm usually at sea."

Edmund stood anyway and gave the man a slight bow, but wasn't sure how deep to take it since he had little idea of the man's status. He had the coloring of the king, but his eyes were clear, his speech distinct.

The man gave a self-deprecating laugh. "You don't know who I am, do you?"

"I'm sorry to say I don't."

The man held up a hand. "I am Obertus, a cousin of the High King's and the commander of his Royal Navy. All this time on land has me bewildered. I'm used to roaming the seas, making certain they're safe from pirates." He gave a cough. "For that reason, I wanted to meet you, Prince Edmund."

Edmund gave another bow, deeper this time. But his leg was getting tired, so he gestured for the commander to sit on the bench beside him. "I remember my father speaking of you and how you offered him great help in learning how to run an able navy to patrol the western Illyan Sea."

"Your father was a great king. I'd like to offer my condolences on behalf of the Navy for the lives of those you lost at sea. I wish we could have stopped it."

Edmund looked over at Gwynndolen. Paul was singing something, but the man didn't really have a pleasant voice for it. He turned back to the commander. "I appreciate it. But it was not merely pirates you would have been fighting, but the sorceress, Camilla."

The man nodded, and his eyes widened. "Yes, I had heard this. And I tell you, we have had no dealings with her out here. We have always left the western Illyan Sea to your father to patrol while we took the eastern half. But now that she's here—" He waved vaguely toward the waters beyond the castle's walls. "Well, out there, we need to be prepared. Instead, the king has ordered me here, to make sure that all goes well."

Edmund leaned in. "Does it worry you to have this many gathered in one place with Camilla about?"

"It does, at that!"

"My father told me you were not the type of man to play the fool—even if you served one." Edmund paused, looking directly into the man's eyes, and waited. Would he call him out for making a slur about the High King?

But Obertus smiled, showing white teeth. "I'm glad to hear he thought so well of me. But I don't know what good I can do as long as foolish men require me to be on hand instead of where I should be."

Edmund lowered his gaze to the staff in his hands and then looked back up. "Does the king count well?"

"What?"

"The king—sometimes he loses track of things, right?"

The man cocked his head to the side. "Yes, quite often."

"So how will he know if the entire fleet is here, crowding the Gulf of Alleria? Surely some able-bodied, trusted men can make certain we are not all penned in here, should a sorceress try to stack us in."

The man gave Edmund a hard look, and the prince

clenched the staff as he waited. "This is quite similar to something the queen asked us to do."

"Then it should be an elementary thing to accomplish."

"Simple, yes, but easy, no." The man rubbed his chin and then smiled at last. "Worth doing? Of course."

"Then, on behalf of my small kingdom, I thank you. On behalf of the many lives you may save, we are indebted."

"If you'll excuse me, Your Highness, it seems I have some work to be about."

Edmund nodded and returned his gaze to Gwynndolen. She and the others were singing. He felt himself smile, watching her work with Paul. Perhaps they were both doing exactly what God made them to do.

# THE REPORT OF SPIES

Jacob heard Father Iohannes approaching before he spoke. The man's feet were quiet on the sandy ground where they slept outside the convent, but the warrior monk had not rested. "Brother Jacob, Abbess Sordamor is ready to see us now."

Jacob rose quickly and, since none of the monks had changed to sleep, he simply rolled up the cloak he had lain on and set it to the side.

"Father, this way," a young nun said, leading them to the abbess's study.

Instead of a dark, sedate study, the room they entered was strangely warm and airy, even without the light of the sun. A young nun had lit two brass candelabras that were placed across from each other in the study. Plants of vibrant magenta, violet, and ochre were growing all around, some suspended in glazed pots from the high beams up above, others planted directly in the wall and jutting out of a raised partial wall, waist-high, that divided the study. Behind the wall of plants, there rested a table with parchment spread out upon it and a quill near a corked ink pot. Out in front of the plant-wall there was a sitting area with colorful cushions spread out on the wood floor, and this was where the woman led them. She sat on a bright red cushion and motioned for the men to sit in the chairs that were brought in for them. "The sisters and I prefer to sit on the floor, as our ancestors did," she said, to Jacob's curious look, "But you may choose which way you prefer."

Jacob elected to sit on the floor and observed as Father Iohannes sat heavily with a sigh. "You know," the father said as he addressed the abbess once seated, "there will be a great deal of distress when we reach the High King."

"I imagine there will be."

"It might have been better had we sent you on ahead."

"I wondered about that, but I know you had your reasons."

Father Iohannes clasped his hands and steepled his fingers. "Yes, he, among all the kingdoms, needs to see us united. The force coming against us will try to divide us, and we must not let them."

Abbess Sordamor nodded at Father Iohannes. "It has always been the enemy's ploy to use division to thwart God's plans. But God is so much bigger than our petty differences. We sisters are with you in our prayers and our cunning. This enemy will not win."

She nodded to the young nun who now brought in an ornate tea set and offered them each something to drink. The tea was strong and sweet, childhood memories filling Jacob at the taste.

Jacob looked at the abbess. She appeared middle-aged, but her body was strong, flexible. She tucked her feet beneath her as though she were a young girl and she sipped her tea, her bright, intelligent eyes missing nothing as she looked over at Father Iohannes and then Jacob. "My sister warriors and I have been preparing for this for many years. We have seen the signs when we have prayed. It became apparent this last year that the War of Sorcery would begin again."

Jacob frowned. "Did you ever take your concerns to the High King?"

"No, I appealed directly to Her Majesty for an audience, but as her health suffered, birthing the heir, she had no strength to see me. I'm sure you're aware they did not even leave for the Winter Castle last fall to ensure a healthy birth. She sent word that I could attend to her after the christening. We are prepared to journey to the High King's Summer Castle, but first I would like you to hear the report on the movements of the enemy across the swamps."

Father Iohannes nodded. The abbess raised her chin, signalling the young nun who went out and brought in a massive man—a giant really. The abbess made introductions. "Father, this is Lord Jahlid, a trusted friend whose rice paddies stretch across much of the Eastern Ports. He has kept in touch with our sisters for a long time, and when things changed recently, he let us know. I thought it best that you hear directly from him."

The gigantic man filled the room, his head ducked under the swinging plants in order to avoid them. "Father, it is an honor to be in your presence."

Abbess Sordamor offered him a seat on the ground, which the man managed gracefully despite his size. Jacob thought he must often sit on the floor when visiting others. There would be so few chairs that fit him without being specially made. Like Jacob, he was dark-skinned and had black, textured hair that was closely cropped. His beard was also black but could not hide a wide mouth that held a hint of a smile despite the gravity of their discussion.

Jacob gestured to the man. "I have heard how you aided Prince Edmund and the Lady Gwynndolen this spring. Without you, they might never have found and captured Amee. Camilla would have more power now and might perhaps have destroyed the High King."

"It was my honor to help the prince and his lady, but I confess I wanted to do more. Which is why I began sending my own spies beyond my rice paddies to see what might be happening."

Father Iohannes nodded. "What have you found?"

"Close to my castle at Pelmont, Camilla met with her forces, making plans for the covens on land and those on sea. She has raised quite a formidable force."

"The sea?"

"Pirates from the Land of Midnight. The dark magic of sorcery has clouded the birthplace of the gospel. The pirates pay homage to Camilla and are planning to blockade the harbor once the royal families have all arrived. There will be no help to arrive from outside once the siege begins."

"So, there is to be a siege."

"I think so. My spies tell me that Camilla alluded there is more than that, but they could not discover what."

"It will be foolish if we all gather in the castle and its great city now. But if we do not, we cannot get the High King to listen to us."

The abbess made her proposal. "We will send a section of our warriors and stand ready outside the city for when the attack comes."

Father Iohannes agreed, nodding his head. "Jacob and I will ride ahead and try to speak some sense to the High

King. We will take a small force with us, but I have my doubts whether it will do much good. The High King only wants us present to preside over the christening and the coronation of the Northland kings."

"There will be no new kings if Camilla has her way." The abbess then turned. "Lord Jahlid, will you lead us so that we can avoid the enemy?"

"Of course."

"Good, then we will leave tomorrow morning. Until then, Father, would you lead us in prayers at Prime? It would be so good to worship together before we ride into battle."

NOFRA GOT out of bed quietly and readied her bowl. She knelt down, breathed in deeply, and waited a moment. Then, she raised up on her knees to look into the bowl.

"Mother?"

Camilla's face shimmered on the water's surface, slowly clarifying. "Daughter, what have you to tell me?"

"I have met Dietz, Amee's son." She pulled her loose hair across her left shoulder, missing the braid she had worn to signify her allegiance to her coven.

"Yes?"

"The powers within him clash."

"Is he divided?" Camilla's inflection lifted at the end. Nofra didn't know anything could surprise Camilla.

"He does not know where he belongs or what he should do."

"Then you must convince him. Gain his confidence. Endear yourself to him." Camilla tapped her red lips with her fingertips. "Tell me, how did you come to learn this about him? Is he confiding in you?"

"No, I don't think he likes me at all. I can just sense things about people."

"Really?"

Nofra tipped her head forward. "It's straightforward. Some people, like Rapunzel, are easy to understand."

"Is Dietz easy?"

"Well, maybe not to everyone, but his frustrations are right on the surface. It's simple to—"

"I didn't know you possessed this talent," Camilla interrupted, her full lips splitting into something like a smile. "I'm glad, but we'll have to develop it alongside everything else you're already learning. You must dig deeper beneath the surface and find what is really driving him. What does he long for? What does he most want?"

Nofra shifted on her knees. "I doubt very much that I will have opportunity to—"

Camilla whipped out in a forced whisper, "If you do not, I will send someone else! Do you not wish to succeed? Reach into his mind and see what you can find—better yet! See what you can do with him."

"What do you mean, *do* with him?"

"Play with him, see if you can make him say what you want."

"He can't even say what he wants."

"What do you mean?"

"He stutters, stammers, can't say anything right. It's part of why he str—"

"Yes! That's perfect! You can help him speak, calm his mind so he can connect his words."

"That doesn't sound simple. I don't know if I can—"

"Stop it! You will do as I say, or I will have you

removed. Didn't you say you wanted to be useful to me?" A quick look assured Nofra that none of the maidservants had woken at Camilla's outburst. Her jaw tightened, but she whispered, "Of course I do."

Camilla took a breath and lowered her voice. "Good. You know what it took to place you there beneath the nose of the cat and keep her from sniffing you out. You are taking care to keep yourself disguised from her, yes?"

Realizing Camilla might not see the slight nod she gave through the waters, she answered aloud. "Yes, I weave the enchantment over myself fresh each night, and all those who defeated Ute now sleep over the sachets in the castle."

"And what of that servant, the one who likes to juggle?"

Nofra could grin at that. "Not difficult at all, Mother. I made my way out to his tent and spoke the enchantment into the tent's entrance and tucked the sachet beneath it."

"Clever girl. You are more than I hoped you would be."

Nofra didn't know what to say to that, but she found her smile widening.

"Now, what of the princess? You said she was reluctant?"

"She was reluctant at first to trust me, but today she left me alone with the child."

"Why was she reluctant? Why wouldn't she want a break from the little brat?"

Helena wasn't a brat, but Nofra knew better than to contradict Camilla. "I think she worries, fears losing control."

"Loss of control? Now that's interesting. How can you use that?"

Nofra didn't know if Camilla wanted her to answer. As

the silence lengthened, she found she was braiding her hair. She stopped and rubbed her palms on her chemise.

"No ideas?"

"Uh, well, I'll make certain that she needs time away from Helena, that she knows she can depend on me. If I do it well, she'll wonder what she did before she had me."

"And what about the others?"

Nofra shrugged, but then remembered to say "no" since Camilla couldn't see.

"Gain their confidence as well, make them accept you as a member of the party. These are uncomplicated people who want to trust that everyone around them loves their God as they do. Care for the child, help the others as they let you, and all will be as it should have been before my sister betrayed us. Now, let's practice your split concentration." And she instructed Nofra again on how to manipulate the maids, all three this time, without waking them up.

# AMIS FINDS A FRIEND

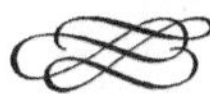

Amis had risen early, which had him hoping that he would be back to his normal self. He had walked around the outer bailey, watching the commoners go about their business as they set up for market day, helping himself to a loaf of warm bread and some fruit with the coin Prince Paul had insisted he take.

But of all the people he expected to see this early, he hadn't expected to see her. How many days had he spent looking for her, and now, here she was? And in the early morn! Most entertainers he had met liked to bed down late after feasts and rise late. He knew himself to be unusual, loving mornings and greeting the sun with boundless energy. There were many times he had frustrated Princess Rapunzel with his happiness, but that had been fun, too. He missed that energy.

Did this woman enjoy the mornings as well? He noted her hooded eyes and how, though she was young, there were dark circles beneath them. Did she have trouble sleeping in tents with other servants?

Amis ambled over to her. "And how are you this fine morn?"

She turned toward him and slow-blinked. Nope, she wasn't quite awake yet. "Aren't you the fool that ruined my performance the other night?" He had thought from her coloring she was probably from the Eastern Ports. Her Latin accent confirmed it.

Amis caught sight of his own limbs in the morning light. Next to her, his skin was blinding! No wonder she was blinking. "Well, I would say the High King ruined both our performances by pitting us against one another. But yes, I am Amis, the prophetic fool at your service."

"Prophetic, you say?"

"Yes, there are times God gives me insight, and I've helped my king."

"Modest, too."

He lifted his shoulders and held his hands palm up. He had nothing to hide. "No need to be. I am who I am. But who are you?" He waggled his eyebrows.

She laughed in surprise at his perusal. "What do you mean?"

"Only that I've never met a maid who's a fool. What's your name?"

"Well, I shall make this simple for you," she over-enunciated. "I'm no fool, but a jester. Name's Mea."

"Call yourself a jester if you prefer, but we are all fools, m'dear Mea."

"Say what you will, I am no fool, nor am I anyone's *dear*."

Amis gave another shrug. The Lord knew what they all were. God would tell her himself in due time. "What are you doing this morning?"

"I thought I would find myself some peace to practice. I didn't imagine that I'd find myself ensnared by you."

"Ensnared?"

"Yes, I have scarcely come out of my tent, and you are following me around the market. I only want to eat my fruit in quiet and then I will find some small corner to practice in before—before the week is up."

"And we will perform together?"

"Yes, what of it?"

"Well, I've looked for you for days, but I'm glad to have found you now. We really should practice together, don't you think?"

"Should we? I don't know that we should. We'll only get in each other's way."

"As we did and will again if we don't practice together—"

She squirmed under his inference. "I know what you are saying is true, but I have no desire for a partnership. What I wouldn't mind is if we took turns in performing. It doesn't have to be something we do together."

Amis furrowed his brow, "Ah, m'dear Mea, I don't think that what you are saying is what the High King intended. I have no wish to bring dishonor on my king or his heir. Therefore, you"—he pointed at her—"and I"—he pointed at himself—"need to work together!" He waggled his eyebrows and was delighted to watch her try not to smile. "Come now, do you juggle?" He pulled three pears out of his stuffed tunic and juggled.

She watched in silence for just a moment. "What jester doesn't juggle? Toss one here." And he obliged. She pulled out an odd fruit he hadn't seen before and began tossing it with him.

"What is this?" he asked.

"Dragon fruit."

"Really? Dragons have fruit?"

"No, you fool, that's simply what it's called."

By now they were juggling six pieces of fruit, but Amis caught them one by one, and tucked all but the dragon fruit away in his voluminous tunic. Hungry and curious, he lifted it to his mouth to take a bite, but saw Mea shake her head. "Only eat the dragon's scales if you want a stomachache. Cut away the peel and scoop out the flesh."

Amis pulled out his knife and cut into the pink skin next to one of the soft, green-tipped spikes. The inside was white and speckled with black seeds. Scooping out a bite, he chewed the tender fruit, wiping away at the juice that dripped down his chin. Ha! It reminded him a bit of a pear. After finishing the fruit, he resumed juggling with Mea.

They were now juggling only five items, and odd numbers allowed for other tricks. "Can you flip while juggling?" he asked her.

"While juggling by myself I can, not sure while juggling with someone else."

He nodded; that seemed fair enough. "How did you come by our trade?"

Her lips twitched and eyes sparkled for the briefest of moments. "My grandfather was a bard, tried to raise his son to be a bard, sing for the lord he served. To his dismay, my father had no talent for singing well. But, he was clever and funny. He found my mother, whose voice was angelic, and they played together. She would sing tales of heroic deed for the lord, and my father would pretend to help and make a bungle it. How they loved to make everyone laugh! Now, their songs and stories are mine, but with only myself —" Her voice hitched, and her face bunched into a scowl, but she kept up her concentration and dropped nothing. Amis was pleased to see this.

"And?"

"It's not the same without them."

Yes, Amis understood. Didn't he miss performing with his own father? "So you can sing like your mother?"

"I can when the occasion calls for it."

"Your lord is lucky to have you. I suppose he is here for the tournament?" Amis caught the items and stuffed three into his tunic, holding out a green pear to her while biting into the other.

Mea took it but shook her head. "I don't have a lord. I've served no one but myself since my parents died. It's a lonely lot, dangerous for a maid. I thought if I came here I might find my place. Surely there are kings and princes looking for entertainment the likes of which I can provide."

"Especially if you can sing. Shall we juggle and flip and sing together?"

She gave him a tolerant smile as she chewed thoughtfully. "Well, now, I can't sing and flip at the same time."

"Then we shall flip into our entrance, juggle, and then we shall sing together."

She took another slow bite, and Amis mentally compared the taste of the dragon fruit to that of the pear. The texture was different. The juices were—

"I think you should choose what we should sing."

Amis grinned in delight. "Do you know the tale of the three sisters of sorcery?"

"Of course, everyone knows that."

"Well, there is a bit more to it now. Let me teach it to you."

# TAMING THE TONGUE

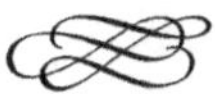

"Hold her for me, please?" Nofra held out the smiling Helena, but Dietz shook his head. He didn't know how to hold a toddler, and this one moved more than he could keep up with. She popped her thumb out of her mouth, leaving a string of drool dripping down her face as she grinned. Why would she grin at him? He wanted nothing to do with her. She was messy, and his life was messy enough.

"Just take her. I need to get something before I can do as the princess requested." This time when she thrust Helena at him, Nofra let go, and he had to grab the tyke or let her fall.

Why had he been told to come up to the bedchambers instead of attending the handfasting of Prince Edmund and Lady Gwynndolen? He was not nobility, but he felt he belonged there more than helping with a toddler. Wasn't Nofra capable of caring for the infant herself?

Helena giggled and clapped her hands, as though it were a game. When he didn't play with her, she whimpered, wanting down. "Why can't I just put her down on the floor?"

"Do you want to chase her?"

"Chase her? She can't get very far."

"Ha! That's what you think. You've obviously not seen how quick she is now."

Dietz shook his head. Of course the child wiggled a bit. But fast? Nofra must be exaggerating. He looked over to see that she was placing several items in a satchel. Then she looked up and smiled at him. Her smile was interesting. It started small and grew outward, her thick brown lips revealing white teeth and one dimple in her right cheek. He looked back at Helena. "What was it Rapunzel wanted?"

"Rapunzel?" she snorted.

His cheeks warmed. "I mean, the p-p-princess."

"I suppose that is difficult for you to say. Can you even say *Prince Paul*? Odd, but I think you can master it if you try."

Dietz looked away from her laughter.

"Oh, don't feel bad. We all struggle with something. I'd much rather struggle with speech than my inability to—"

"T-to . . .?"

She shook her head. "Never mind. The princess wants me to take Helena somewhere and for you to help."

Dietz shook his head and held out Helena.

"Fine, you take the satchel."

He handed the little girl over and nodded at the door. "You s-still haven't s-said—"

"Where we're going? That's because it's a surprise."

Great. That would mean he would follow behind her the entire way to wherever she wanted. He felt his face heat at following a female servant.

Once outside the bedchambers, the maidservant led him down a back staircase that led to an outside pavilion. Two weeping willows stood like women bowing to wash their hair over a glassy pond. Flowering vines grew up the side of trellis. A stone bench rested beside the pond opposite the trees, a thick carpet of spongy moss covering the ground. Nofra set the little girl down on the emerald floor and gestured for him to sit with her. He placed the satchel on the bench but walked over to look at the pond instead of sitting. Was that bright orange swimming creature a koi fish?

"I'm afraid you'd rather be somewhere else."

There was little he could say to that, so he said nothing.

"It's not very kind to be silent when a lady is speaking to you."

He flinched, but replied without looking at her. "Wh-when I am sp-spoken to by a lady, I'll remember th-that."

She walked over to him, touching him on his arm, and he turned, startled.

Her slow smile grew across her face again, and she leaned forward to tell him something, so obviously his words had not hurt her. Her voice was low as she spoke, as though to keep Helena from overhearing them, though the little girl was happily playing with a wooden toy and wouldn't understand, anyway. "I think the princess has the wrong idea."

She waited for a response of some sort, but he didn't want to speak again. Why would he? He always messed up his words.

She pressed her lips together, and her dimple showed again. "I think the princess imagines you have feelings for me."

He scowled, and she laughed. "I know! Imagine you

having feelings for me! You can barely stand to be near me and only do so when ordered to."

He didn't like that she was laughing. Why should that be funny?

She leaned toward him again, and he caught a whiff of the fragrant oils she had worked into her hair. Something exotic he didn't recognize. "It might be my fault, something I said to her."

"Wh-what did you say?"

She smiled again and then stepped back to Helena. "No, little one, don't put that in your mouth." But the girl was faster than fast and popped a cricket into her mouth. She gurgled a high-pitched squeal and scurried away when Nofra swooped after her. Dietz joined the chase and came up from the other side, the little one giggling around her mouthful of insect. "Spit it out!" Nofra laughed, even as Helena grunted.

"You w-were right. She's fast."

Nofra looked at him after scooping up Helena. Her dark lashes fluttered as her cheeks darkened. "I told the princess you were handsome." She looked away, and he felt his chest squeeze. She thought he was handsome?

He shook his head and stupidly opened his mouth, "C-can't even s-speak."

Nofra looked into his eyes again and as he gazed into them, he felt a wave of dizziness overtake him. He sat down hard on the ground.

"Are you okay?"

He tried to nod, but it made the dizziness worse. She moved Helena to her lap as she sat beside him. Placing a hand on his chest, she quietly murmured, "Just breathe."

He did as she said, and a strange calmness came over him as he looked deep into the pools of her dark brown eyes. In and out, in and out. His breathing regulated. The dizziness eased, and he watched as her lips spread into her smile. "Thank you. What did you do?" His clarity shocked him.

"I did nothing. It was all you, Dietz."

He looked down at Helena and then back at Nofra. His face warmed when she finally stood and offered him a hand, Helena on her hip again. As Dietz stood next to her and they began walking around the pond, he wondered why he had never noticed before just how lovely she was.

EDMUND SWALLOWED as he watched Gwynndolen walk toward him. He smirked, noticing she wasn't wearing her short sword. Not that his little warrior would, inside the chapel. But still, he felt as though her coming to him unarmed, in soft layers of golden yellow with the black crest of his family embroidered on the trim of her gown was her own way of declaring allegiance to him and to their union. It was as though she were laying aside her arms for him, even though she would pick them back up to fight for him tomorrow.

When she reached him at last, he wanted to kiss her exposed shoulder, the horizontal neckline allowing him to see a few freckles he had never seen before. After kissing her shoulders, he would place his hands on her waist, feel the onyx belt that encircled her, and then . . . But instead he reminded himself where they were. He would make time for all of that later.

Gwynndolen held out her hand, and he clasped it with his free one, keeping a firm grip on his staff with the other. Her dark eyes burned bright at him, as black as the onyx pendant clasped around her neck. He couldn't help the smile that spread across his face as the priest placed the white sacramental cloth over their hands, uniting them in marriage.

Edmund blinked at Gwynndolen—she was his wife now! He wondered briefly how happy it would have made his mother if she lived to see this day. The day that he gave his life to another. The priest said something else, but Edmund didn't respond to the man until he realized that their few attendants were chuckling.

"What?" He looked up at the priest again, who simply smiled.

"You are free to greet your friends."

As much as Edmund knew he must show off his bride, more of him longed to celebrate alone with her. As though she knew what he was thinking, Gwynndolen's face pinked, and she looked down for just a moment. *Is she nervous about being alone with me?* He squeezed her hands, and she looked up at him, shocking him with a cheeky wink. Oh! "Come, Husband, let's go to our friends." She hooked her hand in his elbow and allowed him to lead her out of the room, ahead of the others.

Several of the nobles had attended, along with King Tasufin and his pouting daughter, and Prince Paul with the fool, Amis. Rapunzel and Katterina had led the bride inside the chapel and spread a layer of petals on the ground before she walked down the aisle, but they now followed along with the others to go to break

fast together. Edmund glanced down into Gwynndolen's face. There was a fierce light in her eyes, but he thought he understood it now. Determination, devotion; it was who she was. They would live their lives together and no one would separate them.

Of course, their eyes were moist. There were people missing. Edmund had never received the gift of his father's blessing; the kindness of his mother wasn't here; and he longed to see his friends and Gwynndolen's siblings, Georgius, Liam, and even Beatrix. He couldn't help missing them. It was wrong that they had died, that Camilla had contrived the typhoon that had destroyed the two ships. Guilt washed over him.

"Edmund—" His wife's voice broke through his reverie. "Don't spoil this day with regrets."

He raised her palm to his lips while they waited outside the Great Hall where they would break fast together. The others went ahead of them, but they would bide their time until the High King introduced them to the entire court. "You are right. There has been enough grief, there should be laughter today." He caught her to himself and pressed his lips to hers. She pulled back with a nervous giggle, looking around as though worried someone might see. Edmund smiled when he caught a grin on one of the normally bored-looking guards' faces. "Careful! That's not the sound of a warrior, my little wife!"

"Little wife?"

He bent his head down to hers as though to kiss her lips again, but stopped there with a teasing smile. "What? Don't you like the sound of that?"

She put her hands on her hips and pulled her head back, but couldn't tame the laughter in her eyes.

"You aren't furious, are you?"

"Just kiss me!"

"Your wish, princess, is my command!" And he closed the distance. When their lips met, he felt a warm rush flow through him like a fire spreading. Their lips moved together and he remembered the first kiss they'd shared. It had been quick, chaste. She had permitted little more at the time and hadn't admitted her love for him for a while yet. But now she was his and would remain his forever. As long as she didn't end up dying for him in the tournament. Or fighting a war against Camilla—!

"Stop it," she warned as she pulled away. "You're thinking of something dire. I can feel it in your kiss."

"How can I not, with Camilla close at hand? Gwynndolen, I don't want you to—"

Placing both hands on the sides of his face, she stared him down. "Edmund, I've married you so that I can fight for you. Trust me! I will not die or even get hurt. Paul has trained me well and I've improved. Wait—" She gasped at the realization, pulling back slightly. "You were the one who asked Prince Paul to help me, weren't you?"

He quirked an eyebrow. "I knew you wouldn't ask for help yourself."

"Our poor children! Between you and me they will be morose, full of regret and pride, and unable to ask for help."

"Or perhaps we will have taught them the hard lessons that we are learning now. It could always turn out that way, you know!"

A young page hurried over to them, his small brown face serious. "The High King and Queen are ready for you to join them in the Great Hall."

"Are you ready, my little wife?"

Gwynndolen arched an eyebrow. "Only if you find a better nickname for me."

"Very well, Warrior Wife."

"Oh! I like that! Yes, let's go."

# A FOOL'S ERRAND

*A*mis frowned momentarily. He was standing behind the raised platform where the High King and Queen dined so they could look out over the heads of the gathered royals. Of course, there was a curtain and the High King's banner that kept the fool and his partner from being observed, but being noticed or not being noticed wasn't what was bothering him. There was something strange happening in his belly, as though he had eaten worms that were now wriggling inside him.

"Is something amiss?" Mea stepped over to him with her lovely brow puckered in concern.

Amis lifted a shoulder. "Well, my name is Amis, so I suppose something is always amiss."

She rolled her eyes.

"But, since you ask, I'm wondering if I ate something I shouldn't have." He patted his belly through the dark blue silk tunic. "My stomach doesn't feel quite right."

"Really? My stomach always feels that way anytime I'm supposed to perform. I used to get quite sick and lose my meal right before I would go out. I learned to not eat until after the performance, and I'm much better now."

Amis shook his head and whispered, "I've never felt this way before. Could I be nervous?"

"You've never been nervous before?" she whispered back.

"No, never. Why, is that unusual?"

Mea rolled her eyes again, but this time she laughed. "You know, you can be quite an infuriating man."

"Me? Why would you say that?"

"Most performers struggle, but you say you don't? How can it come so naturally?"

He shrugged and adjusted his jester's cap, making the bells jingle. The sound cheered him. "My father raised me this way. After all, he was a fool and flitted from kingdom to kingdom after my mother died. But I just don't—don't feel as I normally do. It's the story this time. I've had weighty messages before, but never before a king who is so —so—foolish. It feels as though something—someone—" What was wrong with him? He couldn't even think straight. Couldn't put his thoughts together. He was so glad that he had practiced the tale with Mea enough times that he didn't have to reach far back in his memory to pull the tale forward.

A page hurried over to them.

"The High King will announce Prince Edmund and his bride, and then you will perform."

Amis nodded and wiped his brow. Why was he sweating already? He felt as though he were fighting against some invisible force in order to do what God created him to do.

Mea frowned at him again, no hint of laughter in her

eyes. "Amis, are you sure you're all right? I could try by myself if you like."

The trumpets sounded, and the entire kingdom welcomed Prince Edmund and Princess Gwynndolen. Amis had to shout for his partner to hear him. "No, this is just part of the tale, you know? A fool being distracted before his brilliant performance!" He stretched high and then low.

She followed his lead and limbered up as well. "If you say so, fool."

Doing a quick backbend to limber up, Amis prayed a quick word for God to calm him and take control of the night's proceedings. He ran out from behind the curtain in the opposite direction from Mea. He did two handsprings in front of the raised platform toward the center of the room, while she did two handsprings toward him. Then they both flipped and landed side by side with their hands stretched high. The people were clapping, but it was halfhearted and plodding. Amis could tell that the days and nights of being entertained had lessened the impact of their grand entrance. The bored audience was hungry for the upcoming violence of the tournament, the surprises of who would win and what princes would distinguish themselves, earning greater land holdings or trade agreements. Two jesters, albeit talented ones, were nothing exceptional to them.

*Enough thinking!* Amis chastised himself, and he backflipped away from his new friend and then leapt up onto the dais and launched himself onto the High King's table. Finally, at a gasp of surprise from the audience, Amis cartwheeled his way to the High King himself, who looked shocked. "Your Majesty!" He took a knee in front of his sovereign. "We fools have a tale to tell."

"Then by all means, tell it!" The High Queen's voice cracked.

Amis opened his mouth, and the tale poured out as Mea harmonized, strumming a lute she had preset near the platform. Amis's voice went high while Mea's voice went low, the lute leading the crowd along the tale.

Three sisters gathered their stores of power and, with the aid of a witch and her transformed cat, began forming a plan. Pirates at sea began plundering nearby ships. Covens in the Dark Wood and the Eastern Ports learned their craft of magic and war. The eldest sister called them together, and their spirits met deep in the Soontrisse Mountains, but—Amis's voice thundered, suddenly deep— the name of Jesu killed the great sorceress! The other two sisters lost their connection. Amis's voice rose again, and Mea's alto picked up the mournful strains describing the journeys of Prince Edmund and Prince Paul as they separately found their way to the Eastern Ports. Camilla rose to power and reunited with Amee at Edmund's foolish wish, but they were torn apart again by the name of Jesu when the young prince offered his life, barely surviving. Amis watched as the crowd wiped their eyes and glanced over at the princes and princesses seated together following the handfasting.

Now was the moment, and Mea stopped strumming her lute so that his voice alone echoed throughout the Great Hall as it rang out pure and clear.


"DOWN IN THE dungeons and out in the marsh
   Sorcery strengthens and covens grow harsh.
   Thinking they're safe, the kingdoms all gather

Believing His Highness, trusting his blather.
The High King's a fool, not much unlike me!
But if he'll relent, perhaps then we'll see.
The name of Jesu victorious once more
Only if he trusts God to win this war."

AMIS QUITE LIKED THE GASP, and he stared into the watery eyes of his sovereign, who beckoned him to come closer as the last note of the song hung in the air. "This is Our entertainment? A mockery of your sovereign?"

Amis flipped off the table and hopped off the dais. He gestured first to the king and then to the sitting nobles. "O King, prove me wrong. Will you be wise and prepare us for the war at hand? You have gathered together all the kingdoms, each court with their own armed escort! Why not have them ready for battle instead of the tournament?"

But as the king made ready to answer, silver trays clattered, hitting the ground at the rear of the Great Hall. Servants and nobles murmured in alarm as warrior women and monks began rushing up the aisles.

Guards were everywhere, and one hit Mea, causing her to drop her lute. The guard stepped through the fragile instrument in his rush to defend the king. Amis helped Mea scamper to her feet and shielded her with his body. A young maid like her shouldn't be harmed!

The warriors, holding their weapons in front of them, parted before the High King. Brother Jacob strode to the front of the procession. The High King swayed on his feet and barked, "What is the meaning of this?"

*Well timed, warrior monk!* thought Amis.

"War." Jacob did not shout the word, but said it loud

enough for all to hear. "You know it to be true, but you insist on conducting yourself as though it were not sitting in your dungeon and coming toward you through the marsh."

"We are the king, and you will pay homage when you come before Us!"

Jacob gave a brief bow. But Father Iohannes came from behind the other warriors. "I will not bow to you, nor will you bow to me. We should bow alone to the God and Maker of us all.

"You have allowed the enemies of these kingdoms to thrive in hidden places. Was not your own household plagued by sorcery when your daughters danced their shoes to pieces? Though you had the riddle solved, you did not seek to discover how sorcery was still being implemented in your kingdom, though I warned you that very summer that you must see to it. You did not. Now you have evidence of the treachery that has been under your very nose. One sister of sorcery is here, now!" Amis liked how the man measured his words and emphasized each statement with gestures. Obviously, attending Mass with this man leading it would be interesting! "But I hear you ignore the counsel of your wife, of us, of those who recently fought such evil. You ignore it all and think by imprisoning one you have disabled them all. But Brother Jacob here has foreseen the demise of this kingdom. If you want such a thing to take place, then proceed, dear king, proceed."

Jacob stepped forward. "You must—"

The High King shouted, "We *must* do nothing! You dare tell Us what to do with Our lesser nobles? You do very well in your church, but We will not take orders from a lowly monk"—he pointed at Brother Jacob—"not even a warrior such as yourself."

"Then you must listen to Father Iohannes of the Brotherhood."

The High King shook his head and pushed away the hand of the queen as she sought to beg his attention. "No! This is Our kingdom, and you will not instruct Us. The tournament will continue as planned. These perpetrators of sorcery have not harmed Us, they cannot impede the growth of Our kingdom. You will see! Your visions are the nightmares of imaginative men. We will celebrate the life of Our heir as planned. Either stand down or We will incarcerate you!"

Father Iohannes stood up straight and tall. "You would take holy men into your dungeons? How then can I christen your son?"

The king looked puzzled for a moment, and in that time the queen stood. "No, of course we would never incarcerate you. There must be peace between us to keep the kingdoms safe. His Majesty is overwrought. We have been anxiously awaiting your arrival, fearing we would have to go ahead with the christening without you. We can resolve this amicably, can't we, my love?"

The king looked about to argue, but then stared at the queen. "Well, We know you well enough to know you have a compromise to suggest."

The queen smiled, but there was no sweetness in it. "Only this. Let us finish the feasting this morning and then go ahead with the christening if Father Iohannes feels well enough. We can enjoy more entertainment and feasting for the rest of the day and meet with Father Iohannes and this monk tomorrow."

The High King rubbed his chin thoughtfully and nodded. "We have decided. Let Us have the christening and finish feasting today. Tomorrow We will hold company with Father Iohannes and his monk." The man clapped his hands and sat down.

"Now, finish eating! And bring in the next entertainers."

Amis put an arm around Mea, and they bowed out as the next fool came to amuse the crowds.

# A DAY TO FEAST

Jacob sat quietly through the early morning meal, happy to rise with Father Iohannes when it was time to ready themselves for the christening. This would be a long day if they were to pretend everything was fine. But he knew better than to address it aloud. He looked through the crowds of nobles and at last saw Prince Paul, who caught Jacob's nod and nodded back. Good; they would find each other as soon as the christening was over.

When they had entered the Summer Castle grounds the night before, they had quickly found their way to the cathedral, alerting none of the High King's sleepy guards. The back of the cathedral housed a dormitory for the sanctified visitors, one half for the nuns and the other for the monks. Early that morning they had put on their vestments, green silk tunics over hosen, which looked elegant but allowed for effortless movement in case an enemy ever followed them into worship. They girded themselves with weapons, as always, but prayed they would not need them.

The front of the cathedral was a mere stone's throw

away from the Summer Castle. Whereas the castle had stood for hundreds of years, its foundation giving way and being rebuilt repeatedly, the cathedral was a newer structure, and the foundation had been well planned so it had never yet sunk. Its elegant structure rose toward the sky, its spires pointing to heaven. Inside, the sun lit the stained glass windows depicting the Christ's time on earth, splashing the grey stones with hues of bright yellows, reds, greens, blues, and purples.

Abbess Sordamor and a few sisters were conferring with the priests who served the High King daily. It took little time to set out the sacrament and fill the small gold basin with holy water. The other warrior women were walking in pairs around the outside of the cathedral, as though expecting trouble. Father Iohannes sent several of the warrior monks to do the same.

*Foolish king!* thought Jacob. *He gathers us all in one place and pretends we are invulnerable.*

Father Iohannes turned to Jacob and placed a hand on his shoulder. "The abbess and I want you to stand beside us during the christening. We will bless the child and you will serve the sacrament with Brother Philip."

Jacob looked at the other council members' faces. They did not seem upset by this change, but he could not be sure. He hoped that his elevation was not slighting someone else. He certainly had not asked for this kind of honor.

All the nobles crowded into the massive cathedral, the younger princes looking up high and exclaiming at the unique architecture. Jacob took his place in the front, and as he waited for the crowds to take their seats, he prayed. A bird flew into the building, flying higher and higher into the rafters, its birdsong cooing. A dove! Was it a benediction? Was it a sign from God that he would grant them peace if they continued to seek his will?

AFTER THE CHRISTENING, all the nobles received the sacrament of the Eucharist. Paul knelt beside Rapunzel as he received the wine and the bread that represented the blood and the body of Christ. Receiving Jacob's blessing and that of another brother, they turned to move outside. Paul sighed. Not that he didn't appreciate the significance of christening the young prince. He took his responsibility to pray for the babe, who would one day become king, very seriously. But sitting still for such a long time was tiresome.

"Do I need to elbow you awake, dear son?" Katterina laughed, coming up from behind him.

Paul shook his head, suppressing a smile. "No, dear mother, I'm awake now that we're done sitting."

"Oh, I doubt very much that we're done sitting." Edmund leaned heavily on his staff as he came to join them, a jubilant Gwynndolen practically bouncing beside him. "No, the king is going to make the most of today. Now is the time for feasting and making merry, now that he has christened his son and named him heir."

Paul saw Rapunzel looking around. "What is it?"

"I asked Nofra to take Helena outside today."

"You don't think she brought her outside the castle walls, do you?"

"No—" Rapunzel shook her head, the sunlight glinting off her braided crown. "Of course not. Silly of me. I just hoped if I saw them, I could sneak away to—"

"There'll be no sneaking away on my wedding day!" Gwynndolen laughed. "Perhaps the High King thinks we are only celebrating his son, but I mean to make merry with my friends and new husband. Why are we standing about outside? We should go inside, see if it's time to dance."

Rapunzel's giggle lifted Paul's spirits. "Yes, of course my friend, let's go!" But just as she and Gwynndolen began making their way back to the castle, Lady Florese intercepted the two. Gwynndolen went on ahead, but the lady pulled Rapunzel aside.

"Paul, I must speak with you." Jacob's voice caught him by surprise. He hated to take his eyes off Rapunzel, but he turned to greet his friend.

"What can I do for you?"

"You and the others spoke with the High Queen?"

"Yes, of course. We did the best we could while we waited for you. I'm afraid we have only learned how dire the situation is and have been prevented from fixing things."

Jacob's solemn lips pulled down. "It was my intention to arrive much sooner, surely not on the day of the christening. But Father Iohannes wanted to wait, and then we knew God wanted us to bring the warrior women with us. Forgive me for not coming sooner."

Paul looked up at his mentor. It was ridiculous to feel so put out over something the man couldn't control. "Of course. We are all doing the best we know how."

"It's all we can do. We must leave the rest to God. Still, I would ask a favor of you."

"Yes?"

"When the king speaks to us tomorrow, would you come with us?"

"He hasn't paid me any regard."

"I know, but I would still like you"—he looked over at

Edmund and motioned until the man hobbled over—"all of you to come try with me one last time. I know Camilla seeks to hem us in. We mustn't let her."

Both men nodded, and Jacob continued. "Till tomorrow, I suppose you should make merry as the king desires."

"What will you do?"

A rare smile lit the monk's eyes, before his lips moved. "I will be in my father's house." And he turned and went back inside the cathedral, presumably to pray.

Edmund smiled at Paul, the goofy look of a man besotted by love on his face. Paul laughed and smacked him on the back. "We'd best go find our wives. I can tell you need yours right now!"

Paul's hazel eyes roamed through the crowds of people, at last lighting on the form of his wife as he entered the Great Hall. She stood across the room from him, her arms pulled tight across her chest. Lady Florese was leaning in close and saying something to her, and Rapunzel's lips had pressed into a firm line. Her chin drooped, and Paul crossed the room to her. But just at that moment, a very merry Gwynndolen skipped to her, grabbing Rapunzel's hand and leading her to the dancing floor. Paul felt a smile widen his mouth. Surely a dance would cheer his wife.

During the christening ceremony, the servants had moved all the tables in the Great Hall to create a wide space for dancing. The court musicians took their place up on the raised platform as women streamed forward, forming a circle. The women sashayed as men formed a circle outside them, rotating in the opposite direction.

Edmund sighed as he looked about for a place to sit.

Gwynndolen was so lovely, he longed to take her in his arms, to spin her about. But he didn't let his mood sour. Once he sat, he found himself relaxing, beating the rhythm of the music on the floor with his staff. Watching for his wife's bright-red hair among the dancers, Edmund found himself strangely content. He would hold her soon enough.

The rotating circles stopped, and the women turned to face the outside circle, linking elbows and spinning around. Circles resumed their turn, a full rotation and a half, and then dancers faced new partners. When they had spun around with them, the men clasped hands and lifted them high, while the women ducked under and wove back and forth between the men, a half rotation. Now facing their original partners, they clasped hands and spun around till the women were on the outside. Women clasped hands and tried to lift them high enough so the men could duck under and weave. But laughter filled the hall as several large men, Paul among them, got stuck, and the dance could not continue. Edmund wiped his eyes as he laughed along with the others. The music finished as the dancers began clapping. Servants were running about, delivering refreshments to side tables, and Edmund, feeling refreshed, followed his nose to find meat pasties.

# THE SON

Dietz left Nofra at Paul and Rapunzel's bedchamber, smiling, until he remembered what he had to do now before he could finish the day. The High Queen had sent him a message ordering him to visit his mother. He had avoided it as long as possible.

Dietz descended, feeling the vice around his skull tighten. The guard behind him was keeping his pace or else he would probably have halted here on the spiral staircase, right where the smell of must and waste saturated the air.

But he had to keep walking, he had to keep going. The High Queen had commanded it. What could his mother have done to get in the queen's good graces? Didn't she know what Amee was? It wouldn't be long before the queen learned she couldn't trust her. There was nothing the sorceress could do to redeem herself. Nothing any of them marked by sorcery could do to find redemption.

The guard moved past Dietz to place the torch he had brought in the iron ring, light spreading out over the vast dungeon, reaching up to the high ceiling. Perhaps standing at the foot of the stairs was good enough and he wouldn't have to go further in. He didn't want to get any closer to her. The shadows flickered over his mother's grotesque form. What was she supposed to be? Some sort of horse-duck? Disgusting. She shifted and tried to make an intelligent sound, but it came out as some sort of honking-whinny. His hands fisted at his sides, his jaw clenched tight. Still, he kept his feet firmly planted. He needn't say anything; he only had to stay here, bide his time. That was all the queen required of him. After that he could withdraw, never come again.

The guard turned to him. Dietz had to step down in order for the guard to move past. "I'll be just outside. She can't hurt you."

No, she couldn't hurt him . . . anymore. She had already done her worst.

Dietz stared hard. He hoped she could feel his hatred. It was like a hot fist around his throat. Her eyes were wet, the eyes of a doe who seemed innocent but could outwit a hunter. She was the true hunter. She was the one who would destroy them all if they let her. What was the queen thinking, allowing her any privileges? Why hadn't the king simply put his mother to death when they brought her here? Why had Jacob used the name of Jesu instead of killing her? She hadn't earned God's mercy. Surely now was the time for her to pay for the lives she had taken.

"My son," she finally squawked. "You've come again at last."

"N-not b-by choice." He stumbled over the words, hating his impediment.

"I understand. I don't deserve your forgiveness."

He shook his head. He wouldn't speak anymore. She didn't deserve the effort.

"But I can tell you how to change things, how to make things right."

"I d-didn't d-do anything wrong." Dietz halted. How should he say this? He focused his mind as Nofra had encouraged him to do. Imagining her hand resting on his chest again, his breathing eased a little, making the words a little easier to access. "You were wrong, b-but your guilt stains me."

"I know, which is why I've told the queen some things, but not everything. I have held onto the most important information for you alone, my son. Dietz, be the savior and make it right. You can be the man you've always wanted to be."

He bit down on his tongue, tasting blood. What did she know of who or what he wanted to be? She who had sent him far away. She who had sacrificed his older brother.

"I've watched you, seen you when you were growing in the Dark Wood. Did you know I could sense what you went through, always feeling different from those I allowed to raise you? But you're not so different, not so strange. You just have a greater purpose than most. It is your fate to save the kingdoms, to bring life from death."

He shook his head, his hands gripped in tight fists again. "Th-th-that's not m-my job. I'm no s-savior."

"But you could be. You simply must learn what I have to teach you, and you can defeat Camilla."

"And wh-what? F-free you, I s-s-suppose?" He bit his tongue again. Stupid! He sounded so stupid!

Her frame shook as she morphed once more, this time into a gigantic lizard, her long green tail curling. "Free me or don't free me, I leave it up to you." Her forked tonged flicked in and out of her mouth. "The High Queen has given you leave to come to me, and if you do, I can teach you what you must do. What you must—"

He shook his head fiercely. How much longer till the guard came back for him? Wasn't his time here over yet?

"Please, my son, it is the only way you will be safe. Camilla will still come for you, use you as her sacrifice to reclaim the power she lost when their god struck her down in the swamps. Don't do it for me, don't do it for the kingdoms, do it for yourself. If you don't, all will be lost and all the sacrifices will be—"

Suddenly, it happened again. A strange calm came over him, the bizarre focus he had felt before in Nofra's presence. His mind and his tongue stilled for a moment. He could no longer taste the metallic tang of his blood. His fists uncurled, and a clear voice spoke from his mouth. "They will have earned exactly what she always wanted them to. Won't they? The kings will be dead, the throne will be Camilla's. All will be as she always wanted. She only has to kill me."

His mother blinked at his clarity, her large, dark eyes still those of a doe in a lizard's face. "No, she has to do so much more than that. Please, my son, I know you have no reason to trust me, but know that I have always tried to keep you safe."

He gave one stiff nod. This much was true.

"If you will listen to me, then you will still be safe and the only one who can save the kingdoms."

He heard the door of the dungeon open, the clomping of a guard's footsteps descending. "It's too bad, your time is up," he hissed, smiling.

~

GWYNNDOLEN HELD tight to her composure. She had just wed, and now it was time to fight. The opening ceremony would not overwhelm her! But as the speaker continued to give introductions to each warrior prince or lord, she felt smaller and smaller. As if she weren't small enough already? What had she been thinking? She glanced through the stands to where Edmund and Rapunzel were sitting. Why was she doing this? To save his life. And possibly lose her own.

Suddenly, a shriek screeched from the king's platform. One of his many daughters cried out.

A black tentacle slithered around her and pulled her backward.

The High King stood up, his personal guards rushing in front of him to face the monster before them on the platform. Camilla reared up, towering over them, smacking aside the guards' weapons. She boomed with her deep, raspy voice, "Little king, do you really think you can hurt me? You who deny that I'm even a threat. Silly king, don't you know when you've lost?"

A mighty cry rang out throughout the courtyard, and shrieking women took the field, holding their weapons aloft. Gwynndolen sucked in a stunned breath. These were women like those who had attacked King Purnell's ship. The pirates who had killed her—until Edmund had resurrected her with the power of his wish. Her eyes darted to her love. He was safe in the stands, but she knew he wasn't likely to stay there.

The company of would-be competitors surged forward. Their weapons raised to meet the onslaught. No one could have prepared them to meet such a strange group. Gwynndolen began hacking her way through the throng, beating a path, grateful the women, while tall, were not as tall as most of the men she knew. Nevertheless, they were powerfully built and deadly.

The warrior monks and women came surging out of the castle, their weapons ready, prayers filling the air. But even as they did so, another group came from behind, warriors from Amee's marshes, spouting out strange words in a guttural tone.

Rushing towards her, different from the rest, was a blond man. His face became clear as he neared.

Georgius? *Brother?*

But how could he—no, it couldn't be him! Her brother had died and this figment of her imagination was coming at her with fish-dead eyes and a sneer on his lips.

"Georgius!" she couldn't help sputtering.

He howled when she called his name, making quick strides to meet her with a sword in hand.

Gwynndolen's heart thumped out of rhythm. Now that he was closer, she could smell him, see him more clearly. The rank of rotten flesh clung to him, and his skin was pale, mottled. His eyes were cloudy. He wasn't really seeing her. She had been right: this wasn't her brother. But how could she defeat someone who was already dead?

Hoping the thing fighting her didn't possess her brother's memories, she quickly stepped into a lunge, thrusting and then spinning away at the last moment. But his body reacted the way he had many times before. He met her sword on his shield and threw her back. She needed something new, but her mind felt so tired—

She lunged forward again, but then threw her shield arm forward, turning her foot so that she spun away at the last minute, landing a hard kick to his unprotected ribs. He fell back with an "oof" and she advanced again. He had more power, but she was faster. She jabbed her short sword under his shield, prying it loose, and it fell uselessly to the side. But she hesitated, seeing the face of her brother once more.

"Gwynndolen!" She heard Edmund's cry just in time to push her back into action. She hop-stepped, leaping into the air, bringing her full weight behind her into the thrust of her sword, digging in up to the hilt. The reanimated Georgius fell back onto the ground, his eyes shut.

A scream ripped from her throat as she caught sight of Liam now advancing in the same stiff way that Georgius had. No! She couldn't do this again. She couldn't—

"Gwynnie!" Someone's arms were around her and she was pushing against them.

Darkness covered her. She couldn't see. "Get off me!" she yelled and pushed the person so hard they lost their clasp on her.

She heard a thump and groan. "Gwynndolen, it's me, it's Edmund."

She looked through the darkness, her eyes adjusting. Edmund? What was—

She sucked in a breath. It had all been a dream. A very real dream. What had happened? Why were they alone in her bedchambers? And *why* had Edmund been in her bed?

"Edmund—you know, your husband."

"My husband?" Suddenly it came rushing back at her. The day of feasting, the food, the dancing—the numerous goblets of wine she had consumed. She jumped to the floor and helped him back to bed. "Are you hurt? I didn't hurt you, did I?"

"Not too bad." He tried to laugh, but she could feel him recoil as she tried to help him. "I'll manage, just give me a moment."

"I'm sorry, I don't know what—I don't even remember getting to bed."

"No, I wouldn't think you did. You were quite merry before we came back here, and as soon as your head hit the pillow, you snored."

"I did not!"

He laughed and then groaned again as he settled himself under the covers. "You certainly did. I tried to wake you, but it was no use. So I simply put my arms around you and fell asleep. That is, until you—"

"Threw you out of bed."

"It's been an eventful night. I take it you're still having nightmares."

"Sometimes, yes."

"Want to tell me about it?"

She shook her head, and in the dim light, he must have been able to see her well enough to not continue the line of questioning. "I'm really sorry I fell asleep without you." She reached out and put a hand on his chest, which he covered with his own.

"Well, you're not asleep now."

"No, I suppose I'm not."

"And if you promise not to thrash me, I'd like to hold you again, maybe kiss you, maybe more . . ." He leaned in and kissed her shoulder, her neck, and at last her lips, sending sparks tingling over her skin.

"Mmm—maybe more?" she whispered into the night. "I suppose that sounds all right. I can thrash you tomorrow instead."

# A NIGHTMARE

Rapunzel woke gasping, soaked in sweat. Her hand touched something small and strange beneath her pillow. A sachet of some sort, probably to scent the sheets and keep them fresh.

"Paul?" She couldn't see what she was holding, but it wasn't because of the darkness of the room. An image locked in her mind, and her body trembled. Helena's small lump was breathing calmly next to her, but there was no Paul cuddled to her back. She dropped the sachet.

Rapunzel raised herself slowly. She didn't want to wake Helena. Her head was foggy. The princess blinked, trying to think. But she couldn't imagine where Paul would go in the middle of the night. What was going on? Her mind refused to leave her dream. "Paul?" she whipered as she uncovered herself and stood next to the bed. Why had he left?

"I'm here, by the window."

Rapunzel took in a calming breath. He was here. She wasn't dreaming. She came around the bed to see him, her eyes now adjusted to the moonlight. Things were as they should be. She had her husband and her daughter in one room and nothing would—

The dream crashed in, a voice calling out from below. She knew where to go; she knew what to ask. It was exactly as the High Queen had said: Rapunzel had brought this about, and those she loved were now in danger. She moved closer to Paul in the shadowed room, wrapping her arms around his midsection from behind. Her tears wet his tunic as she cried silently. She loosened her grip only when he turned to hold her. "What is this?" he asked.

"I've had a dream."

He said nothing, but she could sense some movement. She looked up and saw him nodding in the darkness. "Was it of the sisters?"

"Camilla," she confirmed.

"And what was she about?"

"Her pirates. She is teaching them to work with—I don't know. It was all so dark and deadly. They will arrive on the day of the tournament—tomorrow."

"To surprise us as we celebrate?"

"Yes."

"Good. Now that we know, she cannot surprise us."

"But, Paul, it's not as Amee has said. Camilla has changed her plans. She's—she's—I don't know. The dream fell apart when I heard children screaming."

"What do you mean?"

"I don't know, just screaming. But I don't remember what happened to them." Rapunzel pulled away from Paul, her mouth suddenly filling with saliva. Her stomach churned, and her head felt as though it were spinning. She groped for the bed, and Paul came up beside her, guiding her to sit down.

Kneeling down next to her, he placed a hand on her forehead.

"Am I feverish?"

"No. Are you okay?"

"I just feel so sick, thinking about—I don't even know what I'm thinking." Rapunzel swallowed. She didn't want to vomit. "It's more, it's bigger than what I can see. Something about the pirates. They want something back. Camilla has promised them something—they aren't here just for the claim Camilla has on this land, they want something from the High King himself. I don't—I can't understand what it means, Paul. So much darkness. So much blood! And Helena crying, crying. I can't keep her safe from this." She reached over to pat her little one, grateful that when she had sat on the bed, it hadn't disturbed her daughter.

Her hand hovered in the air above where she had left Helena. Cramps clenched her stomach as she twisted around, searching under the sheets. "Paul!" she screeched, "where's Helena?"

Paul jumped to his feet, running to the other side of the bed. "Perhaps she fell off the side and got tangled—" But Helena hadn't rolled off the side of the bed.

"Where is she? Where could she be!" Rapunzel had to turn away from the bed to heave into the chamber pot. The acidic taste coated her mouth as she wiped off her lips. With shaky hands, she lit the candle.

Paul put a steady hand on her brow. "She can't have gone far. I'll look through the room, you just lie down and try to feel better."

Rapunzel nodded, too weak to argue, though her mind was thrashing around, trying to figure out where their daughter could be. Lying on her back made the room spin.

The shadows flickering up to the ceiling made her dizzy. She turned on her side, trying to take in deep breaths to calm the panic and nausea. As she turned over, her fingers found the sachet again, and she raised it to her nose, hoping the scent of dried lavender would help calm her. But one whiff filled her with misgiving. "Paul, what is this?"

Paul halted. He was looking through a trunk, as though Helena could have climbed in while their backs were turned. He came over to the bed with quick steps and shrugged as he picked up the sachet. "Don't the maidservants at home put some sort of nice-smelling things to keep the sheets smelling fresh?"

"And deter bedbugs, yes—but smell it."

Paul sniffed and then stepped back, putting out a hand to grab the bedpost. "What is that?"

"Sorcery."

"What?"

"I knew something had to be wrong. I mean, why haven't I dreamt since we came here? And now, Helena missing? Someone has taken her, something horrible has happened!"

Paul pulled her back to him, pushing her hair off her heated brow. "Shh, quiet, you're not making much sense. We can figure this out together."

She plunged forward. "We need to gather our group together. Perhaps then we can understand what it means. And Amis—Amis will help. He has the sight, doesn't he? And Jacob can help make sense of this."

He stepped back to the trunk, pulling out a pair of hosen. He lit the candle beside the bed. "Of course—I'll find a servant, we'll track everyone down and call them in here. Do you think you can manage until I return?"

She nodded weakly. "I think so. Hand me a cotehardie and I'll put that over my chemise, at least. And, Paul, I need a glass of water."

He nodded and kissed her forehead before pouring the water from the pitcher into a small glass. She took a small sip and waited. Her stomach turned over, and she put the glass down. "Maybe not yet."

Paul's mouth drew tight.

Rapunzel shook her head. "Just go get everyone. And tell them to search under their pillows."

EDMUND WOKE IN A DAZE. Where was he? The soft bed beneath him wasn't just holding him. Gwynndolen was still beside him. He reached over and pulled her close. Nuzzling her neck caused her to wake, taking a gasp. "Edmund!" she said.

"You sound surprised. Not another nightmare, I hope."

"No." She turned to him and kissed his mouth slowly. "I just forgot for a moment you were here. And we were tog—"

A loud knock thudded on the door.

She jerked away from him. "What's that? Why would someone—"

"Wait here." Edmund threw his tunic on, grabbed his staff, and thumped his way across the floor. Opening the door a crack, he started.

Paul stood uncertainly in the hallway, barely able to look Edmund in the eye. "My wife has had a dream."

Edmund stared at him, then slipped through the door. Paul was interrupting his wedding night to tell him Rapunzel had dreamed? "She has?"

"Yes—Helena is missing."

"Rapunzel dreamed Helena is missing?"

Paul grasped the back of his neck. "No, Rapunzel had a dream, a nightmare, really, and then some enchantment broke."

"What enchantment?"

But Paul continued incoherently, as though talking to himself, swaying uncertainly. "Maybe it broke before that, which made it possible for Rapunzel to dream. I should have known something was wrong. She's been so distractible, so excitable, only calming down when we lay down to sleep. She hasn't dreamt since we returned to the castle. I should have questioned that, shouldn't I? Jacob would have." He looked up at Edmund, as though just remembering Edmund was there. "You need to check beneath your pillows. Perhaps you are enchanted, too."

Edmund shook his head and stepped closer. He placed his free hand on Paul's shoulder. "What are you saying? You're enchanted?"

"It's more than that. Rapunzel woke from a nightmare. We both thought Helena was still in bed. But as Rapunzel told me of the nightmare, our vision cleared. Helena is gone—she's not anywhere to be found! And we discovered these." He held up a small cloth pouch. "Someone had tucked them under our pillows. Rapunzel can't make sense of her dream and I think this is the cause."

"Why would you worry over a dream when your child is missing?"

Paul rubbed a hand over his face. "Rapunzel's dreams mean something. God uses them to guide us. I mean, she doesn't dream every night, but not to have a single one? Especially with a sorceress planning our demise?"

A vague memory surfaced: Rapunzel telling Edmund of her dreams. "I see."

"Check under your pillows. I think—I know sorcery has been undermining us. And now Helena's gone. We need to gather, find my child, discover who is doing this to us. Please, come to our chambers, there must be something we can do."

Edmund patted Paul on the shoulder and retreated back to his wife. How would he feel if he and Gwynndolen had lost a child?

Gwynndolen. How could he keep her safe from this? She was likely to grab her sword as soon as she heard—

At that moment, she moved the curtains back, and the moonlight touched her face and form. She was so beautiful. He wanted to savor this first night together. But one nightmare had already interrupted it, why not another? He sighed.

"Get dressed, my love—it seems the Lord has work for us to do."

# AWAKE AND AWARE

Making her way from the swamps to the castle's sewers was quick work for Camilla now that the covens had moved closer in. Her sleek form sped through the waters at such speed that she laughed. The rusted grate that should have impeded her entry into the sewers didn't stop her. She simply shrank through the opening. It was not the cleanest way to enter the dungeon, but Camilla protected herself from the filth by creating a bubble of air about her body. Such rudimentary protection was easy for her. Even Nofra had mastered it before leaving the covens to become a maidservant.

Before emerging from the waters in her human form, she reached out with her mind to see who was watching the dungeons, discovering, to her delight, that they had left them vacant. Foolish High King! How she loved his idiocy. He must have trusted the power of his weak god to bind and safeguard his prisoner. Not wise, but certainly to her advantage. She rose from the waters and made her way through the tunnels, closer and closer to her sister, finding her way inside through the secret door.

Something snorted and shook. Camilla looked around. A torch burned in a ring at the bottom of the steps, and she could see something writhing on the floor. Was that Amee? That creature that was shimmering? Camilla couldn't tell what form she had taken. It grotesquely combined something with scales and fur.

She stepped toward her sister, growing back to her towering height as a massive woman, her head not much lower than the high ceiling. "Amee?" Her raspy voice reverberated against the stone walls.

The creature—her sister—turned a mournful gaze upon her. "What do you want?" she moaned.

"Want? It's not what I want, but what you need —forgiveness."

Amee did not reply, but began shaking, trembling. Her arms stretched out, fingers curling into talons, her head sprouting a mane, and her back end becoming a hind end of a hoofed creature. When she stopped transforming, Amee looked up, her dark, reflective eyes filling with tears. "You wish to forgive me? For what?"

Her transformation fascinated Camilla. What magic was this? How could she best use it? She tried to reach into her sister's mind without alerting her. "For choosing to betray me and your own people. I don't know how you could, after all our work, all our sacrifice—" She paused, licking her lips and waiting for her sister to argue. But the word *sacrifice* had no effect on the creature her sister had become. Was she resigned to this miserable life she now had? She sensed nothing in her sister, no resistance, nothing left.

Amee moved her head in a simple movement. A nod? Perhaps that would be the only acknowledgment that Camilla would get. Amee did not speak.

Camilla hated her for her silence. She needed her to argue, to fight against this. Had her will been taken from her as well?

"Why do you just sit there?"

A hoarse laugh filled the air and then Amee morphed again, this time changing fully into a beautiful phoenix, her bright red feathers reminding Camilla of the flames she had seen at her war council the night before. "I can't just sit here. I don't sit anymore—I change all the time. Constantly. I can't stop myself."

"Sorcery rebels within you, dear sister. Can you not feel it? How it writhes and hates what you have become. That is why you cannot stop changing. That is why you have no control. You betrayed yourself, your people, me, and now you are reaping the consequences."

Amee blinked. "It is as you say. I have been a traitor and now I must pay."

Camilla tilted her head. "Are you all alone here, or do they bring you food?" Weak humans, they would feed their enemies, she knew.

"They feed me, but I haven't much appetite."

"And your son, the one you betrayed us for, does he come and visit his mother?"

Amee's round eyes moistened again, and her entire body shook. Her feathers molted until there was nothing left of her but a frail woman with lank grey hair.

"My, my, sister, how you have changed."

"Leave me."

"How can I leave you? You were all that I needed to win this war, but now they have locked you up. No good."

Amee looked at her. "As I should be for all the harm I have done."

"We didn't finish what we began. They will still persecute the covens unless we—"

"No more!" Camilla stepped back at the sudden vehemence in Amee's voice. "No more, please! I can do no more!"

Camilla gave a low chuckle at how shocked she had been. Her sister was still there; she was just hiding. From herself, perhaps?

"You know, you have it within you to set yourself free, to come back, to be what we require."

"I don't know what—"

"You know exactly what. The sorcery within you does rebel, but it is rebelling against this—against your refusal to fight."

"They placed me under bondage to the one called Jesu!"

Camilla hissed. "He is weak. *You* are weak if you have allowed yourself to find him so powerful!"

"What do you want?"

"I want the power." Camilla surprised herself by speaking the truth.

"Then take it and leave me."

"If I take it—"

"I know, I'll be dead. And this will finally be over."

"It won't be over. It will never be over, not till we win!"

"It will be over, Camilla. It will be over for me."

Camilla hissed again and then lunged forward, her body transforming into a leviathan that slid along the floor, shocked by the invisible barrier. But it could not hurt her in her leviathan form. She quickly covered the rest of the distance and sank her fangs into Amee. But instead of injecting her sister with venom, she simply drank from her victim. The taste of power was sweet to her forked tongue.

Jacob dressed quickly and made his way through the castle to Paul's chambers, trying to hurry the servant along. Woken in the middle of the night in order to meet with the prince? Something was wrong.

Entering Paul's chambers, he saw several others had already gathered. Prince Edmund was leaning on his staff at the end of the bed. His young bride had her arms wrapped around Rapunzel while the princess wept, seated on her bed. Dietz, head down, paced beside the window. Katterina stood staring vacantly next to the bed, face tight and gripping something in her hand. Prince Paul moved away from his wife's side to greet Jacob, but before he could say anything, Amis popped into the room.

"It wasn't under my pillow!" he called out, holding something similar to what Katterina was clutching. "But I realized if I was going to hide something, I'd put it under the threshold of the tent, and there it was!" He turned to Jacob, hand outstretched with the off-white pouch in his palm. "Can you identify the stench of sorcery, Monk?"

Jacob sniffed the innocent-looking sachet. He jerked back at the complex scent of earth, musk plant, and black pepper. The scent recalled to mind lessons he had learned as a young monk, discerning the various plants used in sorcery for nefarious purposes. "Most definitely sorcery. Where did you find it?" He couldn't help looking at Katterina first.

Her eyes were narrow slits of anger. "Under our pillows."

"How did you know to look?"

Rapunzel pulled back from Gwynndolen and wiped at her swollen eyes. Everyone turned to hear her. "I had a nightmare, and it confused me." She leaned forward, head in her hands. "Do you remember how last winter my dreams became clearer, Brother Jacob? You said it was because I had become a daughter of the Most High King, a co-heir with Jesu, my Savior. But after we returned from the monastery, I stopped having them. Until last night. I thought Helena was beside me, but she's not here. As I was looking through the bedclothes, I discovered these beneath our pillows."

"Who would take the child? And who could have put the pouches—"

She straightened her body, trying to hold her head up to answer his questions. "I can only imagine it to be my maidservant. I trusted her lately to help me with little Helena, and she cared for our bedchambers. But why? Why would she do that? And how would she get into the other bedchambers?" She gestured to the other sachets.

Dietz moved backward, dropping his pouch like it was diseased.

"Tell me more about your dream. It's okay if you can't remember everything, but any bit might help us find Helena and stop Camilla."

Rapunzel shrugged and wrapped her arms to hug herself. Though tears streamed down her face, she swallowed and continued. "It was so muddled, like hearing something while you're underwater. I couldn't make out what God was trying to tell me. I only know that all is not right. The High Queen got Amee to tell us about Camilla's plans. But, what Amee told us—that's not all there is. Something more is going to happen, isn't it?" Rapunzel looked around the room, as though hoping someone could tell her otherwise.

Dietz shifted and Jacob looked at him, and the young man wilted under her gaze.

Dietz balled his hands into fists. "Sh-she tried to tell me something yesterday, s-said she could help me if I just t-t-trusted her."

"What did she say?" Katterina pounced.

"I w-wouldn't listen."

"You had the chance to——"

"I w-w-was angry! He grimaced, staring at the floor. "I d-didn't want to s-stay. I left."

Jacob shook his head at Katterina, and she looked away from the young man. He looked back at Dietz. "Do you think you could get her to talk to you again?"

"I d-don't know. M-maybe."

"Then, we'll go together."

Dietz shook his head. "She w-won't talk to m-me with you—w-with anyone. Just me. Said she wants me to do something, s-s-save the kingdoms." He left the room abruptly.

Rapunzel wept loudly. "I can't believe this. Amis or I should have seen, should have known."

Jacob tightened his grip on his staff, grateful for the solid heft of it. "The sachet was binding you."

She clutched her abdomen. "Then why did the enchantment break?"

Katterina stepped forward. "Paul, get her to lie down. She needs to rest. I think I know what will make her well again and help us all make sense of this. I'll be back soon."

Jacob followed her out into the corridor, turning her by the shoulders. "Katterina——" She looked up at him. "Where are you going?"

Katterina licked her lips. "I need you to trust me. There's something I learned, but I don't have time to explain. I think I can find it before dawn—I'll be back soon."

"You shouldn't go alone."

"I can see in the dark, remember? If I take anyone else with me, they'll only slow me down. Please, trust me, Jacob." And she placed a warm hand on his cheek.

He leaned toward her, but then she stepped back.

"I'm sorry, I didn't mean to—"

He shook his head. He wanted to hold on to her, but they didn't have time. "It's fine. Just, please, be careful."

Her head tilted before she spoke. "When am I not?" But she laughed and slipped away.

# NOFRA AND AMEE

ofra was careful as she balanced Helena's weight on her hip and used the torch to lead her to the tunnel into the dungeon. Taking Helena had been simple; making certain everything else was as Camilla wanted much easier than she thought it would be. But now that it was time to leave? She found she couldn't do it. Not until she faced Amee one last time.

How easy it was to sneak in. The guards were upstairs, guarding a door she didn't need to bother with. She used her index finger on the hand holding the torch to motion for the hidden door to open. Silently, she slipped into the dungeon.

Amee was lying prone on the filthy floor, panting. She had taken the form of a frail woman, her stringy hair in a matted mess. Nofra's throat tightened, and she placed her torch in the empty iron ring on the wall, noticing the guards had left another burning near the foot of the stairs. Kind of them to care whether the monster had enough light to see by.

When the little one whimpered, Nofra hushed Helena

by placing her right hand on the little girl's forehead and whispering a quiet chant. The child slumped against her in slumber.

Amee shifted, but she didn't seem to have the strength to sit up. "Nofra?" Her voice creaked. "What are you doing here?"

"For fifty years you were cursed, and you worked to reverse it, but now, look at you!" Spit flew from her lips, and she shifted Helena's dead weight so the little girl was leaning against her more securely.

A shadow outside the stair's torchlight moved.

"Who's there?"

Dietz came into the flickering light, his dark eyes wide and glassy. "W-what are you doing here? How does she kn-know you? W-why w-would you—" He grunted in frustration.

Nofra jerked her free hand in front of her and pointed a finger directly at him. She chanted, feeling the words reverberate in her chest. She could almost feel the beat of her heart slow down as she spoke them and looked up to see Dietz staring at her. But could he see her? She smiled as she realized he was now under her command. She took a breath to steady herself and then hazarded a glance Amee's way.

"What are you going to do to him?" The strain was making Amee's voice crack.

"Don't you know? Can't you tell? You taught me so well my whole life. You, the great sorceress."

"Please, don't hurt him."

"Maybe I won't. It all depends." She clenched her teeth, but did not waver. "I've never seen you look so . . ."

"Old?" Amee hacked a cough.

The rage that had been building for so long rose like a

wail in her ears. She gave vent to it. "What happened to you?" Nofra gasped. "Why did you betray me? I was yours, and you spit me out for him." Her finger remained pointing at Dietz. "Perhaps I shall I hurt him the way you hurt me!"

Amee lifted her head, her pathetic attempts to sit up laughable. "You cannot, please don't! I didn't want to hurt you, but I had to protect my child."

Nofra tightened her arm around Helena. "But you made me believe *I* was your child! How am I supposed to live now?"

Amee's head hit the ground, a satisfying thud on the mildewed hay. "I don't know. It's just, I knew. I knew at last that what we were doing was wrong. What Camilla wants you to do now is wrong. You mustn't—"

"You don't get to tell me what I must and mustn't do. That's not your job anymore, it's Camilla's."

"Do you trust her?"

Nofra locked her jaw.

"You shouldn't. She only wants one thing."

"Yes! To free us from the tyranny of the Church and their weak god."

The haggard woman struggled again; she was fighting her weakness, but it was too much for her. "No, she wants to rule all of you, all of us. The sorceress will dethrone the king and establish a new world—her new world. Don't you see? Camilla wants to be supreme. To be worshipped." Amee's cough rumbled from deep in her chest. Finally, she wheezed out, "Camilla tried to use me to sacrifice my child and take the power she needs from him, but it didn't work, did it? Now she will use you"—the wet cough ripped through her again—"and do what she can to take the power she needs from you. Why do you think I'm lying here? She's already taken mine."

Nofra looked at Amee, but didn't release her hold on Helena or drop her finger from pointing at Dietz. Her mind was also still reaching out, keeping each piece of Camilla's plan progressing. Was it too much? Had she been foolish to add this trip to the dungeon? She kept holding a corner of her mind, focused on each thing she was doing, just as Camilla had told her she could. But she wouldn't be able to continue for long. Her head throbbed with the effort. Even now, the pain tried to overwhelm the anger and the hunger for power. But she concentrated on that hunger, letting the burning flame of desire spark a greater blaze.

That hunger was all that was pushing her forward. To the dungeon, though Camilla had wanted her to leave quickly. But Nofra had to come. She had to confront Amee. And now, she could barely hold all the pieces in place. How was she to escape with Helena and make her way back to Camilla? The young witch should leave the castle before they discovered her with the child. Before parents awoke to missing children and nursemaids singing lullabies to pillows.

Nofra's eyes returned to Dietz. His eyes were still glazed over. When she let him go, he would know about her. He could unravel their plans!

Unless. What would Camilla want her to do? Should she hurt him, kill him, and flee?

She concentrated harder. What if Dietz could help her achieve more than Camilla had asked for? There was potential within him. What if he became what he was meant to be all along? Would Camilla use him to become another sacrifice, as Amee feared, or could he become something more with Nofra's help? Perhaps the next Grand Sorcerer?

She closed her eyes and pulled on her strength. There. Nofra could sense deep within him a well of displeasure. Different. Dietz hated being different. The young man yearned for connection, commonality. He needed under-standing. Thoughts he had kept hidden, frustrations he had buried all came bubbling to the surface. She could feel them, see them. All she had to do was draw from this well.

A laugh burst from her throat, and Amee shrunk at the sound. Camilla had said she had a knack for it, and now Nofra could see her own strength. People often hid things, even from themselves. She could help Dietz bring those hidden things into view, plant them, grow them. Some-thing shifted in his expression; his dark eyes watered. He still wasn't aware of her, as though he thought he was dreaming. But the flicker of emotion gave her hope.

"What are you going to do to him?" Amee asked again, the voice of a broken mother.

"It's not what I'm going to do to him, but what I'll do with him. Together." She could do this. She could change his mind, help him choose something better than the path he was on. He was pliable, just as she once had been.

# THE CHILDREN

"What can we do now?" Paul asked Jacob after Katterina left, when the monk reentered the room.

"I think it's best if we make the queen aware. Camilla had a hand in this, I'm certain."

"Edmund—" Paul's shoulders rounded. He couldn't do it alone. His eyes glanced over at his wife, who looked slightly green. "We'll need you. I wish Katterina hadn't left."

"Gwynndolen can stay with Rapunzel. If we are going to the queen, we'd best also seek the king."

"At this time of night, I only hope they'll let us speak with him."

Edmund furrowed his brow. "They might make us wait till daybreak."

"Jacob, what if you get Father Iohannes? He might request an audience even at this time of night." Paul noticed Edmund was leaning even more heavily on his staff. "Are you all right?"

Edmund grimaced and shook his head. "It's nothing.

We must get to the king, demand an audience. The entire kingdom is in danger if they have stolen Helena for Camilla's nefarious purposes."

"Of course." Paul nodded, though he doubted the young bride would appreciate being left behind. "Gwynndolen—" Paul pulled her aside. "I need to ask a favor of you."

Her dark eyes brightened.

"I need you to stay here with Rapunzel and make certain she's safe. Amis will stay with you—"

A loud rapping beat upon the door, halting his speech. "Paul! Wake up!" came a muffled shout.

Paul ran to the door, opening it to see the face of his brother, Roland, red and sweating. "My son, he's missing—again!"

"What?"

"Yes, he's—you're dressed!" Roland sputtered, just noticing. He glanced at the other occupants of the room. "And—why are all of you gathered?"

"Our Helena's missing, too. When did you discover Eng was gone?"

Roland wiped his sweaty forehead as he walked inside, rubbing his hand on his tunic. "It was the strangest thing. Aalis went to check on the nursemaid in the middle of the night. Nothing unusual—she does that every night. But when she went, she discovered the woman patting and rocking and singing softly . . . to a pillow. You say Helena's disappeared?"

"Yes, we were going to go seek an audience with the king and queen."

"I'm coming with you."

Paul put a hand on his brother's shoulder. "Of course

—we'll go together. Jacob, come with Father Iohannes as soon as you can."

Paul and the others made their way to the royal quarters, not a little disturbed by the dozing guards who barely acknowledged their presence. No wonder babes were missing, with guards not doing their jobs. Edmund stepped toward one dozer and cleared his throat. The man gave a slow blink and then straightened with a look of confusion. "What—what are you doing here? What time is it?"

"I would think you would know, as you have the night watch," Edmund reprimanded.

The guard's cheeks darkened, but his lips tightened. "Whatever it is you need, it can wait till morning."

"I don't think so. The High King will want to know—"

"Once the king passes—I mean, goes to bed for the night, he wants to see nothing and hear nothing, not till late the next morning."

"Then, we need to see the High Queen. She will want to know—"

"The High Queen is not to be disturbed at night. She needs her—"

But a high-pitched shriek broke through the guard's argument. The guard straightened up taller and jerked his chin at the other guard, who had jumped awake at the sound of the woman's cry. He blocked their way with his decorative battle-ax while the other guard slipped behind the massive door that blocked all others from the royal family's wing.

"No!" A woman's voice tore at the air. Shouts, scuffles, and doors opening and slamming shut accompanied the weeping that followed. The guard that had left them returned, his eyes wide.

"What's going on?" Edmund asked.

"The heir has disappeared!"

"What? How could someone take the child while we—"

"Children. The bastard son is missing, too!"

"But that's impossible. They would have had to—"

"What?" Edmund snapped. "Sneak past sleeping guards?"

The guards looked at one other, eyes wild. "The High Queen checked on the babe, but he wasn't there. We are to go get—"

Father Iohannes was padding quickly down the corridor toward them with Jacob at his side.

"Father, you are here! The High King asks you to come inside."

Unruffled as always, the man leaned toward the guard and articulated, "I will come, but only if accompanied by these men."

The elder guard moved his battle-ax out of the way and then waved them inside. Paul followed behind Father Iohannes into what must be the High King's chambers. Inside, the man was comforting a dark-skinned young woman as she sat in a chair. The High Queen was sitting nearby on the side of the bed, a vast robe around her shoulders, her face haggard and weary, her black-and-grey hair loose in waves. Her round eyes narrowed as she glared at the king's back, but she turned when they came in and made herself stand with the support of the bed's post.

"Father, how have you come so quickly?" Her face puckered into a frown. "And why have you brought with you . . ." But her normally powerful voice faded out, as though she knew there was more hard news to hear.

"Your Majesty, your loss is not an isolated event. We

were on our way to speak to you of two others who were taken."

"Two more? What, Princess Rapunzel's daughter and —" Her eyes squinted past Paul at Prince Roland.

"My son, little Eng, Your Majesty."

"The children saved last winter? The ones the sorceress was using?"

"What's this?" The king turned away from the woman he was comforting. The other woman's face was streaked with tears and contorted by grief. Otherwise, she might have been lovely. Her hair, like the queen's was also down, but it hung in coarse spirals of jet black. Though she looked a little older than Rapunzel or Gwynndolen, Paul recognized she must be the king's mistress. "What are you saying?" the king barked.

"My love"—the queen's words were laced with venom —"these children have been stolen for an evil purpose."

He waved a hand in the air. "Of course they have! Kidnapping is evil itself, and those who would do so must have an evil purpose."

"What I am trying to say is that someone has taken them for evil purposes. Dark sorcery is at work here."

The king's jaw unhinged, and he stood speechless for a moment. "No! It must be a jealous king or some such nonsense. We have the sorceress in our dungeon, and she cannot control herself. She couldn't have taken these children."

Edmund stepped forward, deliberately thumping the floor hard with his staff. "No, Your Majesty—forgive us, we meant her sister."

The king's face screwed up in frustration, and Paul couldn't help wondering if the man was still a little drunk from the day's revelry. "You killed her last winter, didn't you?"

"Well, one sister died. But there were three, remember?" Edmund's voice continued respectfully, though he thumped the floor after each point. "Ute died." *Thump.* "Jesu bound Amee." *Thump.* "But Camilla is at large." *Thump, thump.*

"But you bound her to the sea, right? She couldn't possibly—"

"Your Majesty, we explained how she freed herself from the sea and how she can travel unrestricted now. Yes, we weakened her at the swamp a fortnight ago when we fought her, but she is a sorceress with no conscience. She'll stop at nothing to defeat us. To destroy the kingdoms, she would even use these little ones to empower her."

The mistress clasped her hands to her chest and sobbed, but the High Queen stepped toward Edmund as though he could make it go away. "Why would she take our son? Or *hers*?"

He shook his head. "I really don't know."

She stepped over and slapped his face. "Then what good are you?" She turned on the rest of them, now glaring at Paul in particular. "What good are any of you? Fathers who can't protect their children. Warrior monks who can't keep the land safe from evil sorcery."

Paul saw Father Iohannes nod at Jacob, who now stepped toward the queen. "Your Majesty, it seems likely that she will drain them of their life and use them as her power source. Ute carefully groomed Helena and Eng for such a sacrifice."

"And what of my Darras?"

"And my Nymandus?" came the soft voice of the mistress.

"They are the only heirs, are they not?"

The queen balled up her fists. "Someone would have had to help them get to our sons. Someone trusted by the guards."

"The guards seemed drugged—or enchanted."

"Yes, but by whom? And what sort of magic? Guards! Find Princess Qasmuna."

"Your Majesty?" Jacob questioned.

"If both sons die, then her husband becomes the High King's heir. I know my daughter too well. She has hated her displacement since her father has produced not one but two sons to keep her husband off the throne."

# A FLOWER AND SORCERY

Katterina scampered out immediately after talking to Jacob, a satchel tied around her waist. Slipping away from the castle was easy work, given the late hour. The guards were practically asleep in their standing positions, and only a few flicked a glance her way.

She had looked through the apothecary's journal quickly before leaving the castle's light, and she fixed the sketched image in her mind. Her feet carefully traversed the ground as she left behind the built-up roads and headed straight into the boggy marshland. It was dark, but her cat-sight allowed her to see roots and soft spots others would have tripped over. Oh how she longed to travel faster, to make it back to the castle before Rapunzel noticed her missing. She knew her daughter would have cautioned her not to go, but Jacob had understood. A warmth filled her, and she quickened her pace, knowing she could do this. Katterina would help make everyone well before Camilla advanced her plans.

Now, deep in the marsh, only a slight bit of light from

the moon struggled through the branches. But even among the shadows, she could see the colors of the swamp. The air hummed with insects. The sound of croaking frogs joined the chorus. She stopped for a moment to refresh her mind, looking once more at the odd orchid-like flower sketched onto the page of the book. It should be easy to spot, but she hadn't seen anything like it yet. She traveled further in, swatting at mosquitos that attempted to feast on her.

Katterina stepped on tiptoe as though she didn't trust that it would release her feet from the ground if she placed them down heavily. There were stories of people being swallowed by the bog. *Was that sorcery or a natural phenomenon?* she wondered. Bright hues of orange and blue loomed ahead, and she traipsed toward the source, heart racing in her chest. Was this it? She pulled out the journal one more time and noted the description beside the sketch. She stopped and bent low in order to study the plant. It was a delicate, humid-loving species of flower. A crooked smile filled her face. How many had tried to take the flower back to their kingdoms? But lacking the right climate, the poor things never survived.

Her smile vanished. Unless her sister transplanted.

Rapunzel's love of gardens, plants, and herbs all stemmed from how Eufemia had raised her, teaching her to grow things even as she used her witchcraft to supply the right elements to keep things like orchids alive and growing in the Soontrisse Mountains. Or things like the lettuce, the rapunzel plant that lived for months longer than it should have. The plant that Katterina had lost her daughter over.

She blinked. Eufemia was dead. Rapunzel had forgiven Katterina. Despite that, the consequences of past sins lingered. She knew God had brought about her redemption, but—and she didn't understand why her mind connected the two—she worried at the way Rapunzel clung to Helena. Rapunzel had once said she would never let her children be vulnerable, and now it was rare that the girl had been out of her sight. Now that the little girl was missing—what would that do to Rapunzel?

Katterina shook off the thought. They would, by God's grace, find the little girl after Katterina brought back this plant to help mend the damage from sorcery. Rapunzel wasn't like Katterina, trading her daughter for lettuce. It wasn't her fault that they had taken her daughter, and Katterina would do everything she could to set it right!

She refocused her attention on the bright flower. It had four blossoms, three outer petals each, with an orange center that spread out into peacock-blue edges. It was growing between the exposed roots of a giant tupola tree. Such odd-looking trees, with the base of the massive tree swollen and round, thinning suddenly higher on the trunk. Its branches lifted high overhead, where tangled threads of grey moss grew in thick bunches.

"What are you doing, growing here like this?" Her eye caught sight of a movement, and she turned ever so slightly to follow the little animal that was now staring at her. There was something unnerving about the small creature. It was the size of a chipmunk but looked like a lynx. Something about the eyes, the sly twist in the mouth . . . It blinked as Katterina tucked the book back into her satchel and the plant into the bodice of her gown.

Was this a staring contest? It had been a long time since anyone had beaten her at staring, and then only when she allowed them to.

The creature dashed away, and Katterina gave chase, running over the knobby roots of the trees. Dappled moonlight filtered through the leaves and the moss, lighting the ground unevenly, their chasing now in and out of shadows. But to Katterina's cat-sight, she could see clearly all that was ahead of her. The creature turned and then jumped into the water, elongating into a sleek eel-like shape with black and purple stripes.

"Katterina. It has been too long," Camilla's voice rasped.

Katterina recoiled. "What are you doing here?"

"I rule these swamps, now that you have my sister. I should ask what you are doing here."

Katterina blinked. She wouldn't answer.

"What could you possibly want in the swamps, well away from the safety of the High King's castle? What have you been collecting in your little satchel?" She hissed with her forked tongue and then growled words that Katterina recognized, a throaty language Eufemia had been well-versed in. The vines that encircled Katterina sprang from the moist ground, swarming up onto her feet and climbing up her body. But they halted at her neck so she could still turn her head and breathe. And speak.

"What do you want?"

"Only to hear you ask me what I want. To know you care."

"I don't."

"You do!" Camilla gave a laugh. "You worry over the ones you love, the ones you are trying to protect. The daughter you betrayed long ago, the prince she is married to now, even the little adopted grandchild you love as your own. Precious grandchild. If you allowed her to do what she was born for, if Rapunzel had followed through on what she was born for . . ." Camilla let her gritty voice trail off as one tentacle skimmed the murky water, creating ripples that glittered as a shaft of moonlight lit it. "You know, I should thank you."

"Thank me?"

"Yes, thank you. When Rapunzel broke free from Ute, Amee thought we lost everything. But something curious happened to me. Can you imagine what that was?"

Katterina didn't trust her voice, so she shook her head.

Camilla's body transformed into a towering woman, stepping from the swampy water up onto the land and breathing her sulfurous words into Katterina's face. "Power."

Katterina shifted her face away from the sorceress, but Camilla's warm hands grabbed either side of her face and made her look at her. "Power, Katterina, power. It was what my father wanted me to have so long ago, what he sacrificed the life of our mother to give to us girls. I hated him for that, but it was too late. Power so that their weak god could no longer kill our followers. Power so that we could make the kingdoms into what we wanted them to be."

Her voice paused, and she turned Katterina's face to the left and then to the right. What was she looking for?

"You know, I had to cultivate my own little source of power after he cursed us. Ute and Amee did, too. And then, Rapunzel tried to cut us off from all that power. But it didn't work, did it? When Ute died, I received her power. Well, most of it. I watched my sister for signs this spring before she betrayed me. It was apparent she received little from Ute. Fool! I've taken all I needed from her now. She'll die, wishing she'd never betrayed me.

"All of you think that because I no longer siphon power from Edmund's wishes, I am cursed again, cut off once more. But I still have Ute's power and all the power she drained from the people she killed in the Soontrisse Mountains for all those years. And now, Amee's power, too. So much more power than you could ever imagine."

Silence fell between the two women. Camilla turned away from Katterina. Was she done speaking? Katterina felt the vines withering, becoming brittle. She moved, and they snapped, letting her take a step back. But Camilla jerked around and yanked Katterina back to her. Again she put her hands on both sides of her face so that Katterina couldn't turn away.

"You think your monk will save you? That he has the ear of the god you serve? No. Your monk is weak, incapable of making the hardest choice of all. He will lose if he comes up against me. Even if he comes at me with all his warriors. I have all the power I need at my disposal, and your little band doesn't even have the support of the king. I will win, and I will destroy all you love.

"Return to your mountains, Katterina, and make certain no one tries to find me or my followers. We will leave you alone if you leave us alone. Let us have this foolish High King, and you can stay in the Soontrisse Mountains with your happy little family and your precious little monk. Convince them overthrowing me is not something they can win. You can only lose all you love."

Katterina struggled to free herself. "I can't do that."

Camilla's mouth tipped up. "I thought you'd say that." She removed her hand and transformed back into a leviathan so fast that Katterina stumbled backward. Camilla shimmered and grew larger and larger. But it wasn't just Camilla that grew larger—the tree's swollen trunks grew thicker, the branches overhead now far away. Only then did Katterina realize how close to the ground she was now. Her body, shrouded by the dress she had been wearing, was also covered in the fur coat she remembered so well. She scrambled to get free of the gown, disbelieving. How could she be a calico cat of black, white, and tan again?

"What have you done to me?" Katterina knew it was a foolish question.

"You once helped Amee by messaging for Eufemia and serving my sister Ute. You will now serve me. Convince your little group of how powerful I am, how ridiculous their insignificant resistance is to try to keep me from destroying the High King's kingdom."

"I won't do it."

"Are you sure? As soon as you deliver the message, you will return to your proper form."

"I'd rather never speak to them again."

"Now, that's a wish I can grant. You won't be able to speak to your family anymore."

The burning in her throat caused her to hack. Her chest grew tight, and flames spread through her entire being. Katterina looked up at Camilla, shaking her head.

"Still won't do my bidding? Then enjoy the silence. And enjoy your journey back to the castle." Camilla's form slipped back into the waters, leaving Katterina all alone.

# CONVINCING

ofra led Dietz through a narrow back tunnel in the dungeon. His eyes were feverish as they reflected the torches' blazing light. Was his blood boiling, just as she desired it to be? All would be well. She was managing things just right. They just needed to get outside the castle and meet the others. "It's time," she whispered to herself, but she heard Dietz halt behind her.

"W-wait." She turned to look at him, still balancing Helena's sleeping weight. The incantation she had enchanted him with should have brought him into alignment with her purpose. Soon it would also be his purpose —once he understood.

"No, there's no time for waiting or second-guessing. You've chosen your side, and it's with me." She stepped boldly up to him and pulled his face down to hers with her free hand. She pressed her lips to his mouth, parting them slightly. He pulled back, but then leaned in, kissing her back with fire. She broke away suddenly, and he blinked, uncertain. He would be hers to command if she could keep him teetering, his mind confused.

But did keeping things from him make her like Amee? Wasn't that what everyone in her life—in his life—had done? She had told Amee that she would help him choose a different, a better path. He couldn't if he didn't know he had a choice.

His eyes were glazing over again after the kiss, but she snapped her fingers and he blinked again, shook his head. "Wh-where are we and why have you b-brought—"

"I'm leaving with Rapunzel's child, and you can come as well. I must make things right for us. They will never leave us alone if we don't stand up to them."

"Stand up to who?"

"What have you done with your life?" She wished she could set Helena down, but she just shifted her to the opposite hip.

Dietz shrugged.

"Look at me. You have done everything everyone has told you to do. So have I. But it's time we think for ourselves, time we make our own way."

Dietz took a step back, his face crumpled in confusion.

"Your band of so-called friends . . . They aren't really your friends. They aren't looking out for your best interests, only their own. You *know* what I speak is the truth. Come with me, and we will flee with the power to undo all they have tried to build."

"But why the child?"

Her mouth split into a smile. "Not just one child. There are others we will take with us."

PERHAPS DIETZ SHOULDN'T HAVE BEEN surprised when they stepped into a larger tunnel to see three maidservants standing there with blank faces. Each one held a whimpering child. He recognized pale, tow-headed Eng, Prince Roland's son, but the appearance of the other two stunned him. The High King's boys!

He looked over at Nofra and she smiled at him, exchanging Helena for the torch he was holding. "Follow me," she said, and the maidservants blankly lined up behind him as they all traveled a stone path beside the sewer.

Helena was sleeping limply in his arms, but the boys cried in earnest as they were carried. Dietz turned to look at them. The maidservants kept moving their legs but did nothing to comfort their little ones, almost as though they were sleepwalking.

"N-Nofra?" But he couldn't think what else to say. He didn't know what he was doing, where he was going. His mind struggled to connect what was happening when Nofra turned to Dietz and, walking backward, she gave him that slow smile. "Sing to them."

Of course, it made sense to him. He shifted Helena's weight and sang a song from his childhood. Music was strange, for it connected his tongue to his mind differently than speech. The words flowed with no stutter as Nofra led them further and further along the path.

The tunnel stank, guiding them next to the fetid water that carried the refuse away from the nobility. His eyes watered as he sang, and the boys' crying turned back to little whimpers. Dietz tucked Helena close to his chest so if she startled awake, she wouldn't tumble into the nasty water. Nofra picked up the strains of the song he was singing, and her voice blended with his. It was not high like he had heard when Princess Rapunzel would sing, but in a lower range that echoed off the tunnel walls.

Suddenly, Dietz could no longer smell the filth they were walking beside. He could only hear her voice. He was grateful for the torches that lit the way beside the raised stone path. *How many stones had sunk into the boggy ground to build the castle—and then raise it up throughout the years to keep it from sinking?* he wondered as his voice climbed.

Up ahead he saw a door, and Nofra stopped in front of it. She placed the torch in an iron ring so that she could draw a key out of her pocket. Her singing halted momentarily as she unlocked it. When she tried to open it, the door wouldn't budge. Dietz handed her Helena and pried it open, a loud moaning creak filling the air.

Nofra looked up at him, her eyes alight with heat. He wanted her to reach up to him again, to kiss him once again. She laughed then, as though she knew his thoughts, and placed a hand on his cheek. "Follow me—we'll make time for that later." She gestured to the other servants to stay close.

In the back of his mind, something tried to rear up. The memory of following a serving woman had made him feel small, unworthy. But why should he have ever felt that way? Nofra was everything. She would lead him where he wanted to go. He felt a smile slip over his face as the half-moon's light came out from behind a cloud.

Nofra led them to a copse of trees where two horses were waiting, saddled. She drew out lengths of cloth from a saddlebag and began wrapping one around him, securing Prince Roland's son to his back in a sling. With help from the servants, he soon also had the High King's illegitimate son slung across his chest. Nofra similarly had the High King's newborn across her chest and Helena on her back. Though balancing to mount was tricky now with such burdens, they were soon riding off. Nofra led him behind the castle and on past the rice paddies, further into the marsh.

Only once they reached the marsh and they rode side by side did he hazard speaking. "What are we doing?"

"What we must. We will find Camilla and bring her the children."

"We are bringing her sacrifices?"

"Do you think she will really sacrifice four children? No, but they are a source of power. As are we. Camilla and I discussed it. Those of us marked by sorcery will be the power she needs—"

"She will d-drain us. Like she d-drained my mother, left her there in the dungeon to d-die."

He didn't like the look that Nofra shot him. "You believed Amee? She took that form to make us feel sorry for her, to plant distrust between us and Camilla."

"So, you b-believe we should implicitly p-place our t-trust in Camilla?" So many words exhausted him. But he had to know what she could be thinking, trusting another sorceress.

Nofra's jaw jerked, and her breathing quickened. "We're almost there—we mustn't discuss this much longer in case someone is listening." She looked over at him. "Perhaps you're right. We shouldn't take Camilla's word, but we could watch her together. See what she is about. Then we'll know."

Dietz felt pulled taut in opposite directions. He didn't want to go back to the castle—he just wanted to get away. But he also wanted to save the children. He wanted Nofra to see the danger she was in, that she was leading them all into.

Nofra turned her head toward him, her smile softening her jawline and accentuating her wide cheekbones. His eyes traced her lips, remembering how they had felt on his. His breath quickened. What was he supposed to do with these—feelings? It would be better if he had none, if he could rid himself of the constant confusion, the constant motion in his mind, persuading him there was something he was missing, something that could help them if only he noted it. *Oh, God, help!* His internal cry came of its own accord. The need for help smarted. If only he could free himself.

# A PRINCESS DISPLACED

$\mathcal{E}$dmund stared at the young woman as the guards tugged her into the room. During the commotion, he saw Jacob motion to Paul and then slip out of the room with Father Iohannes. Before he could wonder what they were doing, his attention was pulled back to Princess Qasmuna as she stood before the High Queen.

The woman's face was a mask of embittered hatred. Some of the hair had come out of her crowned braid, and the black tuft hung about her face as she struggled against the hands that held her. Princess Qasmuna looked about the same age as the High King's mistress. That couldn't be comfortable. The woman shot a glare from the mistress over to her mother, a gleam in her eye, until the queen walked over and now smacked her face. Edmund winced; his face still stung from his earlier slap.

The princess covered her darkening cheek. "Mother?"

"I am ashamed you can call me *mother*. Why have you done this?"

For a moment, Edmund thought she would refute the queen, but she looked over at the mistress and gave a dull laugh. "You made me marry that man, which was fine and good, so long as he would one day be king and I could be queen. But now, I am to be married to the dolt and never have the throne? No, I would rather have—" But she stopped and turned to Edmund. "There are rumors about you, troubadour prince, how a sorceress empowered your wishes. I had a wish like that once, but Princess Rapunzel ruined all that for me. And now, am I to wait and watch as my brothers"—here she spluttered—"take the crown from me? I think not."

The High Queen grabbed her daughter's face and squished her cheeks between her thumb and fingers. "You? Think? No, foolish girl, you do not think. The crown was never yours to have, no matter whom you married. Your father determined that. No matter how you grasp or manipulate—"

"And who taught me to grasp and manipulate, dear Mother? I have watched you rule my father my whole life, but you couldn't keep him, could you? And now we will all pay for it. Now that he has not one, but two who could inherit the throne. What is he going to do, split the kingdoms between his sons? What will become of us women? Women beneath the feet of men? I'd rather let sorcery return and cast off this patriarchal god who would debase us."

The queen dropped her hand. "You would see your brothers dead?"

"I should say *no*, that the sisters of sorcery misled me, but I won't. You should know that I made this choice to align myself with powers greater than my own. My life will have a greater purpose. When Father dies, he should pass the kingdom to someone stronger, not weaker."

"You don't know what men your brothers will become."

"You call them *both* my brothers? You don't even acknowledge his other son."

"Well, I will do so now." The queen turned and gestured to the mistress, who took a few tentative steps forward. "True power and grace can acknowledge we live in a broken world. Your father"—her eyes flashed at the king—"was wrong to take a mistress, but he has, and now there is a child. Though this child will not share the throne with mine, I will find him, and he will grow to a position of esteem.

"But you, dear daughter, you and your children will be exiled. It matters not to us where you go, but you will no longer live here. And you will have to take your odious husband with you."

The king had held his peace this whole time, but at this last statement, he spoke up. "It is treason, what she has done. And treason requires death! We will put her to death before the nobility instead of holding the opening ceremony to the tournament. Then, We shall require that each kingdom hunt for our sons. We will grant favorable trades for years to come to the kingdom to bring Our sons unharmed to Us." He marched over to Edmund. "You'd best tell your wife that this is the way she can win your island for you. She must find the children, or you will lose Rona forever."

CAMILLA SMILED as she watched Nofra approach, but the smile slipped momentarily when she recognized Dietz.

"Why have you brought— Oh! You are bringing me the sacrifice my sister should have made."

The girl didn't return her smile, but dropped a blanket on the ground. She set about helping Dietz take the children out of the slings. Their docile quietness assured Camilla that Nofra had enchanted them. "I didn't bring Dietz for him to become a sacrifice. I brought him so that he could see that you have a plan that is best for all of us."

Where had this bold confidence come from? She looked over at Nofra, and then observed the young man. "You think I should let him live?"

"I do. I think he can become as great, perhaps greater, than your father ever was."

Camilla smacked her lips and sneered. "He certainly has the bloodline, but he's also spent significant time with the people of the light. You've been with them. Haven't you seen how they try to guide all those they meet into submission to their 'one true God'?"

Nofra nodded, now finished laying the children down. "I know you have grand plans, Camilla, but so do I. I think if we work together, the sacrifices can become something better. A constant source of power to fuel you, Dietz, and myself for years to come."

"You think to rule alongside me?"

"Better than what Amee had planned for me not so long ago."

Camilla allowed her tentacles to grow, creeping out from under the edge of her dress. One reached all the way to the sleeping children, hovering, almost touching them. "Six."

"What?"

"I have six sacrifices at hand, and you want me to alter my plans now to do what?"

"I want you to listen, to hear what I have to say. There is more here than you can imagine. I know it, but it's going to require your trust."

"I trust no one but myself."

Nofra nodded, and Camilla didn't dare look away. What was this young witch about?

# A MOTHER'S HOPE

Katterina found her way out of the marsh as dawn was breaking through the clouds, the flower gripped between her teeth. This, at least, she could do. No one paid attention to a calico cat darting in and out of the throngs of servants rising in their tent village just outside the castle's walls.

She slipped easily into the castle and had to decide. Up to her daughter to help immediately, but she wouldn't be able to speak to them. Or—Camilla said that she had stolen Amee's power and that she would soon die. How much time did the mother have left? Katterina knew she would have to take time to find a way to communicate with Rapunzel, but that was time Amee didn't have. Was there a chance that Camilla hadn't stopped up her voice from being able to reach the dying mother? What if she could talk to Amee one last time? Could she help her?

Down she went into the dungeon, the stench rising to meet her. There, on the damp stone floor, Amee lay prone. Her body no longer quivered from constant shifting. In fact, she didn't change at all. Katterina dropped the flower, hoping she was right to think she could speak with this woman. Hoping she was right in knowing that she *had* to speak to her now.

"Amee?" Her voice sounded normal, even though it came from a cat's mouth.

"Who are you? Did Camilla send you?" But though Amee's eyes were now the grey rheumy eyes of a woman, she seemed to hear Katterina clearly.

"It is I, Katterina, though no longer as woman."

Amee gave a hollow laugh and then a wet cough. "My sister, I suppose, is to thank for that."

"It is as you say."

"Why would you come to me instead of running to your people? I can do nothing for you, but surely they can help you." Amee's voice sounded rusty. Was she dying? Katterina carefully approached where the invisible barrier had kept the sorceress enclosed. She gently pawed the space in front of her. Nothing. Camilla must have destroyed the barrier. Convinced it was safe, Katterina padded over to Amee, careful to avoid the puddles that collected in the divots around the dungeon floor.

"I'm coming to you because a mother should always help another mother. We're not so different, you and I."

"You said that before, but I don't understand."

"I think that's because you don't want to understand."

Amee groaned, her eyes blinking to see better. "She changed you back into a cat. Aren't you angry? Shouldn't you be devising a way to destroy her?" Amee roused herself, lifting her head enough that the curtain of hair shifted, making her face visible.

Katterina pulled back, stunned. "Why do you look like that? What's wrong with you?"

"What do you mean?"

Amee's throat and face were webbed with lines and wrinkles, her mouth full of yellowed teeth, several of them missing. "How old are you?"

The old woman was trying to sit up straight, but there was a rounding in her upper back, causing her to hunch. She strained her turkey-like neck to look at Katterina. "I turned six-and-sixty years of age this past spring."

"You look it now."

Amee lifted age-spotted hands to her face and neck, a frown deepening the folds by her thin lips. "She has drained me of all my power. I have no magic left."

Katterina padded still closer.

"So, why do you think she's returned you to the form of a cat?"

Katterina stopped herself from nodding. Cats didn't nod—they had to use their voices. "She said I wouldn't be able to speak to my people unless I convinced them to leave so she can her have her way with the High King."

Amee shook her head. "She would have kept you from them no matter what. You are a threat to her."

"Me? What sort of threat could I possibly be?"

"She fears any marked by sorcery who bend their knee in repentance to the God you now serve." Amee's filmy eyes gave a slow blink. "How do you trust in this God?"

Katterina sat back on her hunches and peered at Amee. Her tail flipped forward and back as though measuring her moments of time. Time. It had taken time. "I—I was raised to trust him in my small village, but I didn't really know him. He was just some far-off, large thing that I should—I don't know, believe in. He seemed so far away from my insignificant life. But I think—I know— if I had only understood his love for me, his purpose for my life, I could have been the mother God created me to be."

"His purpose for your life?"

Katterina tilted her head, and Amee seemed unable to look away from her cat-eyes. "Amee, I don't understand how it works. But he has a plan for each of us. Even when we deviate from what is best, his purpose is still that none of us should perish, but come back to him and bring him glory. I've made a mess of my life, but he has forgiven me, somehow made me his so that I can tell others how good he is."

"But why should it matter? Why come to me with this news instead of going to your own people?"

Katterina shook her head. "I almost did, but I had to come to you first. I'm trusting there's enough time for them later. But you—you are running out of time. Just as I once was. You must make a choice. You might die now, I don't know. But whether or not you do, you must decide if you want to continue in this life of disdaining a God who loves you, who made you, who wants to set you free—or if you want to accept him. I fear for you—this is your last chance to make that choice."

"But all the horrible things I have done. All the people I have led astray—!"

"I'm not saying there won't be consequences here while we are living this life, but he wants to free you of the consequences eternally so that you might go to live with him forever."

Amee shook her head and let her head droop again, tears dripping from her face to the ground. "I don't deserve—"

"None of us do. That's the point."

"If I do this, if I repent, will Dietz see me differently? Will he forgive me and love me?"

"I don't know. But I know that it can't be for his sake that you do this. If it is, it's not really repentance, is it?"

Amee shook her head again. "I want this forgiveness. I want to be different. But you're right, there is little left in me."

"Then give that little to God. He will take it and make it enough."

JACOB WORRIED that descending would be harder on Father Iohannes than ascending, but the man did not complain. As they traveled down the winding steps into the dungeon to check on the sorceress, Jacob looked back to see how he was faring. But the look on Father Iohannes's face stunned him. What had the man heard? The Father motioned for Jacob to be quiet for a moment, but all Jacob could hear was the sound of Amee's ragged voice. Who was she talking to? He couldn't hear.

Father Iohannes nodded for them to continue their descent, and Jacob saw on the ground the shriveled form of the aged sorceress. She was barely sitting up, breathing out a prayer, while a cat licked her palm gently.

"God in heaven, forgive my sins. Show me how to live better for you. I accept what your son, Jesu the Christ, died in my place. How he died for me and resurrected on the third day to make pardon for all the heinous sins I've committed. Oh, God—" Her voice broke and she panted before continuing, "I know I haven't much strength left, that I'm about to die and don't deserve your love or your pardon. But please cleanse me, make me new. And, please, do so for my son as well. I don't know what happened, where Nofra took him. But protect him from my sister and the evil one. Bring him to you, safely." She lay down, straining to breathe, to form the words. The cat came to her side as the sorceress reached for her. "Will it be enough?"

Father Iohannes startled when the cat made a sound.

The cat jerked her head toward them and yowled, then snatched something off the floor. She darted up the stairs and scratched until a guard opened the door.

"Amee?" Jacob asked, hoping he had time to ask her. "Have you just given your life to our Savior?"

Her head raised slightly, but she had to put it back down on the filthy ground. "I have. Do you think it's too late?"

Father Iohannes took a step toward the former sorceress. "With God, all things are possible."

"My sister—my sister will come to fight you."

"We know."

"But she will use the lifeblood of the children she's stolen. She'll be using everyone she has beneath her power."

"God is greater than she," Jacob stated calmly, now kneeling beside her.

"I—I finally know that. Oh, the time I wasted hating and fearing him, when he could have freed me from my sin so long ago. My son—will you tell my son that he can walk in freedom, too?"

Jacob took her hand. "I will. We thought he would be here. Where—?"

"Nofra—she took him when she took the children." She gasped for air. "They are going—going to Camilla." She took another breath. "When Camilla comes, you must

—" But her breath caught and her eyes emptied of light. Her last breath gone, her hand went limp as her eyes rolled back.

Jacob laid her hand on her chest and stood up. "If Dietz disappeared with Nofra and the children, then Camilla will come in power soon."

Father Iohannes nodded.

"Should we tell the High King about this, too?"

But Father Iohannes shook his head, surprising Jacob with a laugh. "I'm sorry, brother, I know it is no time to laugh, but if we rely on the High King at all, it will all fall apart. Don't you think?"

"You're right, we need to gather our forces before Camilla strikes again."

# THE TALE OF TWO MOTHERS

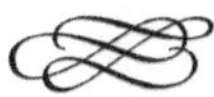

Katterina was a streak of fur as she ran out past the guards.

"What are you doing?" one called after her, running. The chase was on. She darted around the castle, scuttling under tables, past servants, and around other guards. Why were they even paying attention? What had changed to cause them to be alert? Now, panting, she at last made her way up to Rapunzel's door. She dropped the flower down and scratched the door, hoping against hope that someone would hear on the other side. Just as the door opened, a guard came around the corner, his bloodshot eyes wide. He spotted her and went to grab her, but Amis snatched her up first. "Oh, there's my kitty!"

The guard stopped abruptly, his arms out in front of him. He dropped them to his side and stood up. "She's yours?"

"She is, isn't she lovely?"

A humming purr thrummed through Katterina's throat as Amis rubbed her ears. *Oh, that feels good!*

The guard shook his head, looking utterly confused.

"We—we were told to watch out. Just got the word someone took the king's sons. We were to keep an eye out for anything strange."

"Are you calling my kitty strange?" Amis looked away from the guards and made eye contact with her. Was it possible he recognized her even in this state? Surely God had made him a gifted fool!

"She was running out of the dungeon. Who knows what she was doing down there with that thing!"

"Maybe one of you should have been down there to watch that *thing* and, I don't know, guard it?" Gwynndolen stood in the doorway beside Amis, a hand on her hip.

"I'd say it's strange how the guards around here don't seem to guard most anything," Amis told Gwynndolen, who nodded along. "Almost bewitched, I would say." The jester grinned and bounced on his toes, making the little bells on the tips of his jester's cap tinkle. How funny he had chosen to wear it despite the fact he wasn't supposed to be performing, though this certainly *looked* like a performance. "Wouldn't want the High King to hear that, now, would you?"

"No! I mean, of course not!" But the guard trembled. "Do you know which way I should go?"

"I'd say back to the dungeon and make sure the monster does nothing wrong before the tournament," Gwynndolen advised.

Amis shrugged and picked up the flower. "Were you bringing this to me, pet? Better than a dead mouse."

The guard gave them one more look and then stumbled away. Amis shut the door and laughed, but then stopped short at the sight of Gwynndolen staring at him, her arms crossed in front of her chest. "What are you holding?"

"Not what, whom," Amis corrected.

Something stirred behind the net of curtains around the bed. Rapunzel peeked out, her face still as pale as when Katterina had left. "Mother?" She stood, swaying, and Gwynndolen hurried over to offer her arm.

Katterina opened her mouth, but all that came out was a pitiful mew.

"Mother, is that you?"

She opened her mouth again, a moaning whine coming out.

Rapunzel stared up at Amis. "Why can't she speak? Is it just a cat that looks like Mother?"

Amis shook his head and set her down. "No, I think we can safely say this is Katterina."

Gwynndolen kept looking from one to another. "I don't understand—what's going on?"

Rapunzel held up a hand. "I don't really have time to explain, but my mother once lived as a feline. For most of my life, in fact."

"You believe this cat is your mother?" Gwynndolen picked Katterina up and held her close to Rapunzel.

"She looks just like her," Rapunzel traced the swirls of black, tan, and white on Katterina's fur. "Who would do this to you?"

Katterina's caterwauling cry nearly made Gwynndolen drop her. Rapunzel sat back on the side of the bed, and Gwynndolen put Katterina in her lap.

"Only a witch or sorceress could do this."

Amis sniffed the orchid-like plant. "Why do you think she brought us a flower?"

"She said she would return with something to help."

Rapunzel shook her head. "Mother, what is the flower for?"

Katterina stared into her daughter's face. *For you—you need to eat a small bite of the petal.* Katterina struggled to speak. She had been right. She could talk to Amee, but Camilla had stopped up her voice with her own daughter.

"Mother?" Rapunzel placed her pale hand on Katterina's head, scratching between the ears. "You're the only one who knows how to use it. What are we supposed to do?" Katterina mewled. At least God could hear her cries, and she prayed as she had never prayed before.

But when she opened her eyes, Rapunzel simply put Katterina down. "There's nothing we can do. It doesn't matter anyway, now that I don't have Helena."

# THE PLAN

$\mathcal{N}$ofra stepped forward again, advancing as though to teach a recalcitrant student. "I said, listen to me!" she snapped. "The mark of sorcery is on Dietz, myself, Helena, and little Eng. But these other two only make good pawns to get the High King and Queen to do as we wish, which is why I took them. If you ask a ransom for them, then the High King will serve you. He is desperate to do as you will. Just as his daughter would."

"And I take the lives of the rest of you to fill me?" Camilla licked her lips.

"Why should you need to kill us? For years, you siphoned the fuel from Prince Edmund's wishes. You need only be near us, and we can provide you with the strength you require for years. Barter with the king, have him buy back his sons and give you his kingdom in the Eastern Ports and all throughout the Dark Wood. Let him keep his Winter Castle and the Northlands. We don't need them! We will live happily here without fear of the church burning us for our sorcery. We can have everything we want."

"That's not everything that I want! It shouldn't be everything you want. I *want* the Winter Castle, too. I want the Northlands. I want the island of Rona and anything that lays beyond it. I want the Land of Midnight and to extinguish the light of the 'one true god' that has tried to spread his power over all the known world.

"My father exiled me in the western part of the Illyan Sea for half a century. I will not have someone dictate borders to me again. And, yes, I siphoned strength off Edmund's wishes, but I need more than that, now that I don't have my sisters. You show your own ignorance about our craft when you think that leaving these children alive will be enough for all of us to live and rule.

"I thought you could rule beside me, little daughter, but your plan rejects what I hold most dear: power. You want me to leave those to rule with strength to return to power, to one day cast us off. We must destroy them, and destroy them utterly, so that they can never rise like a phoenix from their ashes. It's time for them to pay for all they have put us and our kind through. I will never relent. I will have it all."

Nofra moved back toward Dietz, stepping on his foot. He winced in pain, but steadied her with his hand. "You would kill these children?" she asked.

"All of them. Helena and Eng should have died last winter, and these royal brats could make great bargaining pawns, but they will die whether or not the king and queen do as I say. Don't you understand me yet? I don't compromise. I receive all I desire or I wait to strike later so that I can receive it then."

"How much later?"

"However long it takes. I have lost all of my family in search of this power. Do not think this problem between us will keep me from finding what I desire."

Before Nofra could reply, Camilla's tentacles snatched at her.

~

JACOB SHOWED Father Iohannes to Prince Paul's bedchambers, and they found the princess looking wan, lying still with her eyes shut tight. Next to her on the bed was the cat he had seen earlier with Amee. She hopped off the bed and came over to Jacob as though she knew him, leaning her head against his calves as she circled him, purring. Her tail twined around him and he reached down, picking her up gently.

"I didn't know you had a cat," Father Iohannes said.

"I don't."

Gwynndolen turned from the window and shook her head. But it was Amis who enlightened them. "It's Katterina, Your Holiness."

"What?"

"Camilla must have transformed her into a cat. She brought this flower in her mouth"—he whisked a drooping plant out of his sleeve—"but now she can't speak to tell us what to do with it."

Rapunzel moaned from the bed.

Jacob looked into the cat's small face, noticing how her emerald eyes had a very sad, un-catlike expression in them. "Katterina, is that you?" He knew she had once lived this way, but to see it with his own eyes! The cat nodded, a pitiful sound coming from her throat. He placed a hand gently on her head, closing his eyes tight. He prayed, "Lord Jesu, please free Katterina from the spell that transformed her once again into a cat. We trust you have greater plans than this for her."

He opened his eyes. Nothing happened. Stillness sat awkwardly among the group as they waited.

Jacob opened his mouth to pray again, but Father Iohannes shook his head.

"Perhaps God will not hear you because of your feelings for the Lady Katterina."

Jacob shook his head, but looked hard into the eyes of the creature he held. "Could that be it?" he asked quietly. The cat purred as he stroked her fur. He resolved within himself what he must do. "Lord, if I have somehow wronged you, I freely confess that I never meant to. I made the vows I took to be a celibate monk in the wake of misunderstanding how your love and grace are freedom. You paid the price for the sins of my mother. I never could. I have denied myself love to serve you, but you never required that, and I know the price paid in the woman's family I should have loved as a wife.

"But in you, there is hope and forgiveness. A chance to begin anew. If you would have me stay celibate my entire life, I gladly will do so and deny myself of my feelings for Lady Katterina. But Lord, please free her. Do not punish her because a foolish young man didn't understand your love. Please show us the way to serve you even with the mess we make of our lives."

Father Iohannes stepped over and placed a hand on Jacob's back, adding his voice to Jacob's fervent petition. "Lord God, we know you to be bigger and greater than the forces of darkness. Please return this woman to her proper form. We ask this by the blood of Jesu the Christ who conquered the darkness and returned to life to set us— even this woman—free."

The cat hacked and shook in Jacob's hands, her body

suddenly expanding in all directions at once. Jacob, still holding her, fell on his back, with Lady Katterina staring into his face. Amis whipped his cloak off his shoulders and covered her body. The men looked away as she stood up and covered herself.

Katterina seemed to be laughing at her nakedness as she bent over Rapunzel's trunk and found something more appropriate. Jacob fisted his hands, missing the feel of her. Did her restoration mean that God wanted him to remain celibate, or that now she was his to claim? He would have to deal with the thought soon, but not yet. "The flower," he said, looking into her emerald eyes as she emerged, fully dressed, from behind the screen.

"The flower? Oh, yes." She took the plant from Amis and walked over to the table. She began plucking the bright-orange-and-blue petals, explaining in a rush, "The plant I brought is very special. It helps redeem those affected by sorcery. Those who have been ill-used should take one bite of a petal. With a great deal of water, mind you. But it will cleanse the cursed victim of the effects of the spell."

Each of them who had found a sachet took a small bite and drank an abundance of water. They helped Rapunzel sit up in bed and she consumed the remedy but laid back down. Jacob took a calming breath and sat down at the table, fingering the petals that Katterina set aside for Paul and Edmund. What was taking them so long? He noticed how drowsy they all seemed as the petals worked on them and he prayed that God would move a bit quicker. He grimaced at his impatience. It felt foreign to him.

A sound startled him and he turned to look at the princess. Rapunzel was no longer lying down, but sitting up, her hair a frazzled mess about her head. But though her eyes were open, she seemed to be looking beyond the room.

# THE WAR OF SORCERY

As though she was a bird, Rapunzel could see Camilla's forces moving—she was falling, or, no! She was flying! Swooping low, close to the ships, hearing snatches of conversation. Bitter women, unhappy with their lot.

The pirate ships came in to blockade the harbor, but other ships sailing the High King's purple flags came in from behind. But her sight did not rest on the skirmish in the waters, instead turning to the rising horde that was running headlong from the wet swamps at the castle, surrounding the vast grounds of the High King's domain. She flew inland, and in time she was among the trees, flying near buzzing bugs, overhearing shouting between women's voices. And a child cried. It was her Helena, wailing, calling for—for her?

"You don't understand how this works, do you?" Camilla was saying as she reached her pale, white arms high above her, black-and-purple-streaked tentacles shooting out from her, lit up like lightning. The monstrous woman shrieked, and a storm raged in the sky, ominous grey clouds lighting up as bolts flashed through them. Thunder roared and boomed. The swamp's trees swayed, the wind pulling out the leaves and strings of moss. "These children will be my salvation. They will buy me all that I long for. Give her to me." And she reached for Helena.

Rapunzel screamed, and her cry startled her out of the trance. The waking dream shattered into pieces she could not put back together, shards she could only cut herself on. "Camilla now has them all. She's going to kill Helena! Right now!" She looked outside, but the sky was a cerulean blue, the sun now golden as it warmed the morning. But she had just seen the dark thunderheads—hadn't she?— that were rolling over the land. Oh! It hadn't happened yet. Could there still be time to save Helena, still time to save the kingdoms? "Jacob, please, get to the swamps, before she sacrifices the babes for her power! Oh, where is Paul?"

Father Iohannes leaned heavily on his staff. All the climbing throughout the night seemed to have done him in. He looked across at Jacob. "Find the prince and lead the warriors. I will gather those who cannot wield a weapon and we will prepare to hold the castle, should it come to that."

PAUL AND EDMUND pulled open the door just as Jacob approached it. They stared at each other for half a moment, but then voices erupted, exclamations tearing through the air.

"The High King's sons were ordered abducted by the Princess Qasmuna. She's to be executed!"

"Camilla has the babes, she's about to kill them!"

"Gwynndolen, you must go to the swamps and find the king's sons or we will lose Rona!"

The voices were overwhelming until Amis whistled, a high, shrill sound that stopped them short. "I think we all have places to go, things to do. Brother Jacob, you were saying?"

"Prince Paul, Camilla has the children, Rapunzel has seen it. Come, we can lead the warriors into the swamps to fight the enemy."

Paul looked over at Rapunzel, and she gave him a nod. "Go! Find our daughter. I'll be safe here with Mother."

Gwynndolen finished crossing the room and reached for Edmund's free hand. "Edmund, did you say that I must rescue the king's sons?"

He nodded. "If we are to save Rona."

"I suppose that has more import than fighting in a tournament." She arched a brow.

"Be careful, my love." He touched her face.

Paul could see how difficult it was for the prince to remain behind. "Prince Edmund, Brother Jacob and I will do our best to watch out for her."

"I know you will."

"Prince Edmund—" Father Iohannes strode toward the crippled man. "As I was saying, I will go ready the forces so that we can make our stand here. You will help us?"

Edmund straightened. "Yes, of course."

Amis clapped his hands. "And what shall I do? Where shall I go?"

"Amis, you must tell the servants to be ready. They need to arm themselves with prayer and gather inside the castle walls."

Paul sent one last look toward Rapunzel, who gave him a hopeful look, and he shut the door.

DIETZ STARED at Nofra and then down at the children, still lying as though asleep. How was Nofra any different from Camilla, from Amee? Her thoughts were of power, of using people, even these little ones, to gain power. Perhaps she didn't want as much, but it still would be at the cost of others. The buzzing that had begun in his head when Nofra had spoken to him in the dungeon came to a sudden stop. The little ones on the ground squirmed as though they were waking, and he prayed silently to the God Dorothea and Paul had tried to teach him to trust. *If you are truly the God of light, show me what I must do. These children are yours, and I long to be yours, completely. No more half-measures, Lord. Be God over all of me and show me the way to save these little ones.*

Camilla was raising her long arms and calling forth the powers of darkness. The sky overhead grew dark and stormy, the clouds swirling together. Birds cawed and dove away from the driving wind and the stinging rain that came down in sheets from the tempestuous sky. "Yes, yes!" Camilla cried, and as she shot out her tentacles, the children lifted from the ground, the cloak they had lain on flying away on the wind. The children were now levitating, floating in a circle, much like the clouds swirling high in the sky above. Dietz felt himself lifting off the ground and spinning with them, but he called out aloud, this time lifting his voice in song. It was the song that Paul had taught him to sing, the words drowning out the fear that tried to cut him off from hope.

. . .

THOUGH WE WALK in the flesh,
    We do not war in the flesh;
    Though we walk in the flesh,
    We trust in the Lord's armor.


THOUGH WE WALK in the flesh,
    Our weapons are not carnal;
    Though we walk in the flesh,
    We pull down strongholds now.


CAMILLA ROARED, her white face now blotchy with rage. "Shut your mouth!" Spittle flew out from her maw. She arched and lunged toward him, but she hit something invisible and fell backward. Dietz kept on singing, raising his voice over the sounds of the lashing winds and the crying babes.


THOUGH WE WALK in the flesh,
    We cast down errant thinking;
    Though we walk in the flesh,
    We exalt the Lord alone,


THOUGH WE WALK in the flesh,
    We take captive every thought;
    Though we walk in the flesh,
    Every thought bows low to Christ.

# DAWN BREAKS

*J*acob tore across the lowered drawbridge as Paul, Gwynndolen, and the warriors rushed with him. Weapons in hand, they recited the scripture of the armor. "God protect us now!" They screamed, their voices raised in a plea. Even as his brothers and sisters continued reciting Scripture, he was praying a new prayer.

"Protect the innocent, Lord! Recall to our minds your great goodness. Help us cling to you now. Help us to never let go, never forget, never lose sight of who you are or what you are about. Forgive us our sins as we forgive others. Even this enemy, Lord—if she and her people repent, soften our hearts that we may forgive as well." The hours of reciting scripture and spinning and thrusting his staff had reminded his muscles of what to do. How to run and pray. How to fight again.

Before him, he saw people rushing out of the swamps. "God wants to free you!" he boomed before he was on top of them. "Bow your knee to him. Tell us where we can find Camilla and the babes!"

To his shock, several took a knee. "Have mercy on us. Free us from Camilla!" But those who came behind them ran forward with weapons raised, some turning on those who bent low. Jacob led the onslaught, first pulling off those who were beating the repenters. The cries of the warriors were deafening as sloshing through the swamps slowed their progress. The winds rose around them and crashing thunder shook even the most devout. But one woman stood up from where she knelt and began running back into the marsh. "Follow me!" she yelled, racing further into the swamps.

Seeing an opening between those he was fighting, Jacob dashed through the trees, hoping she was leading him to the children. At last, he came to a clearing. Camilla stood in the center of a strange circle with the children, Dietz, and a young maid spinning around her. Gwynndolen came from behind Jacob, Paul right behind her, and they stopped, staring.

Dietz was singing, crying out to God in a song that Jacob had taught Paul long ago. Paul joined him, and suddenly Gwynndolen's voice rose as she ran directly at Camilla. But the sorceress encircled her with a tentacle. Paul rushed at the sorceress, hacking off the tentacle before Camilla caught sight of him. Immediately, purple-black blood pumped from the wound. Before he could strike again, a burly warrior came at him, but Jacob met the warrior with a raised staff, and as their weapons clashed, a sharp pain radiated up Jacob's shoulder. No matter. He pushed back against the warrior.

On the periphery of his vision, the warrior monk kept track of the others even as he knocked the oaf he was fighting on the head. Camilla was roaring in anger, and those levitating plummeted to the ground, but Dietz grabbed two of the little ones to his chest. Gusts of wind tore leaves off trees, and feathers, too, were plucked out of the flying birds, piercing the fighters with them as though the gales had made them into arrows. Jacob had to shut his eyes against the wind and the sleeting rain that came. "Oh, God, save us! Save us!" he heard the young man cry.

GWYNNDOLEN HAD BARELY UNWRAPPED the tentacle from around her when warriors rushed into the clearing, the noise of their cries deafening. She raised her sword just in time as a woman came at her. Gwynndolen blinked away the rain, trying to see who she was fighting. The woman was broad in the shoulders, holding a sword in one hand and a shield in the other. Her dark skin was a contrast to the bright whites of her berserker eyes. She leered and screamed as she shoved Gwynndolen down with her shield, but Gwynndolen rolled to the side and jumped up.

The sharp sword slashed through the air, and Gwynndolen ducked, slipping in the muck. She felt something sucking at her feet, but she pulled up quickly and tried to avoid the boggy spot. She dodged again as the woman came at her. Paul had said she must press her advantage, and so she would, but she couldn't find one. The woman's long sword kept Gwynndolen's short one out of range, but at last she feinted to the side and then stepped in and stuck it in between the shield and the woman's chest. Her opponent screamed, falling over, ripping Gwynndolen's sword out of her hand. Slipping in the mud again, she lunged forward and pulled at her sword, yanking it out of the woman. Bile stung the back of her throat, but she jumped to her feet and reeled around, barely ready in time to face another assailant. She lurched forward as a man lifted his mace and swung it around.

Gwynndolen skidded a bit again when she ducked, but she stayed on her feet this time. She held tight with both hands on her sword as she tangled the mace, twisting it out of the warrior's hands. Without a weapon, he crashed into her, driving all air from her lungs as she hit the ground and lost her grip on her weapon. She elbowed him in the face and tried to scramble back toward her sword, but he held her down. Large hands encircled her throat.

Gwynndolen felt panic rise, her fear meeting her. She would lose, they would all lose, and the children would die. *Edmund will be lost.* But a thought sliced through her mind just as her vision dimmed from lack of air. Rapunzel had said they must ask for help when they needed it. But how could she? And who could help her now? It was too late, wasn't it? Warrior monks and women now crowded the clearing. But the sheer number of Amee's covens overwhelmed them. Gwynndolen couldn't ask her comrades— but she remembered in the marsh, when she had held Edmund's hand and prayed for help from the God of heaven. Hadn't he provided for her then? And the song that Paul had taught them. It was about relying on the Lord, trusting him to use his might through her. Stars blinked in her eyes as she blacked out. *God of heaven, Lord of life, help! I give you this battle. I give you this war. Use me, don't use me, do as you will. All the praise belongs to you.*

All at once, the weight of the warrior fell on her, and his hands went limp around her neck. She gasped, but then his heavy body rolled off and a powerful hand pulled her up. She coughed, dizzy. Jacob smiled at her before twisting away to ward off more of the enemy. Back-to-back they fought, his staff beating back the enemy, her sword piercing those who meant them ill. She kept looking to the side. They needed to get to Camilla, before she could disappear with Helena and Eng.

CAMILLA'S TENTACLES reached out to grasp Nofra and the remaining children floating about. Losing blood from her severed tentacle had left her dizzy and unable to flee. The water—if she could just take their power and make it to the water! Before she could send an electric pulse through her tentacles to drain those she was holding, the redheaded assailant came at her again, now hacking off the tentacle that held the little boy. Fine! She would make do with Nofra and the little girl. But the current wavered and then shorted out. Her loss of blood must have incapacitated her from gleaning their life source. Her tentacles trembled, losing their hold. Nofra stumbled, grabbed the little girl, and ran. But as Camilla reached out to grab them again, Nofra's eyes widened, and she shrieked, her feet stuck fast. She was sinking.

"Give me the child!" Camilla commanded, reaching for her.

The redhead was now holding the little boy, having unwrapped him from the severed tentacle. The warrior monk stepped forward carefully and reached out his staff. Nofra looked as though she would grasp it, but then looked at Camilla. "You've lost. We could have won together, but you've lost it for us all." The end was sudden and complete, the ground no longer sucking slowly, but in one sickening slurp, the bodies of Nofra and Helena disappeared into the bog.

"No!" Camilla wailed. With only two tentacles left as

she felt herself bleeding out, she reached down into the earth, searching for any source of power. She could not harness energy from those nearby. Their god was protecting them! With her last bit of strength, she electrified herself and touched the wet ground, causing all who were still standing to fall over, spasming. It gave her mere moments, but it was enough. If she could just reach the sea again—She finished transforming into a bleeding leviathan and found her way to the swamp, sinking as deep as she could go. She would need to find her way back to deeper waters, but for now, she would have to heal.

# LOSS AND HOPE

Paul was the first to wake, the first to realize Camilla had fled. How much time had passed since the lightning from her body had rattled their bodies? He pushed back at the weakness and stood on the edge of the bog where Helena had disappeared. Turning, he looked at the bodies of the enemy, dead and dying on the ground. A few of his comrades had given their lives, while others were only injured. The latter slowly woke, shaking in the battle's aftermath.

The air was strangely silent but for the drips of water from the moss hanging from the branches overhead. When had the rain stopped? He could see the skies were clearing, but how could there be a blue sky when Helena had died?

Hours passed as he helped his comrades, as they gathered the children, as they made their way back to the castle, eventually hearing what had happened there and on the water. Impressions tried to penetrate his dull mind. Slowly, he started counting. One, Helena was dead. Two, Camilla had fled. Three, the covens were destroyed. Four, some had repented. Five, the pirates were vanquished.

The High King was congratulating them as he welcomed both sons back into his arms. There would be a coronation now that the kingdoms were safe, and he would bestow great honor on Paul, Gwynndolen, and Jacob. But Paul wanted to hear no more. The counting continued in his head. Six, he had to tell Rapunzel. Seven, they would return home without their daughter.

❧

RAPUNZEL FELT nothing as she dressed and allowed the new maidservant to fix her hair. She had no appetite. No tears to cry. Nothing for days. She went through the motions of eating, of sleeping, of trying to smile as the High King and Queen thanked her and her friends.

But something sparked when her ladies-in-waiting came to attend her. At first she stood listening dully as Ladies Florese and Bazzu instructed her once more on how to conduct herself at the coronation, but she suddenly threw up her hands. "Ladies, if you are still uncertain whether or not I know how to conduct myself as a queen, then I ask you to give up now. I have given everything, even lost my daughter, in order to protect the kingdoms. If that is not enough, then I don't know what is. Now, if you can respect who I am, you may remain to advise me when I ask for help. Otherwise, I release you from your duty and you can find another to serve."

The eyes of Lady Florese ignited with something strange. "Your Highness, I think you are prepared to be a queen."

Rapunzel's mouth almost dropped open at the change in the woman. But she caught herself. A queen didn't gape. "Thank you."

The new maidservant finished straightening the royal blue cape around Rapunzel's shoulders and secured it with a sapphire broach encrusted with diamonds.

Lady Bazzu gave a deep bow. "I believe I will address you as 'Your Majesty' from now on. We will wait on you following the coronation." Both ladies left the chambers, and Rapunzel dismissed the new maidservant. The young girl had a name, but Rapunzel couldn't recall it. She felt as though she were in a cold, echoing cave, and everything felt distant, hard. Today should be a happy day, the day she and her friends would receive crowns and the kingdom's honor. But though she was happy they could save the kingdoms and several children, an ache threatened to bloom in her chest. She gasped and placed a hand over her heart. She couldn't breathe.

"Come in," she could barely sputter at the sound of the knocking on the door. Her mother came inside and, without a word, wrapped her arms around her.

"I know it hurts."

The sobs that she had held off tore through her. "Will it ever stop hurting?" she asked, minutes, or maybe hours, later.

"No, but one day it won't hurt as badly. Sometimes it will ache and you won't know how to think, how to walk, but there will be times when it will feel far away. I know that doesn't help now."

Rapunzel hiccupped as the tears rolled down her hot cheeks. "How will I ever go on?"

Katterina shook her head. "I don't know, but we'll do it together." She wiped the tears away and placed a cool cloth on Rapunzel's eyes for a few minutes. Taking it away, she smiled sadly. "Come, let's go get you your crown."

∼

KATTERINA SAW Rapunzel and Paul leave the celebration hours later and sighed. They would leave in the morning to begin their way back home. Looking around the Great Hall, she could not join in the merriment as the nobles partook of wine and music. She knew it was the same for all their company. Even Amis had declined to perform any longer. Though personally asked by the High King to join his court, the fool had shaken his head and instead recommended his little friend Mea.

Katterina smiled. She was glad the jester would come home with them. They would need his levity in the days to come. Mourning made laughter necessary.

"A word, my lady?" She startled at Jacob's voice and gave him a quick nod. He led her through the castle, to the outdoors, where a weeping willow grew. At last he stopped and turned around, his face sad. *Oh no, Lord,* she thought, *I can bear losing no one else.*

"My lady, you have done me the honor of befriending me, and I thought it best to tell you myself that Father Iohannes has asked me to stay. His health is failing and he would like me to take a position here on the council, possibly replace him when he goes to be with the Lord."

Katterina dropped her eyes. "I didn't know it worked like that. Doesn't the Father usually select someone who has been on the counsel for—for longer than that?"

"Yes, that is usually the way of it, but I think he sees something in me, and he hopes to dissuade me."

She looked up. Why was he looking at her like that? "Dissuade you?"

"From relinquishing my position as a monk."

"But why should you do that?"

"Because I can no longer honor the vow I made. Instead, I would ask to become your husband, if you will have me."

"If I will— But how you can you stop being who God called you to be? Just to be with me?"

Jacob shook his head. "I will never stop being who God called me to be, but now I will be his differently. I will continue to serve the kingdom and God, but I will also love and serve you. If . . ."

"If I say yes?"

He nodded, a slight pucker between his brows.

"I say yes."

He leaned toward her, but stalled for a moment, as though not sure what to do. With a sly smile, she reached up and pulled his head down to meet his lips with her own. And with that kiss, she knew he was hers.

# EPILOGUE

The bog rippled, and a gas bubble emerged, popped.

The bodies of the slain had been carefully removed, the soldiers avoiding the treacherous bog. The ground was no longer a muddy green color, but rusted with the blood of the dead. It would not be long this way, though, for the summer's rains were coming back to wash it away. As the sky crackled with lightning and the air hummed with thunder, the rain came in sheets once more, beating the soft ground.

Beneath the rain, further into the swamps and beyond the blood, the ground was giving signs of movement. A dark man silently moved over the edge of the bog and plunged a long stick into the ground. He dragged the stick through the muck, chanting words unheard above the sound of thunder. A rippling began as something from below surfaced. A bubble coated in the bog's refuse. It rose, climbing higher and settling over more solid terrain before dissolving, leaving its filth on the two beings it had safeguarded.

Nofra coughed awake, the child in her arms startling at the movement. Mauro fell to his knees beside her, and she opened her eyes, blinking at him.

"Camilla is gone."

"Dead?" she managed to ask, unable to sit up.

"No, but back into the waters, at least."

Nofra shook her head. "Mauro," she croaked, "You must hide the child from Camilla. She must never find her. Take her inland, somewhere Camilla can't reach. To the Dark Wood—perhaps there are still followers of the coven there."

"If not, I will find someone I can trust." He took the little girl in his arms, but she didn't make a sound. Her eyes were round, somber, too old for her little face. He looked back over at Nofra. "But what of you?"

Nofra could barely shake her head. "I have nothing left. I gave it all to her."

He nodded again, a tear falling as he watched the sight leave her round eyes. He reached over and shut her eyelids.

What a waste it all was—their many years of secret planning, their fight for power, the dream of returning to a country that no longer wanted them. The Land of Midnight was a myth. They should never have sought it. The sorcery Amee had brought them had also left them powerless and hungry.

The old man stared into the face of the little girl, who simply stared back. Camilla had silenced the girl. He wished the little one would whimper or cry, but he knew she couldn't anymore. Mauro knew he was too old to see this through, to make the journey to the Dark Wood. His mind searched through the names of the dead. Was there anyone who had not fought? Who had not surrendered?

He recalled a man who had refused to fight. He had just taken a new wife with a little boy not much older than this little one. They were not loyal to Camilla, had wanted to leave when she came. But they weren't like the traitors who turned to another god entirely.

Mauro heaved a sigh and stood up, gathering the little girl to his chest, tucking her beneath his cloak as the rain-fall became heavier again. He would place the man under an oath to do this one last thing. Camilla must not revive and find power again.

If you enjoyed *Among the Kingdoms*, please take a moment and leave a review on the retailer where you purchased it and over on Goodreads and Bookbub. Thank you for helping other wonderful readers like you find this series!

~

The Journey series is coming to its epic conclusion soon in *Upon the Throne*.
You can pre-order your copy NOW on Amazon:
www.amazon.com/dp/B09NP551YT
Or read on to discover more.

## Upon the Throne

(concluding soon!)

**She's been living nameless, silent, and unwanted, but Rapunzel has never given up hope of finding her.**

In the Dark Wood a maid has grown up believing she is nothing and no one. The only hope that keeps her alive is the song of the Savior her true mother sang to her long ago. But the maid has no voice and no one can hear her.

Until one day, she discovers an obnoxious prince's shadow that can hear her thoughts.

Before the maid realizes what it will cost her, she makes a promise to help the prince find his body. But his large, intimidating brother is suspicious of her. And his mother, who just happens to be the High Queen, accuses her of sorcery.

It's enough to make a girl wish she was invisible as well as mute.

But returning to her life of obscurity is impossible. She needs to outrun the queen and find the prince's body before it is too late. Only by working with the mouthy prince and his brother will she discover her true name.

And there they will find the remnants of a war fought long ago. Remnants that have entangled their lives and must be severed, for once and for all.

The thrilling conclusion to Rapunzel's Journey weaves fairy tales and faith together in a lyrical retelling you won't forget.

~

**DISCOVER how it all began with this free novella and be the first to hear when *Upon the Throne* is available:**

**ONE CURSE.**
**TWO SECRETS.**
**BETRAYAL IN THE GARDEN WILL LEAD TO RAPUNZEL'S TOWER.**

Get your free book here:
https://dl.bookfunnel.com/wftepfzx96

~

# GLOSSARY

**Chemise** — a slip-like gown that was worn as the first layer of dress for women in Rapunzel's world. It would be naturally colored, typically an off-white color. Often, this was worn as a nightgown at night when the other layers of dress would be removed.

**Cotehardie** — a fitted gown worn over the chemise with sleeves cut to various lengths according to station in Rapunzel's world. The higher the station, the more intricate the sleeves, sometimes tight at the elbows and bell-shaped at the wrist or short at the elbows with a streaming tail called a tippet. The bottom of the cotehardie might also be lined with fur to show off the station of a woman.

**Coven** — in Rapunzel's world, this is a grouping of warlocks and witches that gather in secret to practice the dark arts to return their world back to an acceptance of sorcery.

**Hosen** — leggings worn to protect the legs.

**Sorceress/Sorcerer** — a female or male who has achieved a master status in the practice of the dark arts of magic.

**Surcoat** — the outermost layer of dress a woman would wear in Rapunzel's world, over which she would wear a cloak to go outdoors in cool weather. The gown was side-less and would complement the cotehardie's coloring, often cut a bit short if the cotehardie beneath had a fur-lined hem. The surcoat was frequently embellished with embroidery.

**Tournament** — a series of competitions between trained knights in Rapunzel's world that was held at the Summer Castle when the High King held court. The competitions included, but was not limited to jousting, melee, and the like.

**Tippet** — long, streaming tails extending from the elbows of a woman's cotehardie sleeves, denoting a high station in society. Common throughout the High King's lands.

**Wimple** -- a piece of delicate white linen wrapped beneath the neck and often worn by married women in Rapunzel's time to cover their hair.

# AUTHOR'S NOTE AND THE JOURNEY

The past twenty months have been, forgive me, unprecedented. I'm writing this note at the end of 2021, when I should have already finished. But this book has yet to be put on pre-order and published. Despite all I have done to stay on track, the disruption of the pandemic has hit my health and my writing schedule.

There was nothing about Among the Kingdoms that was simple or easy. Getting to know Nofra and discovering the hardness of her heart was difficult. Watching Rapunzel struggle to find herself and ultimately lose her child was heartbreaking. Journeying with Katterina, Jacob, and Dietz as they struggled to share their hopes and fears took all I had in me.

My husband shakes his head and laughs at me. He has asked me why I just don't make my characters do what I want them to do. But I can't. These characters are real to me and they make some disastrous choices that take us down dark paths.

As I've struggled with writing the book, I know it is a reflection of how I view the world right now. There are so many uncertain as they try to socialize again after lock-down, or wonder where to find new employment, or even how to deal with new health problems.

And, as at other times in my life, I've questioned why God doesn't just "come back and make all things new" as Katterina sighs at the very beginning of Among the Kingdoms. But he delays so that others may still come to him. In fact, we are told to pray that the Son of Man will not return in the winter. We are to intercede for the salvation of many, that they will come to a saving knowledge of a God who loves them so much he allows them to make their own choices that will often take them down dark paths.

He has great plans for our lives and desires for us to grow into the best reflection of him, but somehow, and I don't know how this works together, but I believe it does, there is also freedom. And that freedom is costly. Jesus paid for it with his life. And as I finish writing this, I look forward to bringing you the last story in this series, a final story of redemption, where all things will be made new.

# ACKNOWLEDGMENTS

Sometimes the best part of a book is seeing all the amazing people the author was helped by.

First and foremost, to my God and Savior for carrying me through my life. To my amazing husband who not only puts up with a wife who has crazy characters in her head, but loves her so very well (I'm so glad I get to practice all my kissing scenes with you!). To my book nerdy children; Katie, Sydney, and Caleb, who are not terribly embarrassed by my crazy antics and play along in my bookreels.

To my many, many sisters; Joy will always be missed, Jeanine I'm so glad we both write, and Kess, I'm so thankful you're near. To Allison and Lora, I love that we are now kin and can grow together as family. To Mommie and Daddy, how blessed I am to be raised by you, and to Margaret, thank you for loving us.

Uncle Doug and Aunt Celia, you are still my favorites (shhh! Don't tell!) Heather, Mike, Josh, Travis, and Sean, I love chatting books and other nonsense with all of you! Colin, Tamami, Eris, and Zen, I'm so glad we live near one another and can finally be snarky on the same side of the world.

Jody, you are the business bestie and prayer sister God knew I needed. You make me better. To my besties from college and beyond; Lauren, Heather, and Kevin, you have kept me accountable and made me laugh for decades now. To our herd of children, may we see each other in person soon! Emory, Sophie, Phoebe, Harrison, and Ethan, I praise God for how he is growing each of you to be more like him. Also, you are all hilarious.

To my favorite Dutch family; Bob, Margie, Rachel, and Kelly, I am so grateful to be an honorary daughter and sister. What a gift to know you are praying. Justin, Sarah, and Eva, I love each of you and pray to one day see you soon.

Gwynn and Sherri, I thank God for the gift of your recent visit when I just wasn't sure this book was ever going to happen. What a blessing your encouragement and friendships are. I thank God for prayer warriors like you.

And finally, a huge thank you to Sydney, Mary, and Marrin for helping this book with your wisdom and insight. I thank God for your ability to see things I missed and tease out what needed work.

# ABOUT THE AUTHOR

A lover of books and fairytales, JacQueline uses her faith and life experience with chronic pain/depression to discover new ways of telling old stories as well as her own. She lives in North Alabama with her amazing karate husband and three book-crazy children. She takes every opportunity to drink coffee while wearing dangly earrings and the color purple. Join her newsletter when you download your free copy of *Before the Tower* by visiting https://dl.bookfunnel.com/wftepfzx96.

Find JacQueline at https://authorjroe.com, and you can also follow her on social media:

instagram.com/jacquelinevaughnroe

facebook.com/jacquelinevaughnroe

pinterest.com/jacquelinevroe

patreon.com/authorjroe